FIELDS OF AIR

A STEAMPUNK ADVENTURE NOVEL

MAGNIFICENT DEVICES
BOOK TEN

SHELLEY ADINA

Cover image by Claudia McKinney at Phat Puppy Studios, with images from DepositPhotos.com, used under license. Cover design by Kalen O'Donnell. Author font by Anthony Piraino at OneButtonMouse.com.

Fields of Air / Shelley Adina—1st ed.

ISBN 978-1-939087-46-1 R072623

Created with Vellum

IN THIS SERIES

The Magnificent Devices series

Lady of Devices
Her Own Devices
Magnificent Devices
Brilliant Devices
A Lady of Resources
A Lady of Spirit
A Lady of Integrity
A Gentleman of Means
Devices Brightly Shining (Christmas novella)
Fields of Air
Fields of Iron
Fields of Gold

Carrick House (novella)
Selwyn Place (novella)
Holly Cottage (novella)
Gwynn Place (novella)

Acorn (novella)
Aster (novella)
Iris (novella)
Rosa (novella)

The Mysterious Devices series
The Bride Wore Constant White
The Dancer Wore Opera Rose
The Matchmaker Wore Mars Yellow
The Engineer Wore Venetian Red
The Judge Wore Lamp Black
The Professor Wore Prussian Blue

The Lady Georgia Brunel Mysteries
"The Air Affair" in *Crime Wave: Women of a Certain Age*
The Clockwork City
The Automaton Empress
The Engineer's Nemesis
The Aeronaut's Heir
The Texican Tinkerer
The Wounded Airship

The Regent's Devices series with R.E. Scott
The Emperor's Aeronaut
The Prince's Pilot
The Lady's Triumph
The Pilot's Promise (novella)
The Aeronaut's Heart (novella)

PRAISE FOR SHELLEY ADINA

"She makes hard choices because they're right, because of principle, because of morality—perhaps even out of a need to change her family and her business's legacy: but Gloria's is ultimately the most unselfish path and that is unexpected."

— FANGS FOR THE FANTASY, ON *FIELDS OF AIR*

"It's another excellent chapter in this ongoing epic adventure of this series. I love this world and the story of these excellent women and the saga will never end. No. It will not."

— FANGS FOR THE FANTASY, ON *FIELDS OF IRON*

"I love the rose rebellion, the power of women who aren't just going to be silent. ... All of this comes with some excellent writing—including a really, really epic battle scene that was awesomely well done."

— FANGS FOR THE FANTASY, ON *FIELDS OF GOLD*

For KC Montgomery and Sandy Sliger
and
with perpetual gratitude to Elly and Nancy

FIELDS OF AIR

CHAPTER 1

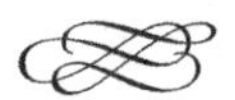

JANUARY 1895

Philadelphia, the Fifteen Colonies

She had not even been home a month, and she'd already had two proposals of marriage. This, it seemed, was the difference between being the heiress to a fortune, and the actual possessor of it.

Gloria Meriwether-Astor, guest of honor at a private ball hosted by the Main Line Hadleys, declined yet another offer of punch from a gentleman whose name she could not remember, and accepted the hand of Mr. Elias Pitman, one of the senior members of her father's board of directors, for the next dance.

"Thank you for the rescue," she said with a smile as he held her very properly and turned her about the ballroom floor in a sedate waltz. "One more offer of punch and I fear I might turn it over the poor man's head."

"You are the guest of honor, my dear, and one of the wealthiest young women in the Fifteen Colonies," he told her. "You could turn the entire bowl over his head and the newspapers would merely report that he had been impertinent to you. Tell me, are you tempted to accept either of the offers presently in hand?"

To shudder would be dramatic, but her rejection of such an idea was real, considering the sources. "Heavens, no. I have far too much to do to be side-tracked by matrimony."

"But you will be twenty-four in the summer."

Gloria struggled to keep her expression pleasant for the benefit of all who were watching. "You speak as though that were the end of the world," she said through a smile.

"Perhaps not, but the quarter-century may mark the end of such fine expectations as you enjoy now."

"Mr. Pitman, I have no doubt that my expectations, as you call them, have more to do with the depth of my pocketbook than of my wrinkles."

"You are a long way from that, my dear."

"Then let us have no more discussion of the subject." He turned her in front of the orchestra and whirled her back down the length of the room. "Instead, I wish to know what to expect on Tuesday, at the board meeting."

"Now?"

"Time is of the essence, and I wish to know your private thoughts, not those you may feel it is appropriate to express in front of others."

He was silent a moment. "Have you heard from your young cousins?"

"Not a word since Egypt."

"The pigeon carrying our notice of the board meeting did not find them in Gibraltar, to my knowledge. Despite quite astonishing advances in technology, one of the drawbacks of traveling so extensively is that communication becomes increasingly difficult. That will work in your favor, I believe."

Gloria missed a step, and he covered for her admirably. "Why do you say that? Do you not like Sydney and Hugh?"

"I like and admire them both. However, Sydney would vote with Carmichael and Adams against you, and Hugh, regardless of his opinions, does not have a vote."

"Do you really believe Sydney would vote against my confirmation as president?"

"Since he has no hope of that position, and the entire board knows it was your father's wish that you take it up, I do not think there will be any difficulty on that score. No, my concern is for the changes you propose to the business once you are confirmed. I observe you have lately been a very busy young woman."

"I have," Gloria said rather proudly. "If we are to get out of the arms business, the foundries and the people who work there must have other employment. We shall turn our swords into ploughshares, as Mrs. Pitman so aptly put it, and the Meriwether-Astor Munitions Works will become Meriwether-Astor Manufacturing and Transport. I have already assigned our undersea dirigibles to trade and transportation on the eastern seaboard, and as I have explained to all the board members, I plan to extend that business further. I have also drawn up extensive plans to redirect the foundries into production of parts for bridges, waterworks, and buildings. Since you, Mr. Stevens, and Mr. Bidwell have agreed in our private meetings over the last few weeks that my plans have substance, I see no reason why Carmichael and Adams should not agree as well."

"Carmichael may not entertain reason," he cautioned her.

"I have been working on him, but he cannot forget the glory days of last year, when, thanks to the Viceroyalty, arms shipments exceeded all our projections by such a margin that he lost his head and purchased a house on the Upper East Side in New York for his wife's use."

Gloria might have been no great shakes at mathematics in school, but her exposure to the business in the years since had given her a keen understanding of profit and loss. And of the dangerous art of speculation.

"He is overextended."

"Yes, and with the failure of the French invasion of England, coupled with the disastrous closure of the English markets to the Meriwether-Astor ships as a result, he stands to lose it before his wife even has a chance to choose wallpaper."

Mrs. Carmichael was a horrible snob who deserved to lose her house and its wallpaper just on general principles, but Gloria would never say so. Instead, she smiled at that lady as they passed, and received a stiff nod for her trouble.

"Can he be won over with a loan to stave off the immediate threat?"

Mr. Pitman's wrinkles creased into a smile above his high collar. "Spoken like a true Meriwether-Astor. How much would you propose?"

"Ten thousand ought to cover the wallpaper, at least."

"If it does not, then it would certainly stave off the jitters until the commercial shipping on the seaboard begins to bear fruit."

The waltz ended, leaving Gloria feeling more informed and slightly more nervous about Tuesday. For she had not confided even to Mr. Pitman about the proposal she planned once the lesser votes had taken place. They all knew of her feelings about supplying arms to other countries, of course. But what they did not know was that she planned to shut down the entire relationship with the Royal Kingdom of Spain and the Californias before the last shipment left the rail yard. She had read in the newspapers of the death of the Viceroy and the accession of his young son to the viceregal throne in San Francisco. Now would be the perfect time to sever ties with that nation permanently. Recompense would have to be made, of course. But there was money in the coffers for it, and to what better use could it be put?

No one but Claire knew of this. And once Gloria was declared president, no matter what anyone said, she would do everything in her power to stop the conflict brewing on the frontier of the Wild West. A conflict ignited and prodded into existence by the pride of one man and the greed of another could not be permitted to flame into open war.

"And here is the Viceroy's ambassador," Mr. Pitman said, "ready to claim the next dance upon your card. He arrived only yesterday, bringing the last payment in order to take possession of the final shipment in person."

"In person?" Gloria's heart sank.

But there was no time to learn anything more. Mr. Pitman bowed and thanked her for the waltz, and then she found herself in the arms of Senor Augusto de Aragon y Villarreal. She had not known exactly who he was, when the young gentleman whom she now realized was his secretary had filled in his name on her card. She had only been amused that his name was so long it had run off into the margin.

She breathed deeply, attempting to convince her galloping heart to calm itself.

Senor de Aragon was a very handsome man in his early forties. He was dressed according to the custom of his country, in a short black bolero jacket liberally encrusted with gold and silver embroidery, a shirt and cravat of dazzling whiteness, and trousers with silver medallions connected by fine chains extending down the outside of the leg. His black hair lay upon his forehead and neck in romantic curls that had never seen macassar oil, and his eyes were so deep a brown that they looked nearly black in his tanned face.

"Miss Meriwether-Astor," he said, his voice a melodious bass. "I am honored to meet you at last in this so beautiful setting, which is still not enough to do justice to such a jewel."

Gloria blushed at the extravagance of his compliments. "You are too kind, sir. The Hadleys' home is very lovely."

"Your father did not tell us that he had a daughter so beyond compare. Please allow me to express my condolences. His death was a great loss to us all—the late Viceroy wore black ribbons for an entire day upon hearing the sad news."

"How very gracious and kind of him. And what a loss for your nation. We have only just heard of his death."

Technically, she was supposed to be swathed in black for another four months out of respect for her father, but what would that signify? She could not honestly say that she mourned him, despite his last heroic moments in giving his life for hers. In England, before Christmas, she had been mistaken for Alice Chalmers by a Venetian assassin sent to kill her friend, and if it had not been for Gerald flinging himself into the path of the bullet, Gloria would not be here now. Nor could she say that the world was a poorer place for his death. In fact, none of her confused sentiments regarding Gerald

Meriwether-Astor could be expressed to anyone—not even Claire.

So as was her habit, she expressed herself through her clothes. Her gown was lilac, the color of the final stage of mourning, with a nod to society's expectations in its black lace and ribbon trim upon the bodice.

She was not even supposed to be out in public. For that reason, because of the recent nature of her bereavement, the ball was a private affair. But Mrs. Hadley, who had been her late mother's closest confidante, was far more concerned about marriage than mourning. And once one had Mrs. Hadley's approval, one had that of all of Philadelphia, and black crepe could go to the devil.

"You were personally acquainted with my father, sir?"

The Viceroy's ambassador swept her into the turns with a flair that suggested the swirling of a cloak rather than a woman. "I was indeed. He was a man of intelligence, of bravery, and of vision. He and the late Viceroy spent many hours together, strategizing, conversing, and shooting. I suspect that in him, His Highness found the closest thing one may to a brother."

Lovely. Two warlike peas in an iron pod.

"Tell me of his vision," Gloria begged. "I am sorry to say that in recent years, I was not with him as much as I wished to be, and I regret the loss of such conversations as you describe."

He smiled down at her. Goodness, he really was very handsome.

"Ah, but lovely though you are, it is not likely a man such as he would have taken a woman into his confidence."

Keep smiling. "But I should still like to hear what he envisioned for the company. If I am to act as its head, I would hope that I might continue his legacy in many respects."

"A noble aspiration, to be sure." He gazed over her shoulder, but whether he was looking into the past or into the crowd, Gloria could not be certain. "You are familiar with the political situation in our glorious kingdom?"

"No, but I am anxious to learn, if you will tell me."

"Let us withdraw from the floor, then. These matters are somewhat complex, and require more attention than dancing will allow. Will you permit me?"

"Certainly. Let us walk in the conservatory."

Propriety dictated that she be chaperoned in the company of a gentleman, but Gloria's need to know as much as possible about the situation in the Wild West trumped such considerations. She hoped that Mrs. Hadley would not miss her for some time—at least until she had enough of the facts in hand that she could make good decisions on Tuesday.

In contrast to the snow and cold outside, and the crowded ballroom with its brilliant lights, potted palms, and chatter, the conservatory was warm and humid and silent, filled with all manner of flowers, vines, and ferns. A row of round orange trees set in the south windows were heavy with fruit that scented the air.

"Please. Be seated." Senor de Aragon indicated white wrought-iron chairs on either side of a breakfast-table, and Gloria seated herself gracefully, her back straight, her expression interested as she arranged her silk skirts.

"I will share with you as best I can what your father learned in his visits to us, and you will see how important his role has been in the safety and prosperity of the people of the Viceroyalty."

Of certain people, at least. Rich people, who want to become richer.

"You have heard of the Texican Territory?"

She nodded, folding her hands in her lap. Alice Chalmers hailed from there—a town called Resolution. Gloria had looked it up and not found it, but she knew it lay south of the capital of Santa Fe. The town's claim to fame was its geography—set in the middle of a flash-flood plain, it had been left alone by settlers and government alike. Alice's stepfather, Ned Mose, found that this suited him very well, air pirate that he was. The town made its living wrecking airships, and the absence of both settlers and law, Alice had once confided, made the uncertain landscape both appealing and profitable.

"Perhaps you did not know that, two hundred years ago, most of the Texican Territory belonged to our glorious King?"

"No, I did not."

"Gradual incursion by movement west from the Fifteen Colonies has resulted in the Territorials setting up their own upstart government, intermarrying with once-loyal Spanish families, betraying the Church, and the entire Territory seceding from Spain. All that is left now of a great kingdom is the thin strip of fertile land down the west coast, into the isthmus between the continents of the Americas, and on to the great southern subcontinent."

"Is that not enough for His Majesty?"

"When one has had the entire plate, it is difficult to satisfy one's hunger with only a slice of bread."

"And is His Majesty hungry?" Gloria asked the question with a twinkle of humor to soften its impertinence.

The Viceroy's representative twinkled back, clearly appreciating her femininity, if he did not appreciate her mind. "In a certain sense—if one remembers the legends saying the Texican Territory is rich with gold."

Gloria's eyebrows rose. If that were so, why was Ned Mose not waylaying miners in the mountains? "Legends?"

"One cannot discover the truth if one is not permitted to mine. Spain must have gold, and therefore it must have its lands back. This is where your father's vision and the late Viceroy's aligned most happily."

"And what of the new Viceroy? Is he a believer in legend?"

A muscle flexed in the man's jaw. "Our new ruler, while a paragon of manly virtue, is of a more studious bent. The way to appeal to him is through books and history, so I have left learned men to educate him while I am gone. An appeal to reason cannot help but bear fruit."

"Is he so very young, then?"

"He is out of the schoolroom, and had been preparing to attend university in Spain like all his ancestors before him, when God called his father to heaven by means of a failure of the heart."

"I see." A bookish young man might see war very differently than his Ambassador seemed to. This could only work in her favor. "The shipments of arms you have received thus far, then, have included guns, ammunition, train cars, articulated loading cranes, and cannon."

His brows rose. "You are well informed."

"I looked it up." She gave him a sunny smile. "But there are entries for armaments I do not understand. The final shipment, which I understand you will take possession of personally, contains many, many tons of iron comprising mechanicals that seem to be parts for larger machines, not those that have been completed."

How pleased he seemed with her knowledge!

"You are quite correct. The Meriwether-Astor Munitions Works has quite outdone itself in supplying the parts for the machinery that our scientists and engineers have designed. Machines that, unlike airships, for instance, do not offend God, but rather emulate His own creation."

"In what way? Does not every creation of man emulate that of God to some degree?"

"I see you are a budding philosopher as well as a great beauty." The warmth of his gaze might have been bestowed upon his own daughter. "I hazard to say that his late highness would have enjoyed talking with you as much as with your father."

"How very kind of you. I cannot agree, I am sure. But the machines?"

"Have you ever seen the mechanical horses upon the—how do you call them? At the fair or the exhibition."

"The carousel?"

He snapped his fingers. "The carousel. Exactly."

"Why yes, I have. I spent many a happy day at the exhibition as a child, and the carousel was one of my favorite amusements."

"Picture those horses then, not affixed to a pole, but made of moving iron and forming the cavalry of an army, invincible, and unaffected by weather or the need for food or water."

"The final shipment contains parts for mechanical horses?" A sudden vision of such a cavalry, thundering across the desert toward a sleepy town, took her breath away with dread.

"*Sí, senorita*. And cannon in the arms of mechanical behemoths. And racing machines built to be faster than a leopard, carrying rockets and bursting through offensive lines to release them into the heart of an army."

"Good heavens." Gloria felt quite winded, her mind reeling at the spectacle. "Would it not be simpler to sign treaties with the Texican government, contribute equipment, and split the yield from the mines equally?"

"There are no mines yet, and there will not be until the land is ours again," he said gruffly. "Land is our birthright—as any Californio will tell you."

"Californio?"

"The noblemen of our country—what the English call landed gentry. Many have titles extending back to the twelfth and thirteenth centuries, and families with roots in the titled nobility of Spain. We do not sign treaties. We own."

"I see," Gloria said thoughtfully, as though the prospect of mechanical war animals and the annexation of perfectly happy territories minding their own business were normal. "And the army is prepared, then, and ready to invade once the final shipment arrives?"

For the first time, his arrogant, proud gaze faltered, and he considered the orange trees with a frown, as though he found them somehow lacking. "The Viceroyalty does not have a standing army. And His Highness is not the leader of men that his father was. But when the time comes, I will see that each landowner raises men from his own acres to go and fight."

Gloria knew her history and geography as well as the next schoolgirl. This seemed rather feudal. "Is this the way they have always done it?"

"We have not needed to—not in two hundred years. Hence the growing necessity to make our will known to the upstarts and trespassers upon our ancestral lands."

"So ... no one has actually fought in two hundred years?"

Gloria thought of the Kingdom of Prussia, where the army was an honorable career choice for any man. Or of England, where airships were registered with the Admiralty and, whether privately owned or not, crewed by trained aeronauts who could take to the skies to defend England's shores at a pigeon's notice.

So these Californios learned about war in school, but no one had actually fought in centuries? Were they mad? Or had legends of pride and grandeur blinded them to their actual capabilities—and even the necessity of war?

"Not physically. But every boy learns the art of war in the schoolroom and gymnasium, preparing him so that at any moment he may obey the Viceroy's will—in the person of his humble servant—to rise up in his glorious name."

Did he mean himself? Was she at this moment speaking to the real power behind the throne, now that a boy who was probably not even in his twenties had inherited it?

"This is why our late Viceroy's partnership with your father has been of vital importance," de Aragon went on, removing his censure from the orange trees and turning his dark gaze upon her instead. "I—we mean to declare war on the Texican Territory and take it back—and the Meriwether-Astor Munitions Works has made it all possible."

She had not missed that slip of the tongue. *He* meant to declare war. Was it possible that the young Viceroy knew nothing of the Ambassador's mission in the east? How widespread were these plans? And what of the gentry—did they support the Ambassador or the studious prince? To say nothing of the farmers and ironsmiths who would be doing the actual invading—what were their views upon the subject? But of course she could not ask.

Instead, she offered as warm a smile as she could muster, and opened her mouth to say something inane and feminine and harmless.

The door to the conservatory opened, and Mrs. Hadley leaned in. "Gloria, dear? Are you in here?"

"Yes, ma'am." She stood, and de Aragon stood with her as Mrs. Hadley rustled over, splendid in burgundy silk. "Senor de Aragon y Villarreal and I were discussing some matters of business."

"Goodness, dear, that will never do. You sound just like your father—and half Philadelphia looking for a dance with you. If you will excuse us, Ambassador." Mrs. Hadley ushered Gloria toward the door with gloved hands that fluttered like birds. When they were out of the ambassador's hearing, she said, "I am bidden to tell you that you have a visitor. She is in here, in the morning room."

Gloria's heart leapt. Claire! "A visitor? Who could it be?"

On the threshold of the morning room she stopped short in stunned surprise, the skirts of her ball gown swirling around her feet.

"Will I do?" Alice Chalmers asked with a grin. She had made a concession to her surroundings by donning a practical navy skirt, and a rather lovely gray coat that Gloria had never seen before. Snow dusted the shoulders of it, and sparkled in her hair, for of course it would never occur to Alice to wear a hat.

"Alice!" She flung herself, laughing, into her arms. "I am so glad to see you. But—is everything well? Our friends—? There is nothing wrong, is there?"

"Now, why would the sight of anyone from England make you think someone was in danger?" Alice asked, rather rhetorically, for they both knew perfectly well it had happened on more than one occasion. "No, everyone is well, and Claire and Andrew send their best love."

"Thank heaven for that." Gloria pressed a hand to her heart to still its thumping. "I must hear all the news, but first —have you eaten? Can you stay to supper?"

Alice listened to the orchestra for a moment, and observed the men in white tie and the bejeweled women in swishing ball gowns passing to and fro through the foyer to the ballroom. "No, I don't think so." Her gaze returned to search Gloria's face. "I do have news, but this is neither the time nor the place. I'll come in the morning, all right? Jake is quite anxious to see you, though he'd never show it and would likely challenge me to fisticuffs if he knew I'd told you."

Jake was the first person in Gloria's life who had actually told her the truth—about herself, about life, about the way people ought to treat one another. He had changed her course forever. They all had. They were her flock.

"We cannot have that," she said to Alice. "Until tomorrow, then. As long as the news is not bad, I can contain my impatience."

Alice nodded, and Gloria saw her out the Hadleys' massive front door herself, despite the chill that blew about her shoulders and neck.

The wind was changing. There would be a storm before long.

CHAPTER 2

Unlike most of the imposing houses along Washington Avenue, Number 50 sat on a double lot, which meant that behind its majestic iron railings and its tall laurel hedges lay not an orchard or an airing garden, but a private airfield, complete with two mooring masts.

It was here that Gloria directed Alice to moor *Swan*. When she attempted to assist her friend by tying off the ropes herself, she was gently nudged out of the way by young Mr. Stringfellow, who seemed to have grown six inches since Gloria had last seen him in Venice, and a gangly, sober individual who had introduced himself as Evan Douglas, a cousin to the Mopsies.

"We've got this, miss," Benny told her with all the gravity of his thirteen years. "No need to trouble yourself."

"Would you say that to Lady Claire, or Lizzie?" she asked him.

"No, miss, but I'm much better acquainted with them than I am with you, and they are better acquainted with ships. Besides which, it is my job."

Perhaps she was merely feeling nettled by the Californio ambassador's obvious belief that not only was she merely ornamental, but lacking in brains to boot. Perhaps this was why she had felt compelled to do something, even if it was only tying off a rope. But one did not interfere with a middy's duties, so she stepped back and waited for Alice to shut down *Swan*'s boilers and emerge.

She was holding to Alice's reassurances that their friends were well, so the news she carried couldn't be that alarming. It was most efficient to have her guests moored here, close at hand, and while Gloria was an admirer of efficiency, she also could not help the warmth that glowed in her heart simply at having her friends near her again.

Alice appeared on the gangway, and *Swan* bobbed slightly as she jumped down. "Is this all right?"

"It couldn't be better." She smiled, and pulled her short wool jacket more closely around her. The morning was bright and sunny, but last night's change in the weather had brought a hard frost and the air held the kind of biting cold that called for scarves and mittens. "Perhaps we might talk aboard your ship. For privacy."

If she had thought that Alice would question her, she was mistaken. She only nodded and waved toward the hatch.

"Mr. Stringfellow," Gloria said to him, "breakfast will be coming out shortly. Might I ask you to direct Mrs. Polk and her staff aboard?"

"Yes, miss."

"And then I hope you will join us."

"If that's all right by the captain, miss."

Alice raised one eyebrow. "When have I ever starved my crew on purpose? Of course you may join us. Jake, Evan, you too. I have a feeling that we'll all want to share our news."

Mrs. Polk, being well used to Gerald Meriwether-Astor's comings and goings, did not bat an eyelash at the prospect of moving an entire meal for five people across the lawn and into *Swan*'s rather Spartan dining saloon. When she and the two maids had gone, Alice fell upon the coffeepot like one starved.

"Colonial coffee," she sighed from the depths of a stoneware mug. "Nothing like it in the world."

"Have some cream," Gloria urged her, and removed the silver lids from the dishes. "And some eggs, and sausage, and baked squash and applesauce."

Evan Douglas made an inarticulate sound that could have been sheer longing, and before half an hour had passed the dishes were empty and the young men finally satisfied.

Alice shook her head. "You'd think I did starve them."

"We have plenty of food, Captain, but it does not taste like this," Jake said, sitting back with his own cup of coffee and belching behind his hand.

"I will admit that while all of us can feed ourselves, none of us can cook," Alice told her.

Despite her assurances the evening before, Gloria could not help but ask again, "Claire and Andrew are well, truly? And the girls? And your fiancé?"

"Very well. The shindig on Twelfth Night was a triumph."

Gloria felt an upwelling of relief. "I am glad to hear it. Did she wear the dress I sent?"

"She did, and the Queen herself complimented her on it—and you, indirectly. She remarked how lucky Claire was to have friends with such taste."

Her cheeks flushed with pleasure. "How very kind." Ornamental she might be, but there were advantages to having an eye for cut and color. And with the House of Worth, of course, one could never go wrong.

"Captain, we did not fly the Atlantic to talk about dresses," Jake grumbled. "Time's a-wasting."

"This is called leading up to it gently," Alice informed him. "I'm trying to think of a way to say this that won't come as a shock. Do you mind?"

"*I* mind," Gloria said, a slight chill replacing the glow. "You said everyone was well. I had thought your news was happy."

Alice looked up, sympathy in her gaze. "Your cousins Sydney and Hugh Meriwether-Astor were in London—at Carrick House, in fact, as well as at the ball."

"Were they?" Gloria sat back in astonishment. She had not expected *that*. "When last I heard from them, they were in Egypt—I wonder if my pigeon ever located them north of Morocco?"

"It didn't need to. Sydney was found in Claire's office, reading her correspondence—in particular, the letter in which you told her you planned to oust him from the board and shut down the deal with the Royal Kingdom of Spain and the Californias."

Gloria's corset hugged her ribs far too tightly. She could not get a breath. Carefully, she set down her cup, and focused on breathing in and out. "Sydney? Going through someone's correspondence? Are you certain?"

"Maggie caught him," Jake said. "But that's beside the point."

"The point is that the gentlemen caught the packet the

next morning and left Paris on *Persephone* on Wednesday," Alice told her.

"Today is Friday. So they will arrive at Lakehurst tomorrow, and be in Philadelphia Sunday afternoon, well in time for the board meeting on Tuesday." Gloria thought rapidly. "Good heavens. You must have lifted the very next morning."

"We did. I wish I could have had an Admiralty speed and altitude recorder aboard," Alice said with some regret. "I suspect we might have broken a record or two."

"I'd like to break something else," Jake muttered. "Sydney's head, for a start. But I'll have to make do with the memory of Lizzie's laying him out on the Victoria Embankment."

"That is a story I am dying to hear," Gloria told him, still a little winded, "but not just now. He will almost certainly vote against me, and here is why." Quickly, yet in enough detail to paint the whole chilling picture, she told them everything that Senor de Aragon had said, right down to the schoolboys learning the art of war along with their arithmetic.

"The devil you say!" Alice exploded. "Invade the Texican Territory? Are they mad?"

"They indeed may be, but the Ambassador at least is deadly serious," Gloria told her. "I am not convinced the young Viceroy even knows of his plans, to say nothing of the ordinary people. But whether they do or not, can you picture men convinced they are warriors ready to fight, while no one has seen the business end of a gun aimed at them in generations?"

"That doesn't make the prospect any less dangerous." Evan Douglas spoke for the first time, and Gloria realized she had forgotten he was there, though he was seated next to young Benny. "One might even posit that fanatics are more of a threat than men brought up to fight, for they have no idea of the danger, and worse, have sacrificed sense to idealism."

"I do not think sense comes into the equation at all." Alice passed a hand over her hair and clutched the neat braided roll at the back. "What are we going to do?"

Gloria's throat closed and moisture sprang to her eyes at that little word that meant so much. *We.* Alice had used it so easily, as though it had not even occurred to her merely to deliver her message, thank her for breakfast, wave Gloria down the gangway, and pull up ropes.

We're a flock, Maggie had once said, and Gloria had rejoiced to find herself numbered among them. She had never been so grateful for it as now.

WITH A SMILE for the men around the mahogany table, Gloria seated herself in her father's chair and arranged her fine wool skirts about her. She had dressed carefully this morning in a midnight blue suit trimmed in purple silk and black lace, with a jabot of matching lace on her silk blouse. Her hat was a delightful confection bearing blue and purple flowers and black tulle, and rested jauntily upon her blond hair, which she had dressed high in order to make herself look taller while seated.

Gloria knew she looked well. And while butterflies might be doing merry dips and dives in her stomach, at least she had the appearance of control here at the head of the table.

"Welcome, gentlemen, to the first board meeting of 1895. I trust you had a good Christmas and New Year's celebration?"

There was a general murmur before Sydney pushed back

his chair, as if he could not remain seated a moment longer. "Gloria, this is supposed to be a private meeting. What is *she* doing here?"

Gloria gazed at him, seated next to Mr. Pitman, who sat at her right hand. "To whom do you refer?"

"There is only one female in the room besides yourself, and that is Miss Alice Chalmers, as you very well know."

"And as *you* very well know, at every meeting of the board we welcome a shareholder representative."

"That is my brother Hugh, Gloria."

"Your brother could not be with us today. The representative is appointed by Mr. Pitman, and today that is Captain Chalmers, by which title you will address her henceforward. Really, Sydney, your manners this morning! Aunt Louisa would be appalled."

But Sydney was not to be put in his place like a schoolboy. "Captain Chalmers isn't a shareholder. I ask you again, what is she doing here?"

"She is indeed, and it is not your business to know everything. It is mine. Now, do sit down. We are now behind schedule by five minutes."

At the far end of the table, she saw Alice pass a hand over her mouth to cover her twitching lips. She too was dressed in the height of fashion in a blue walking suit trimmed in black soutache, with a matching tricorne hat perched upon her hair and trimmed with a black cockade of grosgrain ribbon. Mr. Pitman had sold her ten shares in the company this morning after breakfast, and while she did not have a vote, of course, her presence at the table was both a comfort and a relief to Gloria. If worse came to worst, Alice could always pull out her lightning pistol and shoot the dissidents among them.

Mr. Pitman put on his spectacles and cleared his throat. "I now call to order the meeting of the board of directors of the Meriwether-Astor Munitions Works. The first order of business is the vote to confirm Miss Gloria Meriwether-Astor, our late chairman's heiress, as president. I cannot imagine this point needs any discussion." He glanced at each man, and when he reached Carmichael, the man stood with ponderous gravity.

Oh, dear.

"I mean no disrespect to Miss Meriwether-Astor who, if I may say so, is looking particularly lovely this morning," he said, bowing to her and tugging on his wide brocade waistcoat. "But as pleasing a picture as she makes, I do not believe that she is the best candidate to lead this company into the upcoming century. Mr. Sydney Meriwether-Astor has been on the board of directors since his late father's regrettable passing, and as the closest male descendant of our late president, I feel *he* is the family member best suited to take up the reins of leadership." His gaze met Gloria's. "If I may be frank, this is no job for a woman, who may be taken from that chair at any time by the demands of husband and family, leaving us in the position of having to replace her anyway, at some later date."

Gloria inhaled deeply in an attempt to calm herself.

"Are there any other candidates putting themselves forward for the position?" Mr. Pitman asked, managing to make it sound like a grave social *faux pas*. When no one spoke, he nodded. "Then we shall put it to a vote. All in favor of Miss Gloria Meriwether-Astor as president of this firm, raise your right hand."

Four for, and two against, the latter being Sydney and

Carmichael. Gloria let out the breath she had been holding, feeling a wave of relief, tempered somewhat by regret that her own cousin should not support her. With Alice's news, of course, she had known he wouldn't, but that he would not only not support her, but worse, would put himself forward to take her place, was much more painful than anything else.

"The ayes have it." Mr. Pitman smiled at her. "May I be the first to congratulate you, Madam President, and offer you my fellow board members' best wishes and—" He glanced from Carmichael to Sydney. "—support."

"Thank you, Mr. Pitman." With as little ceremony as possible, she received the gavel of office from him and tapped it upon its cork pad. As though there had been no opposition, as though she had not just been betrayed by her closest living relative, she proceeded to lead the meeting through several points of business, which passed without comment or opposition.

But if she had thought to lull the members into a sense of security with several aye votes, she was disappointed when they reached the seventh order of business.

"In the matter of my cousin Sydney's seat on this board, I move that he be removed and my cousin Hugh take his place."

He had known this was coming—he had read it in her letter. But still, his eyes filled with as much betrayal as if he had not just attempted to vote himself into her chair. What was good for the goose was clearly not good for the gander.

"For what reason?" Mr. Adams said. "Your father was content to have his nephew represent that side of the family, and Sydney has acquitted himself most ably before now."

"Until he voted to oust his uncle's chosen heir and put

himself in her place," Mr. Pitman reminded him. "I must say, this motion should come as no surprise."

"It comes as a surprise to me, since Sydney's motion to be president took place *after* the motion to remove him was put on the agenda," Mr. Adams said. "This tells me she intended to remove him all along. What is the reason for it, Madam President?"

"I knew he was going to try to oust me," she said simply.

She saw the moment the penny dropped and Sydney realized why Alice was there. But to admit it would be to admit he had trespassed upon Lady Claire's trust and hospitality, and read her private correspondence. She saw, too, the moment he realized she was quite prepared to tell them all about his dishonorable behavior if he did not back down.

"Is this true, Sydney?" Mr. Adams turned to him.

"Yes." And yet he remained calm. "I beg my cousin to reconsider."

"I am sorry, Sydney, but the direction in which I wish to take this company is not the same one in which you wish it to go. I feel Hugh to be the better candidate, for greater harmony among board members."

"You mean, you are stacking the deck with people who favor you," he said pleasantly.

"I say!" Mr. Pitman exclaimed. "That was uncalled for, sir. And if I may say so, you are illustrating our president's point admirably."

"I will, of course, allow you to attend the meetings of the board, as your brother has done with you until now," Gloria said a little stiffly. It was difficult to remain polite when her opponent used civility as a weapon with such ease. "But you will not be permitted to speak, only observe."

"In which direction do you wish the company to go, Miss Meriwether-Astor?" Mr. Bidwell asked.

Gloria inclined her head, hoping that the trembling of her knees and the jumping of her stomach was not apparent to anyone but herself. "May I direct your attention to the next motion on the agenda—the matter of the final shipment of arms and equipment to the Royal Kingdom of Spain and the Californias." She took a sip of water to moisten her dry throat. "I move that the shipment be terminated before delivery and the funds already paid be returned to the ambassador in person. I further move that our relationship with that nation also be terminated, with as much cordiality as possible."

Silence reverberated in the room for a single moment, before pandemonium broke out. The board members leaped to their feet, some leaning with both hands on the table, some pushing back their chairs.

"Unthinkable!"

"Outrageous!"

"Are you utterly mad? I move that the president be removed from office immediately!"

But Sydney, to her surprise, did not join in the shouting. Instead, he sat back in his leather-bound chair and folded his arms over his chest, looking grave and thoughtful.

She had met with each of them over the last several weeks, stating her case for the company's new direction as economically and practically as possible. But those meetings had not included this bombshell. She picked up the gavel and whacked it on the cork pad. "Gentlemen," she said. "Order, please."

For a wonder, they seemed to recollect themselves, and fuming and muttering, resumed their seats.

"You all know my plans for this company—that we remove

ourselves from the arms business over time, and focus our energies on producing parts for building materials, for railroads, for waterworks and bridges. We will use our dirigibles for trade rather than spying upon and threatening other nations. I believe that in time, these pursuits will create much more revenue in support of our growing country than arms ever could. This vote will be our first step in this new direction."

She was not so stupid as to believe she had won, since they could be just as angry and obstinate sitting down as standing. But several of them were looking as thoughtful as Sydney—as though they were giving consideration to her proposals in the same way they considered her father's.

"Of course I do not mean that we must decide this critical point in this very meeting. I urge you all to consider it carefully, so that when we reconvene, we may discuss it calmly and rationally. Let us remember that the Viceroy's ambassador is in Philadelphia for a limited time, and we must not draw the matter out. We must be resolute without being insulting."

The noise surged again, but this time, Sydney joined in not to add to the agitation, but to urge calm. When the room had settled down slightly, he raised a hand. "If I may speak?"

"Yes," Gloria said cautiously. He was being awfully decent and cooperative. Perhaps she had misjudged him. But it was too late now—and there was no arguing with her relief that she had done what had to be done. She had a far better relationship with Hugh.

"As my last act as a member of this board, then, let me recommend that we meet again on Friday. We will need to act carefully with the Ambassador, as he is notoriously prickly when it comes to his honor. If the board does agree to stop the shipment, we must frame this delicately in order to avoid unpleasant consequences."

"Will they declare war on us?" Mr. Pitman inquired in all seriousness.

"No, but our esteemed president is of course aware that if we do this, we will have breached the contract. We must be prepared to make it up to them in some way."

"If I have to give them a year's dividends, I shall," Gloria said, and Mr. Pitman's gaze swung to her in dismay.

"Let us not be hasty," Mr. Carmichael said sharply—he of the newly purchased New York town house. "We cannot solve the problem that our president has laid upon us here and now. I have a lunch appointment."

"Very well." Gloria had known that it would be difficult to pull this off, but on the bright side, at least Sydney appeared to be resigned to the loss of his seat and had decided to act like a gentleman. "I agree with my cousin that we should reconvene on Friday, armed with as much information as possible, and having thought out the consequences of each path we propose."

With relief, she saw nods around the table, and then Mr. Pitman moved that the meeting be adjourned.

"Will you join me for lunch, Gloria?" he asked when the room emptied. "I should like to discuss today's meeting with you."

"I should like that of all things, but perhaps I might put it off until tomorrow?" She smiled at him. "Captain Chalmers has never been to Philadelphia, and I am showing her and her crew the sights."

"Tomorrow, then. I will reserve a table at Elliot's."

He departed, and Gloria took Alice's arm. "Get me out of here," she murmured. "How far will *Swan* fly in an hour?"

"A hundred miles or more."

"Excellent. Let us change, point her bow west, and get some air under our feet before I do someone bodily harm."

TWO HOURS LATER, *Swan* floated gently to ground in a wide field formed by the curve of a river. Winter fields, fallow now, stretched away in neat squares like a patchwork quilt, punctuated by houses and barns all painted white. Smoke drifted up from chimneys at the vertical, so still was the air.

"Is this good enough?" Alice asked. "Any idea where we are?"

"There is some kind of Utopian community out here, if I am not mistaken." Gloria gazed out the viewing port as Alice's crew jumped down and did their best to moor *Swan* using trees and a large boulder. "Their religion forbids the use of steam."

They joined the boys at the bottom of the gangway, and strolled over to the steep riverbank. "Forbids steam?" Evan repeated. "How do they live without steam power?"

As though she could discern the answer, Alice gazed with wondering eyes across the fields, at the column of wood smoke rising from the chimney of the nearest farmhouse, about a quarter of a mile away.

"I do not know," Gloria admitted. "But from all accounts, they manage, and keep themselves separate from the world."

The high-pitched sounds of shouting came closer, and below them, on the frozen surface of the river, came five or six children, dressed all in black, bundled up in mittens and scarves, with skating blades tied to their feet. The little girls' heads were covered with starched white caps, and the boys wore black felt hats with sober brims. There was nothing sober about their play, however. They darted hither and yon like water-bugs, playing what looked to be a game of tag.

"That looks like fun," Mr. Stringfellow said with a hint of longing in his tone.

Jake glanced at him. "It does. I miss our lot at Carrick House. Come, let us see if we can join them in their game. With your permission, Captain?"

Alice nodded, and the boys slid down the bank. After the children had recovered from their initial alarm at being accosted by strangers, the boys discovered that the dialect the children spoke was similar to the German they'd picked up over the last several years going back and forth to Munich.

Alice smiled as she watched the game resume, to much laughter and shrieking. "Even without skating blades, Benny is holding his own."

"It was kind of Jake to recognize that he was homesick," Gloria said. "I never can decide whether or not Jake is the hardened criminal he purports to be."

"Not in the least," Alice told her, out of loyalty to her navigator. "But in this line of work, it doesn't hurt for people to think so." This was as good an opportunity to talk things over as any, now that her crew would be occupied for some time. "A reputation as a dab hand in a fight wouldn't hurt either of us, if this morning's to-do is any indication."

With a sigh, Gloria nodded. "There was more than one moment when I thought I would be turned out of the room and another president voted in."

"You'd have had clear sailing if it hadn't been for this business with the Ambassador."

"I know. But how can I live with myself if I do not do something to stop this war?"

"He may still storm the border, whether you send this shipment or not. In fact, from what de Aragon said, it seems likely he will."

"I also know I could let sleeping dogs lie on a train west, fully loaded and paid for. But at least while I am in charge, the company will do nothing to support such a war, regardless of what it has done in the past."

"Good for you," Alice said with approval. "I wish I had your resolution."

Gloria turned to her in surprise. "My resolution? Why, you are one of the bravest, cleverest women I know."

"Not lately," Alice admitted, watching as Evan attempted to organize Crack the Whip. "I suppose you've wondered why it was I who brought you the news of your cousin."

"To own the truth, I have been more concerned with the message than the messenger," Gloria told her ruefully. "Why? Is there something more behind this voyage than that, or conveying Mr. Douglas here?" Of all the times Alice could wish her face were not so transparent … because the next words out of Gloria's mouth were, "Is everything all right at Hollys Park, Alice?"

Her face crumpled with distress. "Is it so obvious? This is why I avoid cowboy poker, you see."

"You've assured me that all is well in Wilton Crescent, and none of the boys are fleeing the law that I know of, so that leaves one subject upon which I have noticed you to be unusually silent. That tends to be one's first clue about a woman's state of mind."

At this, the corners of Alice's mouth tipped up. "You're as observant as Claire."

"I shall take that as a compliment," Gloria said with no small satisfaction. "But I am not as brave as she. I will not wade in and ask what is the matter unless you choose to tell me. I know you are much closer to her than to me."

Alice slipped her arm around her shoulders and gave her a grateful squeeze, surprising not only herself, but Gloria, too. "But without one of us, the other would not be standing here on this bank. I think that entitles us to a certain confidence in each other." Her arm fell away, and she hugged herself protectively, right over the hollow feeling under her ribs. "You're right. I am here for reasons other than the obvious."

"Is it Captain Hollys?"

Alice nodded, and Gloria's eyes filled with sympathy as she said, "You know I have never had romantic feelings in that direction, but I do admire the captain enormously, and feel him eminently worthy of you. Oh, Alice, what has gone wrong? Do you no longer love him?"

Alice's eyes were wet, but that could just be from the wind. "On the contrary. I love him more than ever. But there is an enormous difference between caring for the man and marrying the baronet."

"I don't understand," Gloria said a little flatly. "If I were lucky enough to have secured Ian Hollys's love, I would have no compunctions at all about marrying him."

"Ah, but then you would wake up one morning and realize that there was a harvest festival to be organized, and a church fete, and while you are completely prepared to take on an ambush or fly to the Antipodes to deliver a cargo, you have no idea where to start looking for a festival tent."

Gloria stared at her, clearly trying to translate such babble into sense.

"Exactly," Alice said with gloomy satisfaction. "You don't know either. Well, that makes me feel a little better, at any rate."

"I do not find tents," Gloria said at last. "My housekeeper does, or my butler. But what on earth do these things have to do with marrying Ian?"

"Everything." Alice made a gesture with her hands, as though to encompass the river from bank to bank. Or her future, from mooring ring to vanes. "Lady Hollys has to do any number of things that Alice Chalmers simply isn't prepared for."

Gloria was trying hard to understand. "So you love Ian, but you do not believe you are prepared to be his wife, with all the responsibility that entails."

"Precisely. Got it in one." What a relief to be able to stop explaining!

Gloria frowned, as though marshalling her resources. "Then you are a bigger fool than I have ever met in the whole of my life."

Alice actually stepped away from her in astonishment, and Gloria grabbed her sleeve before her foot slipped down the snowy riverbank. "I beg your pardon?"

Once they had retreated a safe distance from the bank, Gloria glared at her. "You heard me. Do you seriously mean to give up love and happiness because you cannot find a festival tent? Let them have their festival in the open air, for pity's sake, or in the hall, or in the closet! Alice, you are so blinded by the trees that you are completely missing the forest—and it is a beautiful one. One that can shelter you and keep you warm for a lifetime. Are you completely mad?"

Alice's mouth opened and closed a time or two before she finally got out, "One of us is."

"It is not I, of that I can assure you. Honestly, if you weren't two inches taller than me, I should turn you over my knee and spank you for even thinking of throwing Ian over."

"I wasn't—"

"Or for hesitating in such a way. For fleeing here when you should be there! Why, I expected you to be Lady Hollys already, in a double wedding with Claire."

"The chapel at Gwynn Place wasn't big enough." She was still reeling from being lectured to by Gloria Meriwether-Astor, of all people, who to Alice's knowledge had never been in love with anyone.

"There must be more to your indecision than tents and church. What of your ship?" She waved over her shoulder at the sleek, shining bulk of *Swan*, bobbing gently on her lines. "Is Lady Hollys going to give her up too?"

"Certainly not," came out of Alice's mouth without a single thought.

"Are you going to fly for me?"

"Maybe." Alice set her teeth. "If you ever stop lecturing me."

"I shall stop when you begin to make sense," Gloria said crisply. "If Lady Hollys is going to fly, then it follows she will be absent some of the time. Therefore, she certainly must delegate certain of her duties to her household staff."

"She can do that?"

"Of course she can, you goose! She may need to put others

before herself upon occasion, but in the main, she will have people about her whose job it is to assist. Whose life's work it is to assist. My goodness, surely you did not think you were to be mucking about in market towns and lumber yards yourself, and nailing bunting to booths?"

"I didn't know what to think. Claire said that her mother took care of the people in the village with fetes and whatnot."

"I am sure she did—with the assistance of a small army." Gloria's eyes flashed with sudden understanding. "Think of them as your ground crew on the estate, much as you have your crew in the air. They keep the ship running efficiently while you give the orders, do they not?"

"Ye-e-s."

"There you are, then," Gloria said triumphantly. "I suggest you turn your ship about and make good time back to England. Take your fiancé by the hand and march him to church without further ado."

While Alice's brows rose at this familiarity, to her own surprise, she laughed. "I never suspected you were so bossy."

"I never did either," Gloria admitted. "But I suppose I shall have to learn now, and I thank you for giving me some practice in the art."

"You're welcome. Look—the boys are coming." She waved, and in the distance, Evan Douglas waved back.

"I mean it, Alice," Gloria said in a low tone that somehow held urgency. "Do not let the chance for happiness pass you by. You will regret it, and living with regret is worse than all the failed fetes and harvest banquets in the world."

Which rather left Alice wondering if her information about Gloria's romantic prospects had been dead wrong.

CHAPTER 3

Though she had advised Alice to leave at once, Gloria was still thankful that her friend planned to stay until Friday, and see her through the reconvened board meeting. Accordingly, they dressed in their most fashionable yet businesslike clothes (with only a very little appliquéd lace on the jacket, in Gloria's case) and once again took their seats at the mahogany table in the boardroom of the Meriwether-Astor Munitions Works.

When Gloria had called the meeting to order and welcomed her cousin Hugh to his new position—why had someone not told him he was now entitled to sit in his brother's chair, instead of the one at the foot of the table he usually occupied?—she rose to her feet.

"Gentlemen, I will not waste your valuable time, since you have been so kind as to return today. I will simply call for a vote on the matter of the final shipment to the Royal Kingdom of Spain and the Californias. Those in favor of stopping the shipment and recompensing the Ambassador with interest, raise your hands."

She, Mr. Pitman, and Mr. Adams were the only ones to do so.

She stared at Hugh, who looked at his brother and then away. Doing her best to look as though her stomach was not rolling and pitching like a steamship about to go down in heavy seas, she said, "Am I to understand that this company supports the invasion of a peaceful territory by a neighboring nation?"

Carmichael cleared his throat. "We have nothing to do with the use to which our products are put, madam, whether by hunters in the woods of the Carolinas or nations on the western frontier. We simply sell them to customers who have the gold to pay for them, and there our responsibility ends."

"Even though we know our customers have hostile intentions?" Now nausea fought with disgust at these men—men who had no doubt been groomed to this way of thinking by her father. "Intentions that may be spread by greed even to our own doorstep?"

"Are you hinting that Spain may declare war on the Fifteen Colonies, Madam President?" Sydney actually sounded merry. Ooh, if she carried a cane, she would whack him for his impertinence.

"If one rules half a continent, why not take a run at the rest of it?" she snapped. "In any case, you are no longer a member of the board, and have no right to speak. Hugh, your proper place is here, to my right."

"On the contrary, coz," Sydney told her. "A little detail slipped your mind on Tuesday."

"Do not patronize me," she said through her teeth. "Family or not, I allow no one to take that tone with me."

"I do apologize," he said, not very apologetically. "But the fact remains that the board did not actually vote me out of this chair with a legal motion when last we met. As a result, the final payment has been made, and the shipment and the Ambassador left Philadelphia on Wednesday on the specially commissioned train built for the late Viceroy."

The breath went out of Gloria's lungs, and her knees failed her. She sat rather abruptly in the upholstered chair at the head of the table. "I beg your pardon?" she whispered.

He looked so pleased that one would think his next move would be to tip her out of this chair and take it once and for all. "In the absence of a motion to remove, I am still a serving member of this board, and as the nephew of the founder of the company, I had sufficient authority to accept the payment that His Excellency the Ambassador was so anxious to make, and to release the machinery from our warehouses."

"How dared you?" She could barely take enough breath to speak. "You knew my intentions."

"It was the only honorable thing to do, despite the *intentions* of our esteemed but inexperienced president." He bowed in her direction and directed his subsequent remarks to the gentlemen around the table. "The deal having been struck months ago by my uncle, I saw no reason to delay further."

"Well done, Sydney!"

"This is an outrage!"

"Sydney Meriwether-Astor for president!"

"Are you people completely mad?"

Gloria heard Alice's exclamation as though she were under water. She must not faint. She must regain control of herself immediately. Only then could she regain control of the situation—and the company.

Carmichael leaped to his feet. "I move for a vote of nonconfidence in the president. It is clear that there is only one member of the family who steps up to do the right thing, and is therefore fit for the job."

"You just voted her in three days ago, you nincompoop," Mr. Pitman snapped.

"I didn't," Carmichael pointed out with some heat. "I was outvoted."

"By no means—"

"I say again, this is an outrage!"

"Shut up, Adams, you know perfectly well that—"

"Silence!" Gloria shouted, and seven astonished faces turned toward her. She threw the gavel across the room, where it bounced off the wainscoting. "Sit down!"

All but Sydney did. He remained standing, a challenge as strident as if he had spoken aloud—or flung a pair of gloves at her feet.

Gloria leaned into the speaking tube affixed to the wall at her right shoulder. "Miss Ashlock, send our security officers to the boardroom immediately to remove Mr. Sydney Meriwether-Astor."

"Yes, ma'am."

She looked him in the eye, and his satisfied smile lost a few degrees of tilt. "I move once and for all that you be removed from your position—and from these premises. You are never to set foot in these buildings again. If you do, you will be charged with trespassing, if you are not shot on sight."

Four hands wavered upward. Mr. Pitman inhaled sharply, then collected himself enough to record it.

"Gloria, please," Hugh said, clearly trying to smooth troubled waters. "While I disagree philosophically with my brother, you were outvoted a minute ago because economically, we had no other choice. It's business. The shipment would have gone ahead in any case."

"But it would have had the approval of the board, not the cavalier actions of an offended child who knows no one is listening to him."

A rap came at the door, and the security officers came in. "Come with us now, Mr. Sydney," one of them said. "No fuss."

"I move that Sydney be made president, and this crackpot of a girl be sent off to an asylum to mend her soft head," Carmichael blustered. "All in favor?"

This time only two hands went up. The other four members shook their heads, until finally Adams said, "The security men can take you too, Carmichael, as far as I'm concerned. I've never seen such a display of hooliganism in all my life."

"Mr. Sydney? Come along, now." The security men laid their hands on his arms, and when he went to shrug them off in irritation—did he think there was going to be another vote upon the subject?—they only clamped down harder. "Off we go."

"You'll see I'm right, Gloria," Sydney called as he was half-dragged, half-escorted down the corridor. Doors opened as clerks and secretaries stared in astonishment. "I did the right thing, and when you apply your feathery female mind to it, you will have no choice but to agree."

Perhaps he had obeyed the letter of the contract, while flouting the standards of respect, familial duty, and company unity in every other way. Gloria waited until the sounds of his departure faded, and a door closed with a *bang* of finality at the end of the hall. "If there is no other business, I move that the meeting be adjourned."

No one argued.

No one stayed. Not even Alice.

Gloria sat in the lonely chair at the head of the empty table and considered the wreckage of her first week at the helm of her father's company.

And of all her high hopes for it.

AN HOUR LATER, unable to find Gloria in the enormous corner office with its displays of modern and antique weaponry—she hoped redecoration efforts would soon commence—Alice poked her head into the boardroom.

To her surprise, Gloria still sat at the head of the table, having clearly not moved so much as a ruffle since her directors had decamped. Her face was pale, and her gaze seemed fixed upon a view far away, as though mind and body occupied two different worlds. Perhaps they did. Perhaps her mind had taken refuge in a world where men did not encourage others to war, or to arm them when they succeeded.

Alice closed the door, turned the key in the lock, and sat in the chair recently vacated by that nice Mr. Pitman. "Gloria."

She said the name two more times before the vacant stare returned to the room, and the other girl looked at Alice in some surprise. "Are you all right?"

Gloria's mouth trembled for a moment, before she brought her emotions under control. "Physically, yes. But my heart feels as though it has been trampled by a herd of runaway mechanical horses and left for dead."

"That pretty much sums up the board meeting, I'd say."

"Oh, Alice," she sighed, pressing both hands to her face. "What am I going to do?"

"I don't see that there is anything you can do, legitimately, except to close this chapter of the company's history and do better with the next one."

"In other words, give up?"

"I said, *legitimately*." Gloria's gaze sharpened upon hers, and Alice couldn't help a smile. "Did you even notice that I was gone?"

"I assumed your disgust had taken you outside, to prepare *Swan* for lift and a return to a life that must be many times more rewarding than mine is at the moment."

"You're almost right. I found Evan Douglas downstairs, waiting to see if you wished to be escorted home, and sent him to Washington Avenue with orders to my crew to be ready to lift."

Gloria seemed to sag, and she gripped one arm of her chair as though it would hold her up. "You mean to go home, then. I do not blame you. In fact, I believe I told you to do so myself, the other day. But—oh, Alice—I cannot bear it. To lose my cousins—my company—my integrity—and now, my friends—" This time she could not control her emotion, and tears overflowed to trickle down the porcelain-pale cheeks.

Alice laid a hand upon Gloria's sleeve and squeezed gently. "You have not lost the last two, and you're well rid of the first, in my opinion, though I'm surprised at Hugh. He seemed a decent sort. Let me ask you something—can you get away from here?"

Gloria squeezed back, and then with both hands scrubbed the tears off her cheeks. "Get away? From the company, or from Philadelphia? What do you mean? Are you suggesting I go to England with you?"

"No. I'm suggesting that since we cannot stop that shipment of mechanical menaces by fair means, we employ foul."

Gloria's wet gaze held doubt. "I have had enough foul means this week to satisfy me for some time. Possibly for the rest of my life."

"All right. I can do it myself, if you would rather not take the risk."

"Do what? Alice, what are you up to?"

"That train is two days ahead of us—nearly three. But *Swan* is ten times faster than a train. We may not have been able to stop its departure, but we can certainly prevent its arrival."

Gloria stared at her. "How on earth do you propose to do that? Are you trying to start a war in spite of me?"

Alice shook her head impatiently, and a lock of hair fell out of its neat roll. A hairpin pinged off the table and was lost forever in the thick Aubusson rug.

"We are not going to stop it. But we might be able to find someone who will. Someone armed with the ability and the greed to equal those of anyone in Sydney's camp. Someone in the Texican Territory, close to the route the train has to take to get to the Californias. Someone with considerable experience in, er, the removal and redistribution of cargo."

Now her companion looked as though she might call the security guards a second time. "Are you suggesting we employ a *train robber?*"

The solution had come to her in a blinding flash the moment the report of the train's departure had left Sydney's lips, and Alice had barely been able to contain her impatience for the board meeting to be adjourned before she'd fled the room in search of Evan Douglas.

"How on earth would you know such a person?" Gloria demanded.

But Alice noticed that she did not condemn the scheme. She merely doubted the method.

She couldn't restrain her grin now, though she did resist the urge to clap her hands in delight. "Gloria, do you remember me telling you about my stepfather, Ned Mose?"

CHAPTER 4

Dearest Ian,

We reached the Fifteen Colonies safely, having made the airship flight across the Atlantic in two days and 14 hours. Considering this is January and we dodged four storms, I am pretty proud of the way Swan acquitted herself.

I wish I could say all is well. That rascal Sydney Meriwether-Astor has gone behind his cousin Gloria's back and released the final shipment of arms and mechanicals to the Californio Ambassador, whom Gloria suspects is the strong arm behind a threat of war that might have died with the old prince. Sydney said she was contractually bound to complete the deal. While that may be true, she says she is morally bound to stop the war.

So, we are casting off immediately for Resolution to arrange a train robbery. While my last sight of Ned Mose (who despite his relationship with my mother is not your future father-in-law) involved his shooting at me, I believe the prospect of the cargo will induce him to forgive me and assist me in the endeavor.

Do not worry. I will be gone only a few days, and then return to England to plan our wedding with a glad heart.

Your loving

Alice

~

Evan Douglas was used to being disregarded, derided, and occasionally mistaken for a servant, despite the fact that he was one of the foremost scientists in the land in the fledgling field of mnemography, the study of dreams and the processes of the mind. Since escaping the sheer hell of school and finding university a little quieter, though just as lonely, he had graduated with honors and found a measure of comfort in using a small inheritance to open a private laboratory in Exeter. There, he had been quite content to spend his days in research experiments, writing papers, and occasionally accepting a post with a wealthy patron who required his particular expertise.

Life had been peaceful, if one counted the absence of mocking and unkindness as peace, and he discounted loneliness as merely the price one paid for independence.

Until the day his cousins Elizabeth Seacombe and Maggie Polgarth had exploded into his life, and his plans, his direction, and his innermost convictions about himself had irrevocably changed.

He had been some months at the home of Charles Seacombe, who had later been unmasked as the republican traitor Charles de Maupassant, attempted murderer of the Prince of Wales and his younger brother. But before this discovery, Evan had met the girls, whom the entire family believed to be dead, through his patron, whom he had come to respect and even trust. Evan's grandmother and theirs had been sisters, which made them his second cousins ... or was it cousins once removed? He could never remember which. The important part was that the days of their first acquaintance had been stained forever by his blind faith in his employer.

Even now, Evan woke sweating and gasping from nightmares about how close he had come to being the instrument of Lizzie's death. His study of dreams did not need to tell him that his mind still staggered under the horror of it—remembering again and again the moment when he had held up the syringe full of chemicals intended to render Lizzie's body in temporary paralysis, to aid in the recording of her dreams by the mnemosomniograph. De Maupassant had funded the invention of Evan's greatest triumph—his only intention being to use it to discover how much his daughter remembered of his murder of her mother.

Once de Maupassant had his answer, he had attempted to murder her and her cousin, his intent to silence forever the only witnesses to his crimes.

Evan stood at the viewing port in the main saloon of *Swan*, the ship on which he had practically commandeered passage, wondering how in heaven's name he was to live with himself now. Rationally, he understood that one could not live in a state of permanent penance. On the other hand, existing in the hell of the mind in which he had been trapped was unbearable. Deprived of rest, unable to concentrate, he could no longer work with any efficacy, and the rent for his laboratory could not be paid with dreams—only the scientific exploration of them.

His only recourse was to make such an enormous change

in his life that he would not be able to slip back into his previous modes of thought. His mind, shaken permanently out of the slough of despond into which it had fallen, would seize upon new vistas, new experiences, and bring him back to equilibrium again.

An excellent plan, by any estimation. He had not thought it would include the robbing of trains, however.

Gloria Meriwether-Astor rustled into the saloon, the sound of her silk skirts like a finger drawn down the back of his neck. In her presence, he never knew what to do with himself. His feet seemed to grow twice their size and trip him up. His hands, instead of behaving, couldn't decide whether to hang by his sides, plunge into his pockets, or do something sensible, like hold a book. And as for his eyes ... well, she was so beautiful that he still had not plucked up the courage to admire her openly. Instead, he stole glimpses the way little boys stole apples from a forbidden tree—snatching one and running off to treasure it, turning it this way and that before tucking it into memory.

"Have you any fear of heights, Mr. Douglas?" she inquired cheerfully, standing beside him and turning his knees to rubber.

"N-no," he managed. "But I have not had much opportunity to discover whether I have or not. This is my first flight in an airship."

"Truly?" Her brows, fine as the feelers of a butterfly, rose over eyes so blue that whether he fell into their depths or fell into the sky outside, the result could only be the same. "Well, you could not have chosen a better vessel for it, or a better captain. I would trust Alice with my life. Have done, in fact."

"In Venice."

"You are familiar with the circumstances?"

We are having a conversation, some distant voice marveled in his mind. *It is nothing short of a miracle.*

"Mr. Douglas?"

Hastily, he brought his concentration back, and was rocked once again by her scent—lilies and clean cotton—and the glimmer of light upon her golden hair.

"Yes, I am. My cousins have regaled me with the story. If you will permit me to say so, you were enormously brave—commandeering that undersea dirigible and then being kidnapped and held hostage for your pains."

She waved a slender hand as though to disclaim any credit for her part in the adventure, and with a superhuman effort of will, Evan restrained himself from seizing it and kissing it. If he did such a thing, she would either run from the room, or turn upon him that look of disdain that was so often his portion when dealing with young ladies who were not related to him. He did not think he could bear either result.

"For nearly getting Claire and Andrew—to say nothing of Jake and Captain Hollys—killed, you mean. There was no bravery there, I am afraid. Oh, speaking of Jake, he bids me to inform you that we have crossed the eastern borders of the Texican Territory, and will be approaching Resolution within the hour. We may expect to be accosted by sky pirates at any time."

She said it in the same tone in which Lizzie might have said they were expecting orange chiffon cake for tea.

"You are not afraid?"

"Of pirates? Goodness me, at least they are honest about it. It is the kind that hide themselves behind brocade waistcoats, multi-faced pocket watches, and lunches in expensive hotels that I cannot stand."

Evan had a moment to thank his lucky stars that his waistcoat was a rather uninteresting brown herringbone, and held an even plainer single-faced watch that had belonged to his father.

"And you do not mind the pirates taking possession of these mechanicals?" he persisted. "It seems to me that you might want them back, your factories having gone to some effort to make them."

"Alice asked the same question when we talked it over," she said cheerfully. "But really, what does one do with mechanical horses? Pull a landau down the street? No, I do not want them, and if the possession of them convinces this pirate to help us, then he is welcome to them."

"Alice does not really believe the pirates will attack, does she?" he asked. "For I must tell you that I have next to no experience with firearms."

"Oh, that part is easy. With the lightning pistols, one simply thumbs the switch forward, allows the charge to build, and pulls the trigger. Though I would beg you not to fire in the direction of the fuselage unless there is a body in the way to absorb the bolt. I would not want to put holes in *Swan*, after all the effort Alice has devoted to her restoration."

"I will endeavor not to do so, Miss Meriwether-Astor."

"Goodness." She actually smiled at him, dazzling him with such a close sight of the dimple that pressed into her cheek. "If we are to be attacked by Texican outlaws, you must call me Gloria."

He grew dizzy at the enormity of such a privilege. "Then

you must call me Evan. I must say, it will save time if we are to communicate during a firefight."

To his astonishment, she laughed as though he had made a joke, though he had meant it seriously. "You are quite right, Evan. I do like a man of sense. Come. Let us go raid the sideboard. Our friend Lady Claire herself would agree that a person ought not to face a firefight on an empty stomach."

He followed her into the dining saloon, hoping he would not faint, for he had quite forgotten how to breathe.

By common consent, once *Swan*'s captain and crew had eaten the beef pies, carrots, and potatoes with which Mrs. Polk had made sure to stock the galley, everyone gathered in the navigation gondola to watch for the first signs of attack.

"We don't want to kill anyone, mind," Alice reminded them. "I've sent a pigeon to Ned telling him that I'm coming, but it's not likely that will net us much of a welcoming committee."

"If someone shoots at me, he'll get as good as he gives," Jake said grimly.

"But from what you've told us," Evan put in with some diffidence, having no expertise along these lines at all, "*Swan* will greatly outmaneuver any ship they can muster. Since they are made from wreckage and scrap, I gather."

"Don't let that fool you." Alice's gaze did not leave the skies outside the viewing ports, and neither did those of her crew. Evan found such focus a little alarming. "While I'm a pretty good inventor, Ned taught me a trick or two. You might find that the rustiest bucket of bolts hides the biggest gun, or that the one with the patched-up fuselage is the fastest." She paused to ascertain that an eagle balancing in the air currents was not in fact a distant ship. "One thing I know for sure is that *Swan* is probably the prettiest prize they'll have seen since I left. She'll be enough to make Ned lift, even if he had to do it without gasbags."

Evan was about to correct her—a ship could not lift without gasbags—when he realized just in time that she was using exaggerated language. He had been cut adrift from conversational circles for so long that it was taking him some effort to catch up, and he often found himself deciphering the more decorative phrases of English as though he were parsing chemical formulas or a cipher.

Jake had not taken his gaze from the eagle. "Captain," he said, "that bird is not behaving properly."

Alice snapped out a brass telescope. "Your eyes are sharper than mine, but this is better than both of us." After a moment, she located the bird. "Right you are. It seems to be a kind of pigeon, but instead of a container for a belly, it's got great big lenses for eyes. I suspect we're being watched. Mr. Stringfellow, are you armed?"

"Aye, Captain." The boy pulled away his coat to reveal two lightning pistols in his belt, as well as a knife. Around his neck hung a leather thong with an iron ball affixed to each end.

In comparison, Evan felt as naked and vulnerable as a baby bird.

"Arm our guests, if you please," Alice ordered. "I have a feeling it won't be long now."

Minutes later, Evan and Gloria were in possession of a lightning pistol each, and a short knife whose sheath affixed to the inside of the boot.

"I do wish we'd had a little more time," Gloria fretted. "This dress is most unsuitable for a fight, and I have to wear my knife on the outside of my boot." She lifted her skirts to peer at her feet, and Evan swallowed and looked away. "These kidskin ones are more fashion than function, though at the time they seemed terribly practical."

"If it comes to a fight, I won't have done my job," Alice told her. "But still, here's a thought ... any chance you learned archery in school?"

"I did, in fact," Gloria told her. "The headmistress at St. Cecilia's was a strong believer in out-of-doors pursuits. But arrows in the fuselage...?"

"How were your scores?"

"Ninety percent in the inner circle," Gloria said proudly.

"Then we don't have to worry about the fuselage, do we?" Alice grinned at her. "Mr. Stringfellow, hunt up that ancient crossbow in the crew's arms locker, will you? It's old and out of date, but we must use the gifts we're given. Evan, what about you? Any skills we might use?"

He was still recovering first from the sight of Gloria's trim ankles, covered in kidskin though they were, and second from the idea that his idol was to be armed instead of remaining safely in her cabin like a sensible woman.

"I—I—none," he finally got out. "Though I did repair a mother's helper with the parts from a pigeon once."

"That's a start." Alice's eyes gleamed. "I can sacrifice a pigeon if you can take the parts and update that bow. Have you ever seen an articulated crossbow?"

"Once. At Colliford Castle there were a number affixed to the wall of the study as conversation pieces—and, I suspect, to intimidate tenants late with their rent."

"You might have thirty minutes. Do you think you can do it well enough to give Gloria a better chance at defending herself?"

She could not have phrased her request better. He straightened his shoulders. "I do. Lead the way, Mr. Stringfellow."

Twenty-eight and one-half minutes later, he presented the articulated crossbow to Gloria. She took it, sliding her hand into the brass arm bracer, her finger settling naturally on the trigger he had liberated from an ancient flintlock pistol in the cabinet.

"I was not able to test its accuracy," he said a little anxiously, "but I shall be close at hand to make adjustments to the cogs and gears once you loose the first bolt."

Gloria's eyes danced. "I shall look forward to the sight of you with a screwdriver in one hand and a pistol in the other. It will be most exhilarating."

Exaggerated language. It must be, for her to look forward to the sight of him doing anything at all. But still, warmth cascaded through him at the thought of doing something for her that no one else—with the possible exception of Alice, who was an exceedingly talented individual—could do.

"Canvas, ho!" Jake called from the window. "We have company, Captain."

"They are nothing if not predictable. Stations, everyone. Mr. McTavish, our position, if you please?"

"Five miles directly east of Resolution, at the toe of the mesa where *Lady Lucy* was moored," he said promptly.

Jake, Evan had observed, was endowed with extraordinary gifts as well. Over a game of cowboy poker on the first night of the flight, he had told Evan what it was like. "I see the navigation chart in my head," he explained, laying down an eight of diamonds, "and lay it over the land forms below in my imagination. The two become one in my mind, so that the land becomes a map. I don't forget how it lies, once I've been to a place. And Resolution is a place I'll remember for the rest of my life."

When Evan had asked him privately, later, what he'd meant by that last remark, he'd learned a thing or two about Ned Mose. "Flung me out of the hatch at three hundred feet, he did," Jake said grimly. "I deserved to be keelhauled for betraying the Lady and the Dunsmuirs to him and his miscreants, but not killed outright. Lucky for me the season was early and the lake hadn't dried up yet."

Now Alice said, "Since it's not yet noon, they won't attempt a wreck. They'll be looking to harry us down by getting on top of us, so I'm going to do my level best to keep that from happening. All of which means, it would be best if we all wore lines. Things could get a little bumpy."

As it turned out, Mr. Stringfellow, Jake, and Alice weren't wearing belts at all, but leather corselets to which both weapons and a safety line could be attached.

"Are you expecting us to fall out of the hatch, Alice?" Gloria asked as Alice fitted the corselet around her waist.

"It could happen, but mostly I'm concerned about sudden changes in altitude, and maybe some tilt if I take her into a good steep turn," Alice said with far more cheer than Evan felt such a prospect warranted. "*Swan* came equipped with lines, so I figure they're here for a good reason, even if I haven't had the opportunity to test them yet."

"A quarter mile and closing, Captain," Jake said. "They appear to be running out a gun."

Alice snapped the telescope to her eye once more, and nodded. "How very rude," she remarked. "Haven't seen that ship before, but no matter. If they haven't the manners to return a pigeon or even give me a flag, I can only assume the worst, can't I?"

"A flag?" Evan said, buckling his own corselet with fingers that had gone cold.

"Signal flags," Jake explained succinctly. "Certain colors mean certain things—white for peaceful intent, red for emergency or man down, purple for diplomatic personnel aboard, blue for the law."

"It is illogical to signal one's intent to attack," Evan pointed out.

"But they are," Jake told him. "They're flying a black flag."

"What does that mean?"

"A number of things," Alice answered. "It could mean a ship is bearing a body back to the family, or there is plague aboard. But in these skies it means your family will be wearing that color in short order."

Through the viewing port, Evan saw the oncoming airship emit a huge puff of steam, as though it had thrown some engine into action. Alice threw the wheel over at the same time as Jake called, "Vanes vertical!"

Swan, with her automaton intelligence system co-invented by Alice and Lady Claire, rolled lazily and something heavy howled past the keel of the gondola mere yards beneath their feet.

Gloria swore so creatively that Jake took his attention from the ports for a moment of sheer admiration. "Was that a cannonball?" she demanded.

"They must have wrecked a ship carrying antiques for a museum," Alice remarked. "I guess Ned hasn't forgiven me for letting Claire slip out of his grip five years ago. I bet I won't be getting a nice sasparilla and a handshake when we land, either."

The other ship appeared to be taking a moment to rethink its strategy.

"Orders, Captain?" Jake asked.

"I suppose we'll have to return fire," she said reluctantly. "I was hoping they'd just chase us for a while."

"Alice, there's another ship—there, off the—oh, bother, what's it called?" Gloria's nose was pressed to the isinglass.

"The starboard side, miss," Benny Stringfellow said helpfully. "Three of the clock, Captain, hauling around to broadside."

"Those cheating scoundrels," Alice said, apparently not much bothered. "I'm getting tired of this shabby treatment. We shall bob for apples, Mr. McTavish, when they line up."

To Evan's dismay, through the viewing ports he could see the ships take up positions on either side of *Swan*, a thousand feet off her fuselage. Metal glinted in the sun as even he could see guns being brought to bear.

"Vanes vertical in five—four—three—two—one!"

The deck dropped out from under Evan's boots and he found himself ten feet in the air in less time than it took to think about it. Gloria shrieked and collided violently with him, whereupon he clasped her around the waist to prevent her from hitting a bulkhead.

Swan dropped like a stone and in her wake, the volleys of missiles the two pirate airships had loosed arced toward one another, the sounds of the blasts deafening in the thin air.

"Bloody fools," Alice said, hanging on to the helm with both arms while her feet slowly settled back to the deck. "Who uses cannon in this day and age?"

Evan rapidly calculated the angle of their dive and predicted the effects of returning gravity with such accuracy that Gloria's knees only got a little bit bumped as they landed on the deck. Gently, he released her and untangled their lines.

"Thank you, Evan," she said breathlessly. "That was—quite unexpected."

He was not sure if she meant the dive, or his attempt to assist her. In any case, her thanks were more precious to him than any treasure, and his face glowed red with gratification.

"We're not out of the clouds yet," Alice warned them. "I won't be able to get away with that a second time."

"No, since we are now a quarter mile from the surface of the mesa," Jake agreed. "Vanes thirty degrees, please, and engines, slow to five knots, ready for landing."

The throaty hum of the great Daimler engines in the rear of the gondola obediently changed their pitch. Evan had not realized that one could automate an engine to the point where it responded to vocal commands, and his admiration for Alice's skill went up another few degrees.

"Look, that one is going down," Benny said, pointing to one of their attackers.

It dove toward the desert floor with all the grace of an injured pelican, wallowing and jerking and sending a plume of black smoke spiraling up to smudge the sky.

But where had the second ship had got to?

Alice evidently wondered the same thing. "Mr. Stringfellow, I want a report on the whereabouts of our other friends."

He scampered up into the catwalks in the fuselage, and ten minutes later returned, his eager young face reddened with the wind. "It's backed off, Captain, and seems to have lost one of its engines. It's lame, but we haven't shook it, following five hundred yards to the stern, where it thinks we can't see it."

"As long as it has no guns in its bow, it can stay there."

"No sign of ports, but that doesn't mean anything." His voice held disdain. "Pirates."

"My old ship had projectile tubes in its fuselage," Alice said. "I wouldn't put anything past Ned Mose. He's got a bottomless bag of tricks."

The words were no sooner out of her mouth than Evan heard the howl of a projectile. This time, they hadn't been able to see the warning puff of steam, and there was no time to react. With a sound partway between an explosion and a ringing clang, something large, heavy, and deadly struck the gondola in the stern, and the impact knocked Evan clear off his feet.

CHAPTER 5

"My engines!" Alice shrieked. "Vanes vertical—take her up!"

She dashed into the stern, fighting down panic as the frigid cold of high altitude swirled along the corridor and told her they'd been breached. The pressure under her boots assured her that the automatons had obeyed her command—making her doubly thankful that the central intelligence was housed just below the helm, where it was most difficult to hit, and not in the stern where the engines were.

Of course, if something had happened to her beloved Daimlers, no amount of commanding anything was going to help.

She burst into the engine room and saw at once what had happened. Her knees practically buckled in relief and gratitude for the engineer who had reinforced the gondola with iron plates—for there, within a hand's breadth of the starboard propeller, the wall had been stove in. It still held the rounded shape of a foot-wide ball, and the plate had warped away from its rivets—hence the frigid wind blowing in.

"Are the engines all right?" Evan ran into the room, his stride a little uneven as he favored his left leg.

"They're unharmed. We took a shot, but it seems to have mostly bounced off us. Are you all right?"

"Perfectly all right. I landed awkwardly when it hit, that is all. How may I assist?"

"Help me wedge this canvas into that crack in the plating, or we'll all be wishing we had Esquimaux coats before long."

"Will they fire again?" Evan wrestled with the heavy canvas, but he was no schoolboy noodle, all brains and no brawn. For a scientist, he was surprisingly strong, and Alice found the task done much more efficiently and neatly than if she had been alone.

"They will if they can, but it seems my navigator is using evasive tactics to prevent it. Come. I need to take the helm and show that lot how to mind their manners."

No other projectiles had been fired, which told Alice that either they only had the one, or that Jake had outmaneuvered them. And when she gained the navigation room once again, she realized immediately what he'd done.

With a delighted chuckle, she clapped him on the back. "If we were dancing, we would call this the *dos-à-dos*. Well done, Mr. McTavish."

For Jake had taken *Swan* straight up, waited for the enemy ship to pass helplessly below, and then come down upon her stern, where she presented as fat and lumbering a target as any onetime pirate could wish.

"You may fire at will, Mr. Stringfellow," she said pleasantly to Benny.

"Me, Captain?" the boy squeaked, his face turning red in case she was funning with him.

She was not. Their target would make a perfect first lesson for a young gunner. "Yes, you. Into the gunner's pod, if you please, and make it count. Don't forget your lessons in the mathematics of trajectory and arc."

"Yes, Captain!"

He was so elated his feet barely touched the rungs of the ladder as he dropped into the pod below. In a moment, the hum of the Daimlers was joined by a tenor contrapunto. Alice could practically feel in her bones the moment the grand lightning rifle she had built reached its firing charge and the hum took on a businesslike tone, as if to say, *I'm ready, mate—get on with it.*

A bolt of white energy sizzled across the air between the ships. The tub ahead of them was doing its best to pull away, and not maintaining a steady altitude. It dipped and bobbed, but sadly, whoever was at the helm did not realize he had fallen into a pattern.

The bolt caught them on the low end of a dip, passing harmlessly through the fuselage and part of a gas bag. The fuselage folded in on the injured portion, flapping mightily in the wind, but it wasn't enough to bring them down.

"Try again, Mr. Stringfellow," Alice murmured. "Don't be dismayed."

A second bolt arced across the space—too high again—but no! The ship came out of its dip and attempted a bob, just in time to meet the bolt square on the stern. Benny followed it up immediately with a third salvo, and wriggling feelers of energy crawled up the gondola from the stern, sparking and sizzling everything they touched in a web of blue-white light that was as deadly as it was beautiful.

Gloria cheered.

"Merciful heavens," Evan breathed. "I have never seen its like."

"You may thank Dr. Rosemary Craig," Alice said with satisfaction. "She bequeathed the knowledge of how to build the energy cells to Claire, who shared it with me." Something in his face—the awe, the appreciation—made her say impulsively, "I would be happy to share it with you, too, if we ever get a moment of leisure."

In his gaze, Alice saw that somehow she had passed the mighty portals of scientific acceptance, and become not merely a peer, but someone whom Evan Douglas respected.

"I would consider it a great honor." And he actually bent his neck in a bow.

"Captain, you can have the tea party later," Jake said tersely from his controls. "They're going down. Do we follow?"

"The vanes can be operated manually, so they have some steering. Once they run aground, I expect they can take care of themselves. We'll proceed to Resolution. I'm willing to bet my stepfather is still so tight-fisted that he won't waste another ship on us."

When Benny shut down the rifle and emerged from the gunner's pod, she breached the protocols of rank just long enough to give him a hard hug.

"Well done, sir. You're a credit to your ship."

"Thank you, Captain," he mumbled, blushing scarlet. "I remembered what you told me about the trajectory, but that vessel were bobbing about like a duck in a bath. It were a bit tricky."

She held him away from her with both hands on his shoulders. "Do you know what today is, Mr. Stringfellow?"

"Monday, the twentieth of January, 1895, Captain."

Alice fought down a smile and kept her face sober. "Remember that date, for it is the date we will tell the Admiralty that Benjamin Stringfellow, midshipman, was promoted to the rank of gunner, second class."

Benny gasped. "Captain, you don't mean it!"

"I do," she said stoutly. "Congratulations, Benny. Well done."

She took the helm while Jake and the others added their congratulations, and finally allowed herself a smile. Despite the smell of cordite and burned air, and the repairs that would have to be made, they had managed their approach respectably well.

For below were the red cliffs, dusky green pines, and treacherous sands of her godforsaken childhood. As the disabled pirate ship fell ahead of them, in the initial stages of a long, slow descent and a soft landing, she could see the shabby wood-and-stone shacks of Resolution, there in the middle of the flood plain.

The place she'd left under fire while stealing an airship, the guns in the hands of the man she had once called her pa.

ONCE JAKE HAD TRIANGULATED the approximate landfalls of each of their disabled attackers, Alice could choose her own landing site.

"We'll moor there, on that basalt outcropping on the northwest side," she said, pointing it out. "Close enough to get back to the ship if we're chased out of town, and far enough away that anyone thinking to harvest my engines is going to be painfully visible before he gets near them."

Jake took a moment to mark the landing site on the navigator's map, and then they brought her gently down. Benny and Evan jumped out to secure the mooring ropes on the rocks.

When Jake's repeated glances clearly indicated he wondered why she was not going astern to bank the boilers, but remained at the viewing ports watching the town a quarter mile off, Alice relented.

"I don't want the boilers going cold," she said, though he had not been so bold as to question her. "And I want a watch posted around the clock while we're here. I know Ned Mose and the men in this town well enough to predict that even if he welcomes me with open arms—er, arm—that won't stop the more enterprising from taking their chances."

"I'll stay," Jake said briefly. "I've got no wish to be anywhere near that place. I'll keep Benny here with me and we'll start on repairs to the hull."

"We seem to be rather high off this rock pile," Gloria observed from her post at the other viewing port. "We shall have to use a rope ladder to get down, will we not?"

"Clever boys," Alice said with some satisfaction. "The gunner's pod will be high enough that Benny can maneuver the barrel to greet any unexpected company."

Evan climbed back through the gangway, closely followed by the young gunner.

"Well done, you two," Alice said. "Good thinking—though I hope it doesn't come to a full-on assault. Old repeating rifles for one or two men are more likely."

Jake briefly gave Benny his orders, and Evan looked from him to Alice as though expecting his as well. "Shall I stay too?" he asked. "And Miss Meriwether-Astor certainly must."

"She certainly must not," that young lady said with some spirit. "Someone has to go with Alice."

"Someone who isn't worth a fortune and is easy to catch and hold for ransom," Alice told her with no little regret. "I'm afraid I must beg you to stay with the ship, Gloria. If they find out about you, they'll lose interest in capturing *Swan*. With the ransom they'd get, they could buy half Count von Zeppelin's fleet—and then you'd have nothing but a bankrupt company to run when you got home."

"I may have that anyway. I want to come with you—and of course I wouldn't tell them who I am. I shall use the sobriquet that I used before, and be Miss Meredith Aster."

"We'll have to tell them about the shipment in order to bribe them into doing this, and your real name's bound to come up. If you respond by accident, it could tip them off. Better for all of us that you stay at a distance."

Gloria was clearly not used to anyone arguing with her, but the thought of her being captured and at Ned Mose's mercy made Alice feel ill.

"Please, dear," she said softly. "I admire you for your courage, and for your desire to beard the lion with me. But we have come too far to risk everything on a misstep now."

"I wish Captain Hollys were here to go with you," Jake said.

"You're not the only one." Alice had wished it many a time since they'd pulled up ropes in London, but never more so than now. "But he isn't, so we must do what we can on our own."

"I am not the captain," Evan Douglas said humbly, "but nor do I have any value that would put anyone in danger. If you will have me, Captain Chalmers, I will do what I can to help you accomplish your purpose and return to the ship unharmed."

She had known since they'd crossed the Atlantic that it would have to be this way. Jake was the obvious first choice, but she needed him to make the repairs and keep the ship ready to lift at a moment's notice—a task that would be beyond Benny working alone. Taking Gloria into that nest of cranky vipers and cutthroats was out of the question. Which, no matter how you sliced it, left only Evan.

So she gave the awkward, lanky scientist a companionable smile. "I will have you, and gladly, Mr. Douglas. Come. Let us arm ourselves to the teeth. It's too much to hope that all we'll get is an invitation to tea."

CHAPTER 6

Alice knew from experience that when Ned was in a temper, the best way to get through to him was via her mother.

So, feeling a little like a walking armory with two lightning pistols tucked into the waistband of her pants, a set of strangulating irons such as Benny wore draped around his neck in each outer pocket of her flight jacket, and her trusty revolver in its special pocket inside, she walked the dusty track that the river had carved out of the hardpan to the house on the edge of town that the desert flowers called home.

"Alice!" Bonita Suarez exclaimed in astonishment when Alice and Evan walked into the sitting room, where at this time of day the girls were lounging on the sofas, chattering and brushing their hair before the sun went down and business opened for the evening. "We never thought to see you again—we thought you were dead."

"Not me." Alice hugged her, catching the girl's hand before —out of habit—it slipped into her pocket. She gave it a squeeze to show there were no hard feelings. "I always turn up, like a bad penny."

"No such thing." A blond woman nearly her mother's age smiled from the sofa, but didn't get up. "How are you, honey? And who's this handsome man? You looking for a tumble on the house?"

Poor Evan blushed six shades of red before Alice took pity on him. "Don't mind them. They've got no reason to use fancy language to hide the truth, unlike some."

The blond, Lorraine, raised her painted brows. "Ooh. Is this your man, Alice? What's his name?"

"No, ma'am, it's not. Evan Douglas is a friend of mine, and I'd take it kindly if you considered him a friend of yours, too."

"I can be plenty friendly." Bonita caressed his sleeve and batted her lashes. "Friends get a discount."

"No, thank you, miss." Evan hardly knew where to look. "We're here on business."

Lorraine laughed. "Everyone who comes in here is, darling." Then her faded gaze sharpened on Alice. "What is it, honey? If you're looking for your mama, I have to tell you she's not here."

Alice felt a clutch under her breastbone that she had not expected to feel. "Not here, as in over at Ned's place? Or not here, as in out under the mesa?" The town's burial plots lay on higher ground, up under the monolith of stone that formed its own marker.

"Oh, she's not dead and buried, honey—at least, she wasn't last we heard."

"She done eloped, Alice!" one of the other girls burst out.

"Hey, I was going to tell her." Lorraine frowned at the girl in a way that told Alice who was in charge of the Desert Rose now.

"Eloped! With whom?"

"With a man from up north."

"No," Alice said in tones of disbelief. "Not Mike Embry?"

"The very one," Lorraine told her, nodding. "Big man. Has his own saloon in the Northern Light. Came in a company airship and took Nellie away, as romantical as all get out."

"Just like in the flickers," Bonita sighed.

So her mother had given up being Ned Mose's wife and the madam of the house, and started over with a good man who would look after her.

"Well, fancy that," Alice said, smiling in spite of herself—though it was a little trembly. "He did me a good turn, you know, when I was up that way a few years ago. He was an old flame of hers, and when I could, I gave him her direction. I sort of hoped something like this might come of it." She paused. "How did Ned take it?"

Lorraine snorted. "How did the rest of Resolution take Ned taking it, you mean? He ain't over it yet. A more cranky, rage-ridden, howling wilderness of a man I never seen before. We've forbidden him to set foot in here, you know. What few ladies remain in this town need a place to go when he's out shooting up their flowerbeds, and we got enough arms in here to protect Santa Fe itself if need be."

Alice let out a long breath and glanced at Evan, who had not said a word but had taken in every one with wide eyes. "Well, there goes my plan."

"What, to come at him through the back door?" Lorraine's eyes held shrewdness. "Don't think I'm going to take your mama's place, girl. I think the world of you, but it's not worth the risk."

"I wouldn't ask that of any woman," Alice said with complete truth. "Looks like I'm going to have to beard him in his den myself. Does he still live in the same place?"

"Same place. More holes in the walls. Terrible mildew problem when the water gets in."

All the houses in Resolution had that problem, despite the dryness of the air, because of the flash floods. Alice shook away the thought. "I need to get a message to him, at least, to prepare the way. Can you help me with that?"

"For a silver coin."

Alice fished one out of the pocket that didn't have bullets in it. "Tell him I have a deal for him. I need him to rob a train."

Lorraine's mouth dropped open. "And here I thought your mama had raised a girl with some decency. Keep your money. I don't hold with criminal ways."

Criminal ways had been feeding everyone in Resolution since it had been founded fifty years ago, but Alice judged it best not to bring that up.

"Lorraine, girls, all of you listen," she pleaded. "This train is destined for the Royal Kingdom of Spain and the Californias. I need you to get the word out to everyone in town—and farther. If that train reaches the Californias, there are certain men who plan to use its cargo to invade the Texican Territory —to go to war on us. If Ned can stop it, he can keep as much of what's in those cars as he wants. It just can't get to its destination, or everyone in the territory may die."

Lorraine's face froze. "How do you know all this, girl?"

Alice had come up with a story on the way in. "I fly under contract now, and the outfit I'm flying for got double-crossed.

That shipment is stolen goods, so Ned stealing it himself will be its own kind of justice."

"Your outfit might disagree. Who's to say we won't have the Texican Rangers down on us for it?"

"The Rangers aren't going to solve a Fifteen Colonies problem. Besides, once they hear the word *war,* nothing else is going to matter." Alice knelt by the sofa and touched the woman's knee. She'd been her mother's closest friend—or as close as friends could be in a place like this, where the preferences of men were the coin the girls lived on. "Please, Lorraine. We don't have much time and there's a lot at stake. Will you help me, as much as you're able?"

She saw the moment when Lorraine made up her mind. "I don't hold with train robbery, but I hold even less with war. Give me that pen and paper, girl, and I'll send over a note. There might be some shooting, but with any luck, it'll be over by the time you get there."

Evan's eyes widened again, but to his credit, he kept mum. One of the girls took away the note, and in a few minutes they heard the sound of gunshots—a whole fusillade of them.

"I swear by all I hold holy, if he's killed Amarinda, I'll put a hole in him myself," Lorraine said grimly, straightening on the sofa and swinging her feet to the ground.

The shots faded, much the way the popping of corn slows down in the pan. Except for the odd report, there was a long silence. Footsteps ran up the path, and then Amarinda fell through the door.

"He's in a temper," she gasped, holding her side. "But I gave it to him."

"Are you shot?" Lorraine demanded, gazing in horror at the hand pressed to her corset.

"No. I've got a stitch. I ran all the way." She collapsed onto a fainting couch and one of the other girls poured her a tot of something out of the cabinet.

"Thank you, Lorraine, Amarinda." Alice led the way to the door. "I'm much obliged."

"You be safe, you hear?" Lorraine replied. "And if you ever see your ma, you tell her hello from me."

Alice hadn't seen her mother since the day she'd flown out of here, but she promised all the same.

It was a short walk down the street and through a barren field to Ned's house, but it seemed to take forever when you were expecting a bullet in your skull. It was the only building in town with three stories—the topmost of which he used to keep prisoners in. She wondered if he still did, after Lady Claire had escaped by jumping out a window into the raging waters of a providential flash flood. Alice had found her staggering around in the dark once she'd washed up on the bank downstream—and that moment had changed both their lives.

"Remind me to invent some kind of metal plating to wear inside one's clothes," Evan murmured into the dusty, cold silence. "Such a thing saved Maggie's life at Colliford Castle—I ought to look into it more seriously."

"It's not a bad idea," Alice agreed. "Too bad you didn't have it three days ago."

"Do you really think he'll shoot you?"

"Curiosity will force him to hear me out. After that? I don't know. Stay alert and keep eyes in the back of your head."

A gangly figure, five years older and heavier than the last time she'd seen him, guarded the door with a rifle slung casually over his shoulder.

"Why, Perry," she said pleasantly, as though they were meeting after church. "Are you still here?"

"Got any ideas where else I should be?" He sounded belligerent, and very different from the likeable, clumsy boy she'd had to feed every now and again when he got left behind.

"You're where you want to be, it's plain. Ned up for company?"

"Maybe. Maybe not. Leave your weapons with me."

He must have forgotten more than his manners if he thought she'd ever do that. "Who says I'm carrying any?"

"Alice, don't mess me around." For a moment, he sounded less belligerent and more like the frightened boy he'd once been, anxious for acceptance and willing to do nearly anything to attain it. "You know I can't let you in there armed."

"And you know I've always been armed in Ned's company," she said gently. "Neither of us is stupid."

"I can't."

"Then he'd best come out."

After Perry went in to convey this suggestion, Alice only had to wait a moment. With a roar, the windows blew out of the side of the house, scattering glass all over the road, and she was quite sure they could hear the shouting in Santa Fe. She braced herself, wrapping her fingers around the butt of a lightning pistol and thumbing it into life. Beside her, she heard a muffled hum as Evan did the same.

"Alice Chalmers!"

The door was kicked open, and when it bounced back into its frame, Ned Mose shot the hinges out of it. It toppled over flat, revealing the air pirate heaving with rage in the doorway.

"Alice Chalmers!"

He hadn't changed one iota since she'd left—in fact, he'd been shouting her name, black beard bristling and red with rage, the very last time she'd seen him, as though five years had never passed at all. His mechanical eye wheeled as it attempted to focus on her while he was moving, and his mechanical arm ratcheted in and out as though it couldn't wait to grab her and choke the life out of her.

"What did I tell you about coming back here?" he roared, and let off a shot that whistled past her head.

"Hello, Pa."

"I ain't yer pa!"

"All right, Ned, then."

"Captain Mose!"

Captain of what? It would probably be best not to say anything about the two ships she'd downed on her way in, in case they had made up the entirety of his fleet. "Captain Mose," she said calmly. "Did you read Lorraine's note?"

"Of course I read her note, you ninny. D'you think I forgot how to read while you were gone?"

Blam! Another shot, right between her head and Evan's. To his credit, Evan merely flinched and muffled a squeak. He was clearly made of stronger stuff that met the eye.

"So? What's your answer?" she persisted as if the potentially fatal interruptions had not happened. "Are you up for a little train robbery?"

"What kind of a question is that after running out for five years, girl?"

"It's a pretty reasonable question, considering that's why I'm here. I need a hand and you're the only man in the Territory that can give it."

He glared at her, his finger still twitching on the trigger. "So you run out on me, spring my prisoners, steal my ship, and now you're back for more?" His mechanical eye extruded to its full length of about two inches while the organic one bulged with affront.

"I'm not going to take the train's cargo, Pa. You're welcome to it. I just need it stopped and I don't care how it's done."

The *pa* slipped out again by force of habit. She'd never been one to wheedle, or manipulate, or use her feminine wiles to get what she wanted. Ned Mose respected strength, and even though her stomach jumped and her skin was crawling in anticipation of an answering shot from any one of the houses within range behind them, she didn't back down.

Backing down would be fatal.

"What's on it?" The eye retracted a quarter inch, telling her that the pressure on it had eased just a fraction.

"Wonders, Pa." She leaned in a little, as though to exclude Perry, who was watching with the rifle at the ready, just out of arm's reach. "They've got mechanical horses, and parts for great iron behemoths, and panther-shaped missile launchers of some kind, for attacking a cavalry at speed."

The organic eye widened. "Mechanical critters? Are you funning me?"

She shook her head, and with the motion, he took in the fact that her hair was braided up like that of a proper lady, not all over the place for want of a pin or a ribbon—or a brush. "They're all for the Royal Kingdom of Spain and the Californias. There's men in high places who plan to declare war on the Territory, Pa, and the only thing that stands between them and the deaths of everyone from here to Santa Fe is you."

"I don't give a dry fart about Santa Fe."

"But you do about Resolution. This is your town. Do you want to see it ridden down by mechanical horses, and noblemen in black suits putting up their boots and silver spurs on your table?"

His good eye narrowed. "I ain't about to allow that."

"Then you've got to help me stop that train. Got any ideas?"

The mechanical eye measured her, and then swung to Perry. "Stand down, boy. You want my stepdaughter to think you ain't got the manners God gave a goat?"

When Perry lowered the repeater, light glinted in at least three of the windows in the other buildings as the men posted there did the same. Alice wasn't about to breathe freely, though. They weren't out of the clouds by a long shot.

"Yeah, I've got a few ideas," he answered gruffly. "But I'm going to need your handy skills to work 'em up."

She might have known. But better that than being shot out of hand, just for turning up again. She had an idea or two herself, but from long acquaintance with Ned Mose, any plan went more smoothly when he believed it was his own.

"We don't have much time—a day at the very most. Let's put our heads together inside."

CHAPTER 7

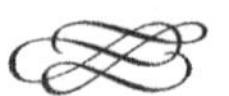

The simplest way to rob a train, as far as Evan could imagine, would be to blow up the track—with dynamite, flash bombs of pyrophoric gunpowder, or by dropping a missile from *Swan*'s stores on it from the air. Ned was all in favor of the last idea, which represented the least amount of effort on his part and the greatest amount of blame on Alice's, to Evan's way of thinking.

But Alice shook her head. "We don't want it to look like an attack—that'll just give the Ambassador more reason to invade with the arms that have already been delivered."

"It would be difficult to make it look like anything else," Evan pointed out, screwing up his courage to the sticking point and speaking for the first time. "How can one rob a train without attacking it? And how can one stop it when it's traveling at full speed?"

Alice nodded to acknowledge the logic of his questions, then said, "Pa, when's the last time the switch at Lizard Arroyo was ever used?"

Ned thought for a moment. "Eighteen seventy-nine? What kind of question is that?"

Alice cocked an eyebrow at Evan in a way that told him she knew perfectly well what kind of question it was—the only doubtful part was whether Ned's greedy brain would pick up on the course it was clear she was setting for it. "Mr. Douglas, I don't suppose you noticed on our way in that there's a rail spur into Resolution."

"No, I didn't," Evan said slowly. He'd been too busy watching air pirates shoot at them.

"At one time our fair town was supposed to rival Santa Fe, but those numbskulls in Houston changed their minds when the line was only partly built, and never finished it. Mostly it's all blown over by the floods and wind, which is a shame, because—"

Ned banged his mechanical fist on the table. "Enough of your history lesson, girl. That's what we'll do—we'll throw the switch and bring that train into Resolution, where we can pick its bones clean right here at our own table."

Alice gazed at him in admiration. "Pa! That's brilliant."

Evan choked down a huff of laughter. She ought to be treading the boards at Covent Garden.

"Of course it is. You take me for one of them numbskulls down south?"

"I'd never do that. Because you know what will happen? That train will seem to vanish into thin air. Who remembers there's a switch at Lizard Arroyo? Nobody within a hundred miles except the switchman—if he's still even there."

"If he is, he won't be for long," the young man she'd called Perry put in from the door, where the other members of Ned's gang were milling about, craning their necks to see the map spread on the filthy table. "We'll look after him, won't we, boys?"

Ned banged the table again. "Ain't no call for killing, you idiots. This is a job requiring brains and stealth, none of which you got. We're going to make that train disappear—but to do it, we gotta clear the track at least far enough that the engineer and brakemen don't suspect they've gone wrong until it's too late to reverse her."

"And when she doesn't arrive in Reno on schedule," Alice went on as though thinking her way through a thicket of difficulties Evan was quite sure she'd already solved, "they're sure to send a train of their own out this way. No matter how many inquiries they make, as long as there are no witnesses to the switch, there will be no answers for them once we switch it back and cover our trail. And no damaged track or scattered iron to tell tales."

"That means you boys got work to do," Ned told them. "Alice, how fast can you modify your old tower to blast the track clean?"

"Two hours," she said promptly. "With Mr. Douglas's help. He's a specialist in that kind of thing."

Which was a bald-faced lie, but with any luck it would allow them to stay together. Evan had no desire to go anywhere with this rough bunch in case he never came back. And he had no intention of allowing *Swan*—and its precious cargo—out of his sight for as much as an hour.

As if Ned had detected his very thoughts—now there was a course of scientific inquiry he might pursue, if he survived this voyage—he said, "You got anything on that fancy ship that might help us, girl?"

"Not much other than gasbags and enough steam to fly,

Pa," she said absently, as though it didn't matter as much as the rail spur she was tracing on the map with her finger. "I can't afford much more than that. Not like the kind of devices they'll have on that train."

"You sure?"

She raised her gaze to his. "Pa, I'm bringing you a train full of more plunder than Resolution has seen in a decade. You can build engines to your heart's content and even sell some of those mechanicals to buyers in Santa Fe and the Idaho Territory. In fact, if you play your cards right, you might even sell some to the Texican Rangers to defend the border once they figure out there's going to be an invasion."

With a bark of laughter, Ned roared his appreciation of the irony.

"So I'll thank you to not get any rash ideas about my ship. It's plumb near empty, like I told you, and such as it is, I earned it fair and square."

"Aw, simmer down, missy, I was only making inquiries. Come on, you lot," he shouted at the men by the door, making Evan jump. "Perry, take someone who can tell a wrench from his own behind, and go examine that switch. Take grease and some extra bolts. I want it working as well as when it came out of the factory by sundown. The rest of you, grab picks and shovels and see how deep you have to go to dig out that spur."

The men scattered, and Ned rolled up the map. His mechanical eye swiveled toward Alice.

"You're being straight with me, ain't you, missy?" he asked in a tone that made a chill tiptoe up Evan's spine. "You ain't got plans to loot that train yourself and leave us to the Rangers?"

Alice shook her head. "Of course not, Pa. I told you.

Those men took what wasn't theirs, and I'm simply giving you an opportunity to right a wrong and make a little profit by it."

"Don't seem right."

"I didn't think so, either."

"Not that. I got no interest in who stole what from who. I meant it don't seem right that you ain't invested in such a sizeable scheme."

But Alice merely shrugged. "Sometimes you just have to do what's right, even if there's nothing in it for you."

Ned snorted and whacked the table with the rolled-up map. "Never took you for a fool, girl. Don't make me start. Now get out there and get your engine working."

Gloria Meriwether-Astor was possessed of much wealth, some beauty, and few skills. Among the latter, such as they were, one could include flawless taste in clothes, some talent for the arrangement of flowers, and the ability to make anyone, no matter their social standing or background, feel comfortable in conversation. She was also an excellent shot, her father having deemed it practical that his daughter should be able to use the products of the family business in demonstrations without embarrassment. In his more optimistic moments, he had hoped she would demonstrate such skill while riding to hounds and grouse shooting in Scotland and as a consequence, bag herself a title.

She had disappointed him in that last, but she could recite the specifications for, load, and shoot nearly everything the Meriwether-Astor Munitions Works produced in its factories, with the possible exception of the cannon. The balls were too heavy for her to lift.

Among the qualities she wished she possessed were those that Claire and Alice had in spades—namely, a mechanical aptitude that had saved their lives on several occasions. Gloria might be able to shoot a gun, but she could not build one with her own hands, though she had seen enough design diagrams that she was quite sure she could learn if she had to. Another quality she often wished for was patience—the ability to wait for something without fidgeting and flibbeting about a room. Waiting was agony, even when she'd been a child at Christmas, when the presents were right there before one, and one could not have them.

Now she stood at the viewing port aboard *Swan*, hours after Alice and Evan had gone, and while she might have a gun in her pocket, she had no patience left whatsoever.

"What has become of them?" she groaned, her forehead on the cold isinglass as though sheer will would bring the sight of them walking back along the dry riverbed.

"Do you expect me to give you the same answer as I did the last three times you asked, or are you looking for a different one?" Jake inquired through his teeth. Patience was not one of his attributes either.

"What if they've been captured? What if they're dead, Jake?"

"If they'd been captured, the Captain would have fired a bolt from the lightning pistol straight up to tell us so before they took it from her, and we'd have attempted a rescue already."

"And if they're dead?"

"They're not."

"How do you know?"

"Because the captain is too smart to be dead, that's why."

"It will catch up with her someday," she said darkly.

"Don't say such things, you ninny!" he snapped. "Are you trying to bring down trouble on us?"

"I am not a ninny, and I'll thank you to be civil." While this crushing setdown might have rendered one of her Philadelphia swains into apologetic jelly, it had no effect on Jake except to make him crankier.

"And I'll thank you to give the captain credit for the brain in her head. Now stop flapping your trap and give a man some peace."

Affronted, she turned her back on him and did not mention that since he was pressed to the other port with just as much concern as she, there was not much point in wishing for peace. Until they saw the return of their companions, neither of them was likely to get it.

Benny Stringfellow came in from the engine room, where as ordered, the boilers had not been shut down and therefore needed periodic attention. "What do you suppose they're *doing* out there?"

Gloria and Jake both turned on him with such glares that he retreated a step.

"I'm just asking. No sign?"

"If there had been, we might have lifted by now." Jake's uncompromising gaze returned to the empty view.

"But it's been three hours."

Three hours in which nothing had moved among the distant buildings except slinking, dust-colored creatures that Gloria suspected were not dogs. They'd seen Alice and Evan go into a building on the edge of town, and then emerge to go into the taller one a few hundred yards away, and then nothing.

"Captain hasn't fired the signal," Jake said. "Our orders are to stay put."

"It's two o'clock," Benny pointed out. "Sun's on its way down soon. If they don't come back before dark, we must go find them."

"They'll be back."

"We must have a contingency plan if they are not, Jake," Gloria said with what she thought was a very reasonable tone, considering he had just accused her of flapping her trap. "What do you suggest?"

A contingency plan meant that they might not survive, and it was clear Jake didn't want to think about it. He ground his teeth and said nothing.

"I believe we have two contingency plans to consider," she went on. "What to do about Alice and Evan ... and what to do about the train if they are not successful."

"Don't wish them dead!" Jake blurted, his face reddening with rage.

She would have snapped an equally angry retort if she hadn't seen the slightest hint of tears in his eyes—if she hadn't suddenly realized that he was not angry at all.

He was terrified.

Her stomach plunged as the depth of the danger was borne in upon her in a way it had not been up until this moment. "I do not—could not," she said softly. "But I see now how brave she was to go alone, with only Evan at her side, so as not to risk all of us." She swallowed. "Me."

"You don't know what it's like down there," Jake rasped, his throat clogged. "They don't value anyone's life—your only value is in what you have, and how fast they can take it from you. They're wreckers, Gloria—do you know what that means?"

"I do. Alice told me."

"They make their living on the deaths of others," Jake said bitterly, "and I don't aim to let them make it on ours. Do you think I haven't been standing here running contingency plans through my head these three hours past?"

"Of course you have," she said. How foolish she had been to think otherwise. How foolish and childish.

Claire would never have acted like this. Gloria straightened her spine. "What are our best options?" she asked again.

But before he could reply, a roar beat against their eardrums, as though a locomotive and a lion had combined. Benny flung himself against the viewing port next to Gloria and, mouth open, watched the strangest vehicle imaginable trundle out of a barn behind the tall house.

"That's Alice's tower," Jake said in tones of disbelief. "I didn't think it would ever run again."

It chugged down the street. It had once been a train locomotive, but the wheels were now mounted on a circular track that propelled it forward. Bolted on top was a tower, and mounted to the front was a huge assembly that seemed to bear an enormous propeller of the kind usually found on airships. Gloria did not want to speculate on which unfortunate vessel that had come from.

"The propeller is new," Jake commented. "What is she doing with it?"

They could not see who was steering the monster, but it was clearly heading out of town. Behind it came a ragtag group of various chariots and vehicles piloted by a rough lot of men, some of them bearing picks and shovels.

"You're sure it is Alice piloting that thing?"

"I believe she's the only one who can," Jake said, watching it crest a small hill and labor down the other side. "They used the tower for unloading passengers and cargo—they don't let captured ships moor on the ground."

"The captain helped take prisoners?" Benny sounded as though he couldn't believe it.

"Aye, in years past, if it meant staying alive," Jake told him.

In the distance, the tower stopped, and in a moment, with a grinding roar that reached them half a mile away, a huge cloud of dust and sand puffed up around the machine, nearly engulfing it.

"What in the name of ...?" Gloria said in wonder.

It moved slowly across the desert floor, groups of men working ahead of it and behind, well out of the way of the spewing, roiling dust storm. After a quarter of an hour of watching the spectacle, Gloria could see that they worked in a line that was unnaturally straight. How could that be? The only features in this inhospitable landscape that were straight were the tops of the mesas and the railroad tracks to—

"Is there a rail spur buried under there?" Gloria asked suddenly. "Can it be that they are clearing the track?"

Jake shot her a glance that might have held admiration if that had not been completely unlikely. "You could be right. I do remember mention of a railroad into Resolution that was never finished. I wonder if they mean to bring the munitions train in here."

"It's a brilliant plan if they do," Gloria said. "If there's a switch off the main line, that is. There must be, mustn't there?

They would have to have built it in the beginning, to run supplies to the end of the line."

"How do you know so much about trains, miss?" Benny asked.

"I suppose I must have picked up a thing or two in my travels," she said, feeling rather pleased and trying not to show it. "Papa was not a railroad baron, but he made me act as hostess while he entertained any number of them, and their conversation tended to include things like that."

"If you're right," Jake said slowly, "there will be an almighty battle a lot closer than we thought. If we're making contingency plans, we ought to think about what we'll do when the shooting starts. I've no desire to have *Swan* shot full of holes. Who will be on that train besides the Californios, Gloria?"

At last, something she could contribute!

"If they treated this shipment as they did the others—and I read the manifests—there will be a full contingent of mercenaries to defend the cargo. There were twenty on the last payroll six months ago."

"Ned has at least that many miscreants under his thumb here," Jake said, "so odds might be even. Who else?"

"The Ambassador did not come all this way without a full escort," she said. "I do not know precisely how many, but easily a dozen, plus his personal entourage. They are all trained in the arts of war, but how much experience they have in the actuality of it is up for debate."

"So there could be as many as forty armed men on that train?" Benny asked, his tone uncertain. "Do you think Alice knows that?"

CHAPTER 8

"No," Gloria said. "I do not think we got as far as counting heads. It was enough to reach this side of the world ahead of the train—we did not have time for further speculation before she went to find her stepfather."

She could see now the mistake they had made in taking the journey a step at a time, and not thinking about what lay at the end of it. But how was it possible to take absolutely everything into account? Gloria herself had simply assumed they could drop an explosive on the track, stop the train, and that would be that. The manifests had not even entered her head until now.

How very shortsighted of her. "They are going to make the train disappear," she said aloud. "We thought they would simply blow it up, but do you see how dangerous that is? And how easy to discover?"

"What difference does it make?" Jake asked gruffly. "We're still up against forty men, whether it's blowing it up five miles from here or bringing it right to the doorstep."

"But they can allow none to escape if they do not want the

Viceroy to find out and send his army into the Territory seeking vengeance. If the train simply disappears without a trace, it will be much more difficult to find the responsible party, since it could have done so anywhere along a route thousands of miles long."

"The captain must have come up with the plan," Benny said with satisfaction.

"She may have indeed, but someone needs to tell her and her accomplices that the train will be manned and well armed by men who know their business. I do not think the air pirates are expecting a fight—and we just downed two of their ships."

"You won't find me sorry for that," Jake said. "But the fact is that even if we throw in our lot with the pirates, we are undermanned."

"We have bombs," Benny pointed out. "Twelve incendiaries and half as many pressure bombs. I counted."

"The trouble with bombs is that if you drop them in the middle of a melee, you're as likely to kill your friends as your enemies," Jake told him, ruffling his hair. "Me, I'd be happy to collect the captain and Mr. Douglas and scarper before the train realizes where it's going, and let Ned Mose and his lot fend for themselves."

"I agree," Gloria said promptly. "The question is, how shall we tell them of their danger without being taken prisoner?"

"I'll go," Benny said promptly.

"You will not," Jake told him. "The captain would never forgive me if I sent you out there to be shot."

"Nobody's shooting yet," Benny pointed out with what Gloria thought was admirable logic. "I can go out to the tower, climb up, and tell Alice, quick as a wink."

"They're two miles off, Benny. There's nothing quick about it."

"The longer we sit here arguing, the farther away the captain will get." Benny's young face set in stubborn lines, and for an instant, Gloria had a glimpse of the man he might someday become—brave, loyal, and resourceful.

"If anyone goes, it will be me," Jake said quietly. "I've had some experience with this lot, and they know I'm flying with the captain."

"That won't save you if someone wants a bit of target practice," Gloria pointed out.

"But it's a leg up over a stranger they've never seen," Jake said. "And a youngster at that. At least I can pretend to offer my services as an ally, if push comes to shove."

"I can too!" Benny wasn't going down without a fight.

"I know you can, lad. But they don't. No, it's got to be me. I'll take a rocket rucksack—that'll land me closer than two miles off, I hope."

Fuming, Benny gave in to his superior officer's greater logic, but Gloria could see how much it cost him. She wanted to slip an arm around him and assure him that time would take care of everything that irked him now, but a female passenger presuming to put herself between two crewmen would likely net her only the disgust of both.

Jake wasted no time. He fetched the rucksack and ignited it, and in less than ten minutes was blasting through the air in the direction of the far-off plume of dust smudging the sky. The rucksacks were notoriously difficult to control, being old-fashioned and unwieldy, but it was all they had, and for short distances such as this, Gloria hoped it would do well enough.

"So now we are down to two," she said, gazing after the trail of burned air that was all that remained of Jake's departure.

"Miss?"

"We began with five, and now we are two," she said. "I hope you are able to teach me how to pilot this ship if the worst should happen, Mr. Stringfellow."

His eyes widened. "The worst, miss?"

"If our friends should not come back."

"Don't put about ideas like that, miss. I've never been one to borrow trouble, and I don't intend to begin now." As though for emphasis, he turned and made his way back down toward the engine room, no doubt to check on Alice's boilers.

So much for contingency plans.

Gloria chewed on her lower lip and turned back to the viewing port, unable to reason away her anxiety.

THE SUN WAS two hours off the horizon, the track was cleared, and Alice and everyone else in the rail crew was covered with a grimy crust of red dirt. It ground between her molars, turned into mud in the corners of her eyes, and she was quite sure it would still be irritating her for days to come, no matter how many baths she took.

As she and Jake clambered down from her poor old tower, turned into a giant bellows for today's purposes, she saw Ned Mose and the boys waiting for them on the ground.

"Can you move any slower, missy?" Ned shouted as she edged past the firebox to the iron ladder.

"What's your hurry?" she demanded, the dirt making her a

little less gracious than was probably wise. "There's no sign of them yet." She jumped to the ground and swatted at her canvas pants and blouse. Puffs of red dust settled slowly but left her feeling no cleaner.

"I was just informed that I'm short two ships," Ned shouted, though she was within speaking distance. "And that I've got you to thank!"

"They were firing on me, Pa," she said reasonably. "I sent you a pigeon, and I didn't take kindly to being held up, especially when they didn't answer any of my flags."

"You didn't have to crash them, missy. I've a mind to take your ship in exchange."

"You can fix those boats as soon as look at them," Alice said, settling both hands on her hips, comfortingly close to her pistols. It would take a little doing for Ned to bring the dead engines back after the lightning cannon had done for them, but now might not be the time to mention that. "Maybe the boys will mind their manners next time."

"Don't backtalk me, girl." She didn't like the look in his eye. "Since I've got no ships and no indication of when this mythical train might arrive, I'm going to send a couple of my boys up in yours to spy out where it is."

"I can do that, Pa."

"Sure you can. You'll lift and sashay away, leaving me with an angry bunch of Californios with a train full of mechanical monsters in who knows what stage of readiness to fire on an innocent man."

"And you think one woman, her passenger, and her navigator will make much of a difference to those odds?" Evan, being thus named, did his best to fade into insignificance in the shuffling, stinking group. Which was quite easy, since except for Jake, who had brought news of what they were up against in direct contravention of her orders, they were all covered in dust and looked much the same.

"I think a military-grade airship will make a dadburned big difference. Now you take Perry and Melvin here, and pull up ropes pronto. If that train's coming, the boys will go down in the basket and throw the switch. If it's an ordinary freight, let it go. Either way, I want a report in an hour."

It was three against eighteen, and Alice was no fool.

"All right, Pa. Jake, Evan, Perry, Melvin, come along."

"Your passenger stays here."

"What?" she and Jake said together. Evan's face was covered in dust, but if it was anything like hers, the color was already draining out of it.

"Call it insurance," Ned said smugly as two men took Evan by the arms and culled him from the group. "We can have a cup of tea and talk about engine repair—and you won't be tempted to toss my boys out the hatch and run for the clouds."

"Let go of me, sirs!" Evan snapped, dodging and kicking with no effect whatsoever. He was outweighed by a good two hundred pounds, and in a moment, he was facedown in the dirt with somebody's knee in his back.

"Get a move on, missy," Ned told her. "We'll take good care of your friend until you get back."

"What happens then?"

"If we don't see that pretty blue fuselage on the horizon by then, we shoot him. I don't want no lollygagging."

She had no doubt he'd do it. Hatred of this man welled up inside her like the huge waves she'd seen off the coast of the Canadas, in the country where the Na'nuk carved their spirit poles in the mist and where legend lived a little too close to the surface for comfort. If she could have commanded an eagle to stoop from the sky and rip his guts out, she would have done it without hesitation.

He must have seen it in her eyes, for his organic one narrowed. "I said, get a move on. You know I'm a man of my word."

"I know," she spat. "When it suits you."

Here was an almighty conundrum, and as they tramped back along the dry riverbed to *Swan*, Alice tried to tamp down her rage and fear long enough to work it out. She could only pray that Gloria would have the sense to hide when she saw out the viewing ports that the wrong crew was returning with Alice. On the other hand, they needed Gloria to identify the train. It would do them no good if the next thing along the railroad was some unsuspecting freight out of the Louisiana Territory. She was not about to let Perry and Melvin throw that switch and doom the innocent.

But revealing to Ned Mose that a millionaire heiress was aboard would be fatal. But who else would know one train from another? Certainly not Miss Meredith Aster, passenger of no particular family or consequence.

When the party boarded *Swan*, she found her lone crewman armed to the teeth and standing on the gangway. His feet apart in classic shooting stance, he held the lightning pistol steady with both small hands, sighting down its flared barrel past Alice's ear.

"Say the word, Captain."

She would promote him if she hadn't just done so. If Evan's life did not hang in the balance.

"Stand down, Gunner," she said wearily. "We're going to

spy out that train, and Ned is holding Evan as insurance that we come back with a report."

"We can come back with two less," he said, and her heart was pierced with grief at this evidence that her young middy had left childhood behind him forever.

Perry and Melvin exchanged amused glances, and she saw that they had already drawn. If Benny moved, they would cut him down with less effort than swatting a fly.

"Stand down, all of you," she snapped, and jerked her arm out of Perry's grip. "We have less than an hour, and a few miles to put under the hull. Mr. Stringfellow, Mr. McTavish, prepare the ship to lift."

"Aye, Captain." Jake sounded grim, but she did not miss the brief squeeze of Benny's shoulder as he passed him on the gangway. It had been bravely done.

Futile, but brave.

"Nice boat," Perry said with admiration as he followed her to the helm, trailing red dust on the polished floors. "Ned needs to see this."

"He's seen as much as he's going to," Alice said shortly. "Now go man the ropes. Mr. Stringfellow, are the boilers hot?"

"Aye, Captain."

"Ignite engines, please. *Swan*, vanes full vertical." The familiar vibration hummed in the soles of her boots, and she felt the moment when her ship was ready to take to the air. "Cast off, Perry, Melvin."

They did so, scrambling back up the gangway as though they thought she'd lift before they were aboard.

"Up ship!"

Swan lifted with silent ease and fell up into the cold sky.

Oh, if only Evan were with them! If he were, she could give Perry and Melvin one chance to change their ways, and if they didn't, she'd tip them into the lake.

But there was no point in daydreaming. Evan was in peril, and goodness only knew where Gloria was, and she absolutely hated feeling like a prisoner again after so many years flying as free as a gull. Because even if they succeeded in stopping the train and Ned looted it right down to its bolts, she knew in her bones he wouldn't let *Swan* out of his clutches. The depth of his greed had no bottom, and *Swan* was too new, too beautiful, too powerful for him to resist.

Alice was going to have to make some hard choices in the hour before sundown. The kind that meant bloodshed. And betrayal.

GLORIA LAID a hand over her heart, which was pounding half out of her chest with fright. At the sight of the pirates marching Alice and Jake along the riverbed at gunpoint, she had fled to her cabin and locked herself in, and now she had to decide what to do.

For it had finally been borne in upon her that this was no lark, no adventure. Through the speaking horns, she'd heard what Alice had said, about Evan being held as insurance against their return. Because Alice had not allowed Benny to shoot the varmints, it was clear that her concern for their friend was as great as Gloria's. And she could not be the only one looking ahead to the coming battle, when every man would be needed.

Gloria had gone to her room like a good girl, but someone

had to identify the train. Surely Alice must have concluded that as well. But how could Gloria do that without revealing her identity and plunging them into even greater danger? She'd never seen Ned Mose, but his gang's casual disregard for life was terrifying. What was to stop them from taking *Swan,* holding Gloria for ransom, and shooting everybody else?

She must not reveal herself.

She crossed to the porthole and gazed down. They were passing over a small lake, and in the distance the sun glinted off the steel rails of the track. The arms and mechanicals were on cars hauled by a shiny new steam locomotive with curving brass trim and an aerodynamic, bullet-shaped front capable of speeds of up to ninety miles per hour. *Silver* something, its name was. She had seen Jake's charts, had calculated the time and distance. The train would pass through here soon—twelve cargo cars, two passenger sleeping coaches, and a luxury lounge car given to the Ambassador as a courtesy acknowledging his rank and the amount of money he had spent.

It would be easy to identify from the ground, where one could see the M.A.M.W. badge on the sides, and the silver numbers and sheer style of the front of the locomotive. But from the air? She was probably the only one aboard who could do that, having seen the cars from above in the railroad offices, on the flying bridge over the cargo yards.

She must think.

Swan sailed gently eastward, following the ribbon of track far below. And then Gloria's stomach clutched as she saw a smudge in the sky, rising from behind a mesa.

"Gentlemen," Alice voice came through the speaking tube, sounding slightly tinny. "I see a plume. Stand by."

In moments, the train wound from between two mesas and chugged smoothly onto the flat.

"*Swan*, decrease altitude three hundred feet."

The ship, by some miraculous means Gloria didn't quite understand, obeyed her captain's command. She felt herself rise onto her toes a little as the deck dropped out from under her. Nose pressed against the isinglass of her porthole, Gloria stared anxiously at the train as they approached it from above.

Blast it all, she couldn't see! There was nothing for it. She was going to have to find a salon with a proper viewing port, not one of these tiny windows only good enough for checking the weather.

Quietly, she unlocked her door and slipped into the corridor. With any luck, the pirates would be with Alice and no one would notice her heading astern, to the engine room.

"Miss!" Benny exclaimed when she stepped over the threshold. "Get back in your room! Do you want them to see you?"

"I am the only one who can identify that train, and I can't see out of the porthole," she told him crisply. But at the viewing port, she realized they were still too far up for her to make the identification properly. "We have to go lower. *Swan*," she said to the room in general, "decrease altitude by two hundred feet."

"Oh, the captain's not going to like that," Benny said, his eyes wide as the decks obediently dropped once more. "Not one bit. Your voices are too alike."

It had never occurred to her before to attempt to command the ship. It was Alice's, and it was clear even her crew believed that its automaton brain would respond only to her. Or possibly to Claire, who had been its co-inventor. Gloria didn't know whether to be elated or terrified.

"Everything all right astern, Gunner?" came Alice's inquiry, its tinny quality now augmented with a touch of iron. A loss of altitude like that was not normal, automaton intelligence system notwithstanding.

"All right, Captain," Benny said, with a glance at Gloria. "We're just getting a closer view, is all."

"We, Gunner?"

"Aye. Seem to have picked up a sparrow here, Captain. I'll set it free as soon as I catch it."

"Carry on, then, Gunner."

"She knows it's you," Benny said urgently, shoveling coal into the boiler. "She'll be here in a minute, and them pirates will come too. Have a gander at the train and scoot, Miss, if you value your life."

Distinctly shaped locomotive, lounge, sleepers, and—yes, twelve cargo cars. And a scarlet caboose, smoke cheerfully issuing from its stovepipe, which had been added somewhere along the line.

"It's our train," she said to Benny. And she picked up her skirts in both hands and fled back to her cabin, expecting at every moment to be grabbed from behind.

CHAPTER 9

Their efforts to clear the spur had turned the windless desert air red—dust, cliffs, scrub pines all glowed as though it were sunset, and dust hung over man and machine, impossible to escape. Evan stood with his captors in an open patch of ground, while Ned Mose watched both horizons, one with each eye. Evan caught his breath so hard he choked on dust, and pointed voicelessly toward the southeast.

"Right on time," Ned said, with what Evan was sure was disappointment at not having the excuse to shoot him.

Swan was moving at a good clip, and within five minutes she hovered over the rise in the ground where they had first moored her, out beyond the edge of town, and settled onto her ropes.

"Durn fool woman—why didn't she moor here on the airfield?" Ned hollered, as though she might hear him.

But Evan couldn't help but think Alice was merely being prudent. The ship was neither out of sight nor out of mind … but she was certainly out of easy reach, and at the moment, that was good enough.

And then Evan saw something that pushed the ship out of his mind altogether. "Look!" he shouted at Ned, and shook himself loose of the hands that held him to point to the south. "Train's coming!"

The plume of steam from a locomotive rolling down the spur line followed *Swan*'s arrival so closely that Evan wondered if the two pirates who were to have thrown the switch had even had a chance to fling themselves back in the basket and be winched up again. But no, in the distant dry riverbed came four figures at a dead run—the same four who had left an hour before.

Evan hardly dared hope that Gloria was still safe, still hidden aboard, and that no pirate could get close enough to sully her pristine sleeve by so much as a grain of red dust.

"Get the bomb on that tower and get it moving!" Ned shouted. "Arm yourselves for a fight, boys!"

For a single moment, Evan hesitated. Could he run to Alice and Jake, and the three of them overpower Perry and Melvin? Could they make it to *Swan* and lift before the train ran off the end of the spur and derailed—and unholy hell broke loose?

In the next, he realized that the calculations he had unconsciously been making as to the train's imminent arrival were wrong.

No locomotive burst over the rise to crash at full speed into the riverbed, where the last ties of the spur terminated—presumably the rest had washed away in a flood. Instead, the plume rose into the sky at about a tenth of its previous speed, and in a moment it stopped altogether, ascending at the vertical and colored faintly pink with the dust.

"They've figured it out!" he shouted to the crowd of men

leaping on their cobbled-together machines. He could barely hear himself above the roar of steam engines and the shriek of tortured metal. "They're going to reverse up the track!"

He did not know whether anyone had heard, but at least one or two had eyes in their heads, Ned Mose first among them. At the top of his lungs, Ned yelled, "Cut them off! Blow up the spur before they reach the main line!"

For no one would know or care that the spur had been damaged, since it had been covered in dirt and rocks for decades. The main line would remain as pristine as ever, and the train's disappearance just as mysterious ... if the pirates could win the race.

Evan was heaved unceremoniously into the back of a wagon bearing the most enormous carousel-shaped gun. It lay in pieces for transport, but that did not make it any less ominous. He had never seen one of Mr. Gatling's creations—and the actuality was much more frightening than the drawings in magazines could ever be. He gripped the running boards for dear life and tried to keep his balance as the great iron wheels of the conveyance jounced into and out of holes and fissures in the rocky ground. Where were Alice and Jake? In the dust and roar, he could see nothing, only squint against the barrage of small rocks and dirt thrown up by the machines ahead, and try to protect his face with a filthy sleeve.

The wagon seemed to be bringing up the rear, the lighter engines flying along the ground ahead. But Evan could not imagine that any vehicle, no matter how swift, could outrun a locomotive when its crew was motivated by their own danger.

The wagon topped the first rise, the dust cleared a little,

and Evan peered into the distance. In a moment, he saw the second error in his calculations: the weight of the cargo in the cars. Slowing the train and then stopping it in order to reverse had taken enormous amounts of energy, to say nothing of time, and until this moment, it appeared that while the train's crew might have suspected they had taken a wrong turn, they had not suspected it to be life-threatening.

They seemed to know it now.

A huge gout of steam issued from the engine's raked stack and its dozen wheels began to turn in reverse, pushing more than that number of heavy cars behind itself.

Puff ... puff ... puff puff ... puffpuffpuff ...

Evan could just imagine the tenders shoveling coal like madmen, and as if to punctuate their distress, the whistle blew in a long, lonely scream of warning.

A flash of red light silhouetted everything for one hellish moment—train, pirate machines, even scrubby pines—and then Evan's ears popped a second before he clapped his hands over them and flung himself into the bed of the wagon. The explosion ripped through the air, deafening him and lifting the heavy wagon clean off its wheels for a couple of inches before it thumped to the ground again and knocked the breath from his lungs.

Pressure bomb, his brain told him.

My friends, his heart cried.

As though from a great distance, he heard cheering and the crashing of metal, and when he lifted his head to see the reason for the cacophony, someone hauled him to his feet.

"That's done it," the pirate seated in the pilot's chair shouted with satisfaction. "Look, they're coming back this way—they think they can make a run for it." He threw a glance over his shoulder at Evan and his two companions. "Don't just stand there, you dumb coyotes—assemble that gun!"

He hauled the wagon around and they rolled back down the hill, and soon Evan could see the pirates converging on the trapped locomotive like wolves on the head of a dying beast. There was nowhere for it to go, and as the train screeched to a long, unwilling halt on the last quarter mile of track, men poured from the doors of its coaches, bristling with arms.

They were not going down without a fight.

The wagon driver brought his vehicle to a rocking stop on a promontory, slewing it around so that the bed pointed toward the train. "Good enough," he said, leaping into the back. "Hurry—they'll be needing us to lay down cover fire. Hurry, dadblast you!"

Crouching in their pocked, rusting vehicles, the pirates rushed the train, bullets ricocheting off the iron hides. Evan had no idea if they had practiced such a maneuver before, but two men fired round after round at the Californio soldiers while a third maneuvered the vehicle. As Evan worked, fitting bolts into the gun's legs and putting his back into it as they tilted them into their housing, and then lifted the iron carousel high enough to load, he looked frantically over his shoulder to the battlefield for any sign of Alice's curly golden hair.

"That's not how it goes!" His captor smacked him on the side of the head with a leather-gloved hand, and he stumbled. "This plate goes on top of that one."

"How do you know?" The round plates were toothed, as though multiple plates locked together and caused the carousel to turn, but without a single moment to study them, his mind could not comprehend the assembly just like that.

"I done this once before, to show Ned when we brought it in."

"You mean you've never fired it?"

"I'm firing it now—and you'll be my practice shot if you don't get your sorry behind up here to hold this!"

On the great brass central cap of the carousel were engraved the initials *M.A.M.W.* Dust and scratches marred them, but there was no mistaking the manufacturer. The whole world, it seemed, had been armed by Gloria's father. No wonder she wanted nothing to do with it. What kind of legacy was that to leave one's children?

Evan heard a scream as, directly below, a pirate was knocked out of the pilot's chair of his vehicle. It careened on its iron wheels straight into another one, and both overturned, flinging men to the ground. A mercenary crouched in the door of one of the cargo cars picked them off like a chicken picks spiders off a wall, with ruthless efficiency, before being shot himself and tumbling in slow motion out onto the track.

Evan focused his mind and redoubled his efforts to assemble the gearworks that turned the carousel of the mighty gun. Should he be glad the pirate numbers were down by four? Or should the fear he was barely keeping under control be all in anticipation of capture and execution by the Californio forces? At least if the pirates proved victorious, they were a devil he knew. If the Californios won, what would they do, with a disabled train and no track to run it on, stranded out here in outlaw country with no means of finding help?

No means ... except for *Swan.*

~

TRAPPED in the navigation gondola with Benny, Gloria pressed her nose to the isinglass to watch the battle as best she could. They could not make out faces, but they could see the vehicles clearly, snarling and feinting as the pirates attempted to get close enough to some part of the train to board it.

She didn't even see the wagon with the big Gatling carousel until Benny grabbed her sleeve and exclaimed, "Miss! Look at the size of it!" She followed his shaking finger up to the promontory not a quarter of a mile away, where four men wrestled the gun into position.

"Why, that looks like one of—"

A puff of smoke issued from it, and one of the men was thrown backward, off the wagon, cartwheeling over the pilot's brace to the ground.

He did not get up.

Benny gasped. "It shot him! What are they doing?"

She snatched up the telescoping spyglass and focused on the gun. Yes, it was one of theirs—a Model CG-36, which meant it had three tiers of twelve cartridges each in the carousel. Each cartridge contained a dozen lethal projectiles that would detonate in secondary explosions on contact with the target, increasing the destruction for a distance of—

She cried out in horror as a familiar figure became clear in her field of view. "Benny, it's Evan! They're dragging him back into the wagon. If they make him operate that gun—and they haven't assembled it correctly—no, they mustn't—" She flung the spy glass at him and fled down the corridor to the crew's quarters.

A jacket—leather, sturdy—would offer her some protection while it obscured her form. She tore off her skirt and yanked on the first pair of canvas pants that came to hand—Jake's. She hoped he wouldn't begrudge them. She stuffed her lightning pistols into the pockets.

She bundled her hair up into an aeronaut's cap and pulled the goggles down over her eyes. They were so big they rested on her cheekbones, but that was all to the good. Her corset was already concealing her identity papers and several gold coins, and a gold locket with her mother's likeness inside lay under the shirt she buttoned with hasty fingers. There wasn't time to leave any of it—she had to save Evan from his companion's fate.

"Miss, no, come back!" Benny shouted as she dashed for the gangway.

"Evan's going to be killed if I don't fix that gun!"

She plunged down the boarding ramp and remembered too late that *Swan* hung some ten feet off the ground, so that Benny could maneuver the underbelly guns. At the last second she grabbed the rope handrail and her own momentum swung her feet out into space.

When she swung back to the vertical, she let go and dropped ungracefully to the ground, landing flat on her posterior. She scrambled up and took off at a dead run for the gun in the distance, where she could already see Evan's unwilling form being pushed into the gunner's brace.

CHAPTER 10

The locomotive was the most beautiful Alice had ever seen. Steam curled up from its three raked stacks and leaked out from between its six pairs of wheels, and the sun glinted off its brass trim and smooth blue-gray snout. *Silver Wind,* it said on the side. Why had Gloria not told them? Blowing it up would be like shooting an eagle, or harpooning a goddess whale.

If Alice had known she was to be the instrument of its destruction, she'd have found another way. Dadburn it, they could have dropped Perry and Melvin out of the basket on top of one of the moving cars and had the coupling pins out and the cargo cars sitting pretty while the locomotive went safely on its way.

No matter how you sliced it, though, the mercenaries would have noticed eventually and they'd still have a fight on their hands.

Her poor old tower had been blown to bits by the pressure bomb, having been sent rumbling to its doom with the acceleration bars tied in place. The train couldn't go back to the main line, and its engineer had been brave or foolish enough to make a run for it, not seeing the spur wasn't finished until it was almost too late.

And here came the mercenaries out to defend it, big as life and bent on death. Perry brought the steam chariot to a skidding halt and tossed her a carbine. A Colt. Not too many years old, either. "Get behind the machine!" he shouted. "Use it for cover."

"How are we going to fall back if they're too much for us?" If the boiler were punctured by a bullet, the chariot would be about as useful as a rock for getting away.

"Fall back to where?" Melvin demanded, lying flat and shouldering his rifle. "There ain't no fallback, missy, resign yourself to that."

She'd do no such thing.

Jake flung himself down beside her. "The minute we can, we cut and run," she told him under the blast of the guns.

"What about Evan?"

Here was the hard decision—the one that meant betrayal. "Don't know where he is. We've got to get our little sparrow out of here. Our job is done. What happens to all this is none of our nevermind."

Jake frowned as he sighted down the barrel of his gun and fired. Across the gully, a mercenary spun and fell. "That's hard, Captain. He's a good sort. Won't last a day if we leave him."

"He's a scientist. Whichever side wins, they'll find a use for him, which will keep him alive until we can get the sparrow to her nest and come back."

"What's that, missy?" Melvin hollered down from his position standing behind the bulk of the machine. "You ain't falling back from here, I told you."

She racked a shell, appreciating the smooth pump action of the Colt. Ned had wrecked someone who knew his guns. "I said, someone has to watch our backs in case they circle around. I ain't got eyes in the back of my head like some people."

"They won't. The boys got the Gatling gun fixed up. Any minute now they'll start mopping up these Californio fancypants."

Any minute now.

But with every passing minute the dust got thicker, the sound of explosions more deafening, and the screams of dying men more horrible. And then a shout went up.

Alice, lying on her belly firing as fast as she could load, felt the earth tremble as though a huge rock had broken away from the mesa and plummeted to earth.

For a moment, everything went still, and the breeze blew the dust and smoke away to the east.

The earth shook again, and Jake whimpered. Jake, who to her knowledge had never been afraid of anything except disappointing Claire.

His eyes widened until the whites showed, and standing above them, Melvin croaked, "HolyMaryMotherofGodbe-withusnow."

Slowly, Alice turned her head to follow their line of sight.

Towering above the scattering mercenaries and the Californio Ambassador's escort was something out of a nightmare. Even in her craziest absinthe-ridden dreams from the hard years, Alice would never have thought this up—it had to have come from the mind of someone well acquainted with hell. The massive mechanical was the size of a manor house—nearly as tall as the tower at Hollys Park. It might have been shaped like a man, if a man had been hulked over, head lowered like a bull's and a pilot's housing embedded in it. Thick, articulated iron legs with steam-powered pistons and feet as big as her tower's locomotive base shook the earth with every step ... and its arms were not arms at all. One appeared to be a rotating gun, and the other a cannon. Viewing ports in its chest showed glimpses of its crew, frantically busy with levers and wheels so that the thing might move forward and shoot without overbalancing.

"HolyMaryMotherofGod—"

How had they assembled it so quickly? Or did it simply fold up, ready to be activated when needed? But there was no time to speculate. Behind it, the Californio troops regrouped, and the behemoth began to fire on the pirates' machines as it advanced.

Somewhere off to their right, Alice heard Ned scream, "Where in tarnation is my Gatling gun? By heaven, I'll have your heads!"

Unfortunately, heaven was a long, long way away.

THE MEN at Ned's stolen Gatling gun had frozen in horror as their minds attempted to make sense of what they had never seen or imagined. Evan felt his insides loosen, and fought to control his body's perfectly sensible instinct to flee. For there was nowhere to go—except up into the gunner's brace of a machine that had already killed a man.

There was a rush of movement beside him, and a voice

shouted, "You've got the turning plates in upside down, you idiots! You there—get down and help me!"

If he had been afraid before, it was nothing compared to the sheer cold terror that engulfed him now as he recognized the voice of the boyish figure wrenching at the clamps of the carousel assembly. Goggles covered her face, but there was no mistaking the porcelain skin or the delicate fingers that made a ludicrous contrast with the dirty iron and brass of the gun.

"Who in the Sam Hill are you?" one of the pirates snapped. "And what do you mean, upside down?"

"That's why it's turning backward, you stupid fool," she shouted. "Why that poor fellow was shot. Help me!"

Two of them lifted the cartridge carousel off while Gloria wrenched at the plates, turning them over and re-ordering them. Suddenly the mechanism that had seemed so stiff and unwilling before began to turn with all the smoothness of superior engineering, and the mathematics of it clicked into place in Evan's mind.

Of course. The bottom set of plates and cogs turned about the central shaft, with a set of transfer gears between them and the plate that moved the carousel. Three sets of moving parts comprised the head of a gun that was practically all that stood between them and imminent annihilation.

Gloria leaped into the gunner's brace and flipped two levers forward and one back. Evan did not wish to speculate on how a young lady who belonged in a drawing room pouring tea could possibly know how to operate a killing machine of this size.

"What in the—get away from there!" The pirate who had been driving the wagon had finally found his tongue.

But Gloria ignored him. Instead, she took hold of the

guidance posts and lined up the sights to accommodate her smaller form. Evan watched her mouth settle into grim concentration as though he were watching a flicker—a moving picture of someone he hardly recognized.

Whom he did not know.

Then a cartridge clicked into place and she fired.

The missile flew across the flat where the battle raged, emitting fire as it went, and exploded on contact with the behemoth's gargantuan body. Like a Roman candle, secondary explosions went off all around the impact point, bullets pinging off the behemoth's arms and legs. The arm containing the cannon halted in mid-aim. Dropped. Rose again, halting in the same place.

The secondary shot had got into the gears and they'd seized up.

The pirates cheered, and cut off abruptly when the second arm rose and took aim.

Gloria fired again—and again—and the Californio forces seemed to realize their danger. They heard a sound almost like a trumpet and the behemoth turned its impassive isinglass face in their direction, where they'd thought they were safe up on their promontory. Evan squinted to see a bugler—of all the antiquated things—beside an elegant man standing in the door of a luxury car directly behind the locomotive. Wearing a black suit of clothes with a short jacket and silver brooches running down the sides of his snug pants, the man clung to the brass railing of the stair, waving commands with his free arm that the bugler translated into sound. Evan had not met him during his stay in Philadelphia, but this could only be the Ambassador.

Each side was down to only a few men, but the behemoth was sure to turn the tide.

"They're running!" screamed Ned Mose below them to his decimated gang. "After them! It can't turn fast enough!"

Gloria hauled on the wheel to fire the gun at the behemoth and give Ned some cover. Once again, the explosions peppered the thing, but its carapace seemed even harder than iron. Even the double-acting missiles did not penetrate it. Shells fell sparkling to the ground, only doing damage when they worked their way by accident into the piston mechanisms that made the thing walk.

And it was walking inexorably toward them.

ALICE COULD SEE through a grindstone with a hole in it. "We're outgunned," she said to Jake, flat on her belly as the two of them fired round after round at the mercenaries from behind the lifeless hulk of their machine. "There's no beating that thing. Ned is just too stubborn to see it."

Jake glanced at the body of Melvin, who had been hit by one of the Gatling gun's secondary bullets ricocheting off the behemoth's body, and died before he'd hit the ground. The same flurry of gunfire had put paid to their steam engine. "Time to fall back."

Three pirate machines remained of the crowd of more than a dozen snarling, jury-rigged crates that had originally roared into battle. The mercenaries hadn't fared much better. Bodies littered the ground, but the Ambassador and his bodyguard were still holed up in the train, using its iron bulk for protection. They had the advantage, for unless someone could circle around behind the train and board it, they could sit in comfort and the behemoth's protected crew would pick off anyone who approached.

Except it was heading for the big Gatling gun on the ridge, where its crew had finally gotten itself together and started firing the thing. Even now it hadn't given up, clearly going for disabling the legs instead of fruitlessly bombing the giant body.

"We could try to board the train," Alice said.

"And be shot by the men on it?" Jake shook his head. "Time to cut our losses and do as you said before Ned notices we're gone."

"That Gatling gun could shoot *Swan* out of the sky. Whoever is manning it knows what he's doing."

"We'll take our chances." Jake's tone was bitter. "Better that than dying here in the dirt with a Californio's boots in my face."

"Or Ned's."

"Aye. Or his. Again."

She plucked a sack of shells from the tilted floor of the chariot, and tucked the Colt carbine under her arm. "All right, then. Head for that pile of rocks, then over the bank of the arroyo to the riverbed."

They scrambled to their feet and, heads low, began to run. Behind them, someone screamed and Alice threw a glance over her shoulder, expecting to see a man go down.

Instead, she saw Ned Mose in a cloud of dust, riding his chariot into the dirt as it died under him. "Alice!" he roared. "Git over here and cover me!"

Ducking lower, she ran for the rocks as though the hounds of hell were after her. A few more yards—

"Alice, you yellow-bellied whelp of a whore! Where are you going?"

Just a few more and she'd be safely out of range—

"Alice!" he bawled, crimson with rage. He hefted his rifle—

—just a few—

The bullet slammed into her and spun her clean off her feet. She landed flat on her back, her head caught a rock, and she lay there, stunned.

"Captain!" Jake scrambled toward her on all fours—at least, she hoped it was Jake. She couldn't seem to move her head.

"Don't you run out on me!" Ned bellowed.

Alice couldn't see. Couldn't breathe as the pain swamped her. But she heard Jake rack a shell into her Colt carbine. She heard the bark of the rifle.

Another scream.

Rack. Fire.

So many screams. So much death.

And then the dark closed in and took her to hell with it.

CHAPTER 11

Gloria didn't let up on her attack on the behemoth. The carousel clicked into firing position time after time as she emptied the first layer of cartridges into it, and when she threw the next lever up to drop the second layer into place, she took out a squadron of four men in black uniforms sneaking up on a pirate chariot for good measure.

She was fed up to *here* with being discounted and hidden away and treated like a Dresden shepherdess when by George, she had knowledge that could help, and the skill to put it into action.

"Boy!" Evan shouted up at her. "It's no use—we've got to fall back!"

"No!" she shrieked over the roar of the gun. "I can do it—just give me time!"

But they had run out of time. The behemoth raised the arm containing the cannon and for one frozen second, she looked straight into the eyes of the gunner in his isinglass chamber. He touched the brim of his black cap in acknowledgement of her ability, and then lowered it to grip the firing lever.

"No!" Evan screamed, and with an almighty yank, pulled her out of the gunner's brace and rolled her off the back of the wagon. They tumbled down the slope like a pair of fighting wildcats while the behemoth fired. The missile detonated on the wagon, blowing the gun straight up in the air, tearing it to pieces along with the bodies of its crew. Brass parts and wood and flesh and unspent cartridges rained down on the slope, on them, pummeling them in a mindless attack.

Gloria screamed as they went over a bank into a small canyon maybe five or six feet deep, and she landed face down in its sandy bottom a second before Evan landed on top of her.

"Oof!" The breath went out of her and she lay stunned, her lungs laboring to take in air.

Pieces of the wagon and the gun were still raining down, as though they had been flung hundreds of feet into the air.

"Evan!" She pushed herself to her knees and tugged at him. "Get out of the way—closer to the bank!"

But he did not move.

"Evan!" And then she saw the side of his head, awash with blood seeping through the thick dust, and the slackness of his mouth, and the marionette sprawl of his body. "Evan! Oh, no, dear heaven, please, no—"

She looked up as a shadow crossed the sun. The behemoth! It had found—

A circular brass plate bounced off her head and knocked her back into the dirt, and the world spindled up and went out as though someone had blown out a lamp.

~

"I SAW him go over the back, Captain Escobar. The fall would have taken him—ah. There, down in the arroyo."

Voices. Men's voices. Not screaming, not shouting over the cacophony of engines and guns, but conversing in normal tones. Feet scraped on a rock, and then two thumps, as though men had jumped down a few feet from where Gloria lay.

How strange that she could hear, but could not move her eyelids by so much as a flicker. Nor her body. And strangely, she did not care. If she had any luck, she would die before they got to her.

"Are they alive? It would be a shame if the gunner were not. Such skill and presence of mind. I vow if he is dead, it will be a waste of talent for His Highness's forces."

"The taller appears to be dead," a voice reported. "Head wound."

Despair pressed down upon her. Poor Evan, so gallant and brave. His death was her fault. If he had not tried to save her, he might have been able to get away uninjured.

"And the gunner? He wore an aeronaut's cap and goggles. Is that he?"

"*Si*. Still breathing." Someone pressed fingers to her throat, then hefted Gloria into the air and tossed her over his shoulder as though she were a sack of potatoes. Again the breath went out of her. Her nose bumped his back as he climbed the bank. He smelled of sweat and gunpowder and wool.

"Ah, what luck. *Volvamos*. The Ambassador will be pleased —as am I."

The blood rushed into her head as she hung lifelessly, and

it felt as though it might swell up and explode, like a ripe melon. Her entire life faded away, to be replaced by a hellish, painful journey across goodness only knew how many hundreds of yards, before she was unceremoniously dumped on the ground once more.

"Where is the doctor? If the explosion has damaged this one's brain, there is no hope for him. We will simply leave him with his companions for the coyotes and the vultures."

Leave? Gloria attempted to open an eyelid, but the effort was too much. Was the battle over? Had the pirates lost, then —was that why these men were so unhurried and deliberate? It must be. But if they had won, how could they leave with their train disabled and the track destroyed? Had they captured *Swan*? Where was Alice? And Jake and Benny? Were they dead, too?

A rush of urgency filled her, and she cracked open an eye. A man knelt beside her and set a doctor's bag on the ground next to her head.

"Ah. He wakes," said someone hovering behind his shoulder.

The kneeling man chuckled. "Captain, you must allow me to fit you with spectacles. This is not a he, but a she."

"She?" the other man said incredulously, to the point that Gloria thought she ought to feel offended, but could not muster the strength. "This is the wrong person. A woman could not have operated that gun at all, much less with such familiarity."

"There were no other survivors wearing a flight cap," said the man who had carried her, a little defensively. "You did see a person in a flight cap, did you not?"

"*Si, si,* I have said so," said the gunnery captain impatiently.

The man who had saluted her—who had shown her respect when he thought she was a man. "This will not do. I must consult with His Excellency on the matter. Doctor, see what you can do for him. Her. *Madre de Dios*."

Muttering, he strode away, while Gloria struggled to manage her other eyelid.

"Are you in pain?" the doctor asked, pressing her middle and finding only the corset. He examined arms and legs, turning her booted feet this way and that. "Have you any broken bones?"

"No," she croaked, suffering quite sufficiently, thank you, from all the bruises his fingers had found. "Ow!"

His hands froze on her scalp. "You have pain here?"

"Hit. Something fell."

"Ah. We must hope the skull is not fractured." He pulled off the flight cap and her hair, which had been pinned up at some time that seemed like ancient history now, fell down around her shoulders and into the dust. The two men who seemed to be watching the proceedings murmured between themselves in the Californio tongue while the doctor's businesslike fingers pressed and prodded her scalp.

"I do not feel a depression—the opposite, rather. You will have an impressive lump on your forehead and some spectacular bruising. But it will pass, thanks to the padding in your cap. I have an ointment that should help."

"Evan," she whispered.

"Pardon?"

"Evan. The man with me. You must not leave him." The thought of the coyotes and vultures made her sick with horror.

"I understand there is nothing more to be done for the

other man, unless he is a child of Holy Mother Church. In any case, here is the Ambassador. Can you sit up, *senorita*?"

She struggled to do so, and fell back with a cry as the pain blinded her. But she could not face Senor de Aragon y Villarreal while lying in the dust like a corpse. She was Gloria Meriwether-Astor, the toast of Philadelphia. Perhaps she might appeal to him to give Evan a Christian burial, regardless of Holy Mother Church. If she could do nothing else for her poor friend, at least she could do that.

The second time she attempted to sit up, the doctor assisted her, and offered her something foul-tasting from a silver flask. She swallowed, coughed, and this time movement did not hurt quite so much. She squinted up at the Ambassador, but could not see more than a black silhouette against the burning sky.

"Dios!" he exclaimed. "I never thought to see you again!"

"You know this young woman, Excellency?" the doctor said in astonishment. "How is that possible?"

"It is magic. Incomprehensible. A miracle of God." Senor de Aragon moved to the side so that Gloria got a better look at him. He was still dressed in formal black, the only concession to having led a battle being the slight disarray of his hair. "It does not seem possible. Yet—"

"Who is she, Excellency?" the gunnery captain demanded. "She dresses like a man, shoots like a man, and yet faints like a gently bred *genta de razon* from one of our own *ranchos*."

"That is because she *is* gently bred, and a woman of high *casta*, Captain Escobar," the Ambassador said reprovingly. "This is none other than Gloria Meriwether-Astor, whose father was such a friend to the late Viceroy that His Highness wore black ribbons for an entire day when he was informed of his death." Boots scraped in the rocky dirt as the men shifted and looked from each other to her and back again. "What is the matter with you, allowing her to lie in the dust?" he snapped. "Carry her into *Silver Wind* at once, so that *el doctor* may attend her there."

This time, she was not slung over someone's back like a sack of food. This time, the gunnery captain himself slipped an arm beneath her knees and shoulders, and lifted her as gently as though she were his own daughter. The man was very strong; she was no fragile miss with a seventeen-inch waist, yet he carried her past the behemoth's motionless bulk and the burning hulks of several pirate chariots as though she weighed no more than a small child.

The least movement jostled her head, making her feel as though her brain were made of jelly, slapping and wobbling against the walls of her skull. But she had enough presence of mind to glance over his shoulder in the direction of the town and the cluster of rocks where *Swan* had been moored.

No blue and silver airship floated above it.

The harsh landscape was as empty as if Alice had never been there, as if nothing had existed before pain and battle and Evan's death except the low winter sun, the red mesa, and the scrubby pines.

Gloria's eyes closed under the weight of her despair. There was no one to help. No hope of rescue. For the second time in her life, she was utterly alone and in the company of those who had no reason to wish her well ... and every reason to wish her ill if they realized for an instant the meaning of her presence.

At least this time she had walked into it with her eyes wide open. That was an improvement.

She had less than a minute to rouse her poor brain to decide how much of the truth to tell ... though it seemed quite clear that nearly every word might be grounds for execution.

Silver Wind was much bigger and more imposing from the ground than it had looked from the air. Despite having been fired upon and its braking and reversing systems taxed to their limits, it still looked as beautiful as it had sitting in their rail yard in Philadelphia.

She wished she could say the same of herself—but perhaps the pathetic, injured approach was best. Not that she felt capable of anything more. Claire Trevelyan Malvern had told her once that sometimes a woman's greatest weapon was the fact that she was often underestimated.

A second man assisted the gunnery captain to carry her up the wrought-iron exterior steps at the rear of the great locomotive. And here Gloria saw what she had not known before —that within the great engine were not multiple steam boilers and coal boxes, but a luxurious saloon meant to house the owner of the train, providing the maximum in comfort with the utmost in safety. The lounge car that had been coupled behind was merely for the entertainment of guests. It was inside the locomotive that the most important members of the party would sleep, safe behind iron walls.

Comfortable bunks were set from floor to ceiling, three to a side and two at the front, with sliding cupboard doors that might be drawn across for privacy. A mahogany dining table did double duty as a navigation table, and as they laid her on a sofa, Gloria looked up to see that the roof of this half of the engine was not in fact iron, but some kind of impermeable, translucent material that arched overhead, allowing in the sunlight while keeping out the weather.

Whoever had designed this engine was a genius. It was a crime to abandon such a beautiful thing in the desert. For surely they must do so—unless the Californios proposed to walk home.

"*Por favor,* Miss Meriwether-Astor, drink a little more of this." The doctor had followed them inside, and obediently, she drank again from the silver flask. Whatever the liquid was, it possessed great powers of restoration, for her head began to clear and she was able to focus both eyes on his kind face. The doctor nodded in satisfaction. "That's better. Your Excellency, the young lady may be able to answer your questions now."

And here she had thought he might be concerned for her health because of the vow he had taken. With a sigh, she prepared herself to be the frail sort of woman who could rouse the protective instincts of a man. At the moment, it would not be much of an act.

The Ambassador pulled up a chair covered in brown and purple brocade, his black eyes limpid with concern. "Do you feel well enough to speak? For though I am anxious to hear your tale, I will not press you. We have many days ahead for the telling of tales."

"Many days?"

"*Si, senorita.* It is a full seven days' journey to San Francisco, even without the weight of the cargo cars."

Gloria could not grasp it. Perhaps the liquid in the flask was not as restorative as she had supposed. "You can walk across the Wild West in a week? How is that possible?"

He laughed as though she had made a joke. "We will not be walking, my dear young lady. We will proceed in comfort aboard *Silver Wind.*"

She had believed this man to be arrogant, and far too convinced of his countrymen's skills in battle. But this went far beyond that—hubris so great that it would power a locomotive across several hundred yards of broken track to reach the main line?

Never mind. She must stick to her decision, and to facts. "Please, Senor de Aragon, I beg you for one favor before I tell my tale."

"Of course, my dear. Would you like another cushion?" He tucked it behind her back as though she had answered in the affirmative.

"Thank you. How do you say it in your tongue?"

"Gracias."

She repeated the word, so similar to Italian. Her pronunciation was identical to his, which she saw pleased him. All to the good.

"My request is not for me, but for my companion—the young man whose body lies in a shallow canyon behind the promontory. Please, could you give him a Christian burial? He died bravely, to protect me, and I cannot bear the thought of —of the coyotes." Tears sprang to her eyes.

He gazed at her sadly. "If it were any other favor, I would grant it, and gladly. But we are already a day behind schedule. It is bad enough that we will arrive without the cargo His Highness paid for, and have to return with another train. But to arrive late when his son is anxiously waiting?" He shook his head, then said, as though he had had an excellent idea, "I will have the padre say a prayer for the soul of your companion. We pray regularly for the heathen, so this would not be unsuitable."

"Gracias," she said weakly, wishing she had the strength to

strike him with the cushion. "But many fell today—would His Highness not understand if we took a few moments to see if any live?"

Was Alice's body out there under some piece of scrap metal? Or Jake's? Could she not at least be given the opportunity to see for certain, and say a prayer of her own for her friends?

"To what purpose? And why such concern? They are only despicable pirates. The bodies of our own men, of course, have been retrieved, and the injured seen to. A contingent of men has taken control of the town nearby, which fortunately seems to be populated mainly by women, who will care for our men until a company returns to retrieve them. We cannot house everyone on *Silver Wind*." His gaze settled on her with finality. "Perhaps my questions will be answered during the telling of your tale. But for now, please make yourself comfortable."

He rose and crossed the Turkish carpet to a speaking tube in the front of the saloon. "You may depart, Senor de la Vega. We have not a moment to lose."

"*Si*, Your Excellency."

How could they depart? It was impossible. In dreams, people said and did impossible things; therefore, she must be dreaming. That was it. No wonder none of this seemed real.

She was still lying unconscious in that arroyo, Evan was not dead, and Alice and Jake would come looking for her at any moment. It was the only explanation for her present companions' complete disregard for reality. Gloria sat back, immensely cheered, and interested to observe what fantasy her own unconscious mind might now produce.

Through the glass above, she saw gouts of steam as the

engineer began the ignition sequence and the great boilers responded. *Silver Wind*'s iron body shuddered, and a series of heavy clanks underneath her made the polished floorboards vibrate. Then, with a scream of her whistle like the embodiment of bereavement itself, the locomotive shifted abruptly sideways, clanked, and began to move.

"What . . .?" Gloria struggled to sit upright on the sofa.

Slowly, the panorama of desert through the viewing port wheeled to the north as the locomotive turned—there were the destroyed pirate chariots, the bodies, the resting behemoth—the west, the promontory where the CG-36 had been mounted, behind which the sun was setting in blood-red glory—and then to the south.

With another scream of the whistle, huge gouts of steam billowed upward, and *Silver Wind* began to make way across the broken landscape.

"How—how is this possible?" Gloria whispered, clutching the arm of the sofa. "This is a dream!"

"I regret the necessity for contradicting you, *senorita,*" Senor de Aragon said with a smile, "but it is neither dream nor miracle. It is simply the excellence of our late Viceroy's imagination, and your father's partnership with the Stanford Fremont locomotive foundry. Between the two, we have been able to make his vision a reality."

She gaped at him, and then watched in disbelief as they passed the crater where the pressure bomb had destroyed hundreds of yards of track, staring until she could see it no more.

"*Silver Wind* is aptly named," he went on. "She is the first of her kind. Along with the standard twelve wheels for the rails, she has a secondary set of wheels for land, which adjust as necessary to the topography. It is upon these that we presently make our progress. The rails, of course, are much more efficient. We will resume our journey once we reach the main line."

"I am not dreaming," she said flatly. As Resolution faded into the distance—and the past—she realized belatedly that while she had been lying comfortably on this sofa in denial, her only hope of escape had faded, too.

"No, you are not," he assured her. "I am delighted you have the honor to be present at this unexpected demonstration of the engine's abilities. Now, *senorita,* while we journey these few miles to the main line and pause to transfer to the rails again, I believe you have a story to tell me."

CHAPTER 12

"I don't see why we ought to care for the same men who killed our own. In fact, now would be a fine time to finish the job—while they're half mad from pain or passed out altogether."

The voice seemed to come from a long distance away, distorted as though transmitted through a blocked speaking tube. Evan had heard the appealingly accented feminine tones before, though he couldn't place exactly where.

"For land's sakes, keep your voice down, Bonita! Those soldiers wouldn't think nothing of shooting us where we stand just for having such thoughts. Bad enough we're out here at all. If they ask, we're looking for plunder."

"But what do we do if we find someone alive? If Ned's alive? Dadburnit, Lorraine, he's your man! You going to let one of those black jackets shoot him?"

"It'll take more than a bunch of dandies to kill Ned Mose," came the grim reply. "He's out here somewhere, and I aim to find him. Now, look. That arroyo's full of blown-up parts and pieces. Could be we'll find someone in there."

In a moment, above the scrape of boots on stone and the flapping of cotton skirts, someone gasped. "Lorraine! It's that nice boy Alice brought. Oh, say he ain't dead!"

Evan felt warm fingers at his throat, then in his pockets with light-fingered skill. There was nothing in them, though, except perhaps a few shell casings. Everything he owned was on *Swan*.

Swan.

Gloria.

Memory cascaded in like a landslide, and he moaned.

"He's alive," Lorraine said. "Boy, can you hear me?"

He tried to speak, but his mouth wouldn't form words. A gutteral sound came out instead.

"He ought to be dead," Bonita observed doubtfully. "All the blood—it looks awful."

"Head wound. They look worse than they are." Capable hands felt his skull, and while it ached as though it were one giant bruise encasing his consciousness, there was no sudden screaming flash of pain, either, that would have indicated a more serious wound.

His medical degree had given him more than a passing acquaintance with the frailty of the human body, and the wards of hospitals had given him an understanding of pain both mental and physical. Now he knew even more on that head than he had before. He opened his eyes, expecting to have to squint against the noon sun, and met the soothing apricot gray of early twilight instead.

Gloria. Oh Lord, help me.

"Can you hear me, I said," Lorraine repeated. "Can you talk? Move? What's broken?"

He took inventory, moving feet, legs, fingers—nine out of

ten—and arms. Then he rolled his head from side to side. He appeared to have sustained no broken bones except for the smallest finger of his left hand, which had swollen to the size of a plum in an effort to protect itself. And it was difficult to breathe without pain, which told him he had probably cracked a rib.

Lorraine watched him, clearly having seen this procedure before. "This is a fine kettle of trout," she said. "What are we going to do with you?"

"Leave him here for the moment," Bonita suggested, rather callously, in his opinion. "We have to check over the hill. If anyone is alive, they won't last the night. Not with the coyotes and the pumas."

Evan didn't know what a puma was, but if it was anything like a coyote, he didn't want to find out.

"Glo—" he croaked, and stopped himself. No, he couldn't say her name, could he? What was the other one she had said she would use?

"What's that?" Lorraine was already standing, but now she bent to him.

"Meredith."

"Who's that? Never heard of her."

"Another—body—here? Woman?"

"Was someone with you? Was Alice? Bonita, have a look around. It might be Alice—and she might know where my Perry is."

But while there were others, none were alive, or whole, and before long, the two women scrambled up the wall of the arroyo with instructions to stay put until they got back, and the sound of their departure faded.

How could Gloria have deserted him?

Misery swamped him, and it took a good ten minutes to weather the storm of grief, lying there in the sandy bottom of the wash as the twilight thickened, wishing his injuries had just killed him and been done with it. But at last, good sense swam to the surface to reassert itself. The truth was that she would not have left him had it been up to her. For she had come running from the airship to save him from the same fate as the air pirate, who had fired a gun incorrectly assembled.

His heart would have warmed at this possibility of a change in her regard for him, had the situation not been so dire.

For the fact was that they had landed together in this arroyo. He distinctly remembered falling over the edge with her in his arms. Had she been injured, and been taken somewhere? Not by the pirate contingent, that was certain. By the Californios? A chill of foreboding prickled his skin. She could not be dead, for they would have left her as they had left him. If those men had touched a single hair on her head, they would answer to him. And while he was rescuing her, he must look for Alice, and Jake.

Grunting with the pain, he rolled to his knees, and then, with the help of a sinewy juniper, pulled himself to his feet.

The vertical walls of the arroyo nearly defeated him, until he found the draw where Lorraine and Bonita had climbed out. Half stumbling, half crawling, he gained the slope of the promontory and skirted around it until the flat where the fight had been came into view.

Off to the left, he sensed something had changed, and with an effort, turned to look.

Above the pile of rocks where *Swan* had been moored, there was only empty air.

She had not been shot down, for no deflated fuselage lay on the ground. But she could have been stolen. She must have been. For Alice and Jake to have lifted while leaving him and Gloria behind was so unthinkable that it defied possibility. It could simply not have happened.

He turned back to the field, and reality shimmered into doubt a second time. He stared at the track, where he would have staked his life the great locomotive had been standing, steam curling up around its wheels and mercenaries pouring out of the doors of its cars. The cars were there. The bodies of several mercenaries strewed the ground, along with wrecked chariots and broken lumber and shells and guns.

But the locomotive was gone.

It could not be gone. There was no longer any track for it to run on. But it was as gone as Alice's airship, leaving behind the lounge car to which it had been coupled, the cargo cars, and the caboose.

Had the airship carried it away? Had it been rendered invisible by some alchemy of war? Was he dreaming? For every moment since he'd regained consciousness had been wrong somehow, from murderous grieving women to disappearing people to vanishing conveyances.

But he would not be in this much pain if he were dreaming.

Perhaps this was why they called it the Wild West. The rules of physics and mathematics and logic simply did not seem to apply here. Perhaps there was even magic at work, and if he were himself, he might be tempted to explore that possibility in the name of science. But he was not himself. Doggedly, Evan resigned himself to a reality that had lost its ability to make sense, and staggered down the slope.

Along with the cars full of mechanicals and arms, the Californios had left behind the behemoth. Reality took another blow. These munitions had cost their country a fortune. And yet, there stood the behemoth, bent over, the weight of its trunk resting upon its extended arms—or arm, in this case, since the other was still cocked at an angle because of the exploding secondary rounds that had jammed its pistons. In this position it would be less likely to fall over, for heaven only knew how one would set it right again if it did.

The head of the behemoth was lost in shadow. It was nearly dark, twilight being much shorter here in the desert than he was used to. But he could hear the voices of the women somewhere over toward a small rise crowned by rocks, and then one of them gave a sharp cry.

"Ned! Aw, Ned, they done for you—I never would have believed it." And then a sob. Was there really someone who would grieve the death of Ned Mose? "Dadblast you, Ned, now what am I going to do? You left me alone with these Californios and you know darn well our lives ain't worth a plug nickel to 'em."

Evan turned away.

Evidently not.

A slow, agonized walk across the field of battle in the fading light showed him that neither Alice nor Jake were among the dead. That was something. If Lorraine did not know where she was, then perhaps she and Jake really had lifted. Perhaps they had found Gloria close to death, and had taken her to a larger settlement, where there was hope of a doctor.

One who was alive, and had actually practiced medicine. Perhaps they had taken their chances, and run while they could, leaving him where he lay because, like Bonita, they thought he was dead.

The dearth of facts in this place was likely to drive him mad. Could he not fix on one solid thing?

For want of a better plan, he made his slow way over to Lorraine and Bonita, still kneeling disconsolately next to Ned's body. Bonita was already disconnecting the mechanical arm.

"I have not been able to find Alice or Jake," he told them. It was difficult to take a deep breath. "Have you?"

"No," Lorraine said. "Them Californios were thorough, I'll give them that. They brought all the survivors from their side to us. We got no doctor here, so me and some of the girls have learned a thing or two about binding up wounds, but these injuries ..." Her voice faded. "Could be they just shot any who couldn't be patched up, including our men, and were done with it."

"How many are among their wounded?" Evan asked.

"A dozen or so. The girls been wasting good whiskey on bullet wounds, and we've got some broken bones. They set two healthy men to watch us, so I s'pose we'll have to feed them on top of everything else."

"They will not hurt you as long as you are useful to them," he ventured.

"They won't hurt us as long as we ain't there," Lorraine retorted. "I got no reason to stay here, and my Perry ain't nowhere to be found. He wasn't on the dadburned locomotive when it left, so I'm betting he's with Alice on that airship."

"Wait—what did you say?" He must have sustained a brain injury of some kind, for the world kept spinning farther and farther away from rationality. "The locomotive *left?*"

She nodded, felt in her pockets, and produced a stubby cheroot and a lucifer. She scraped the latter alight on a piece of sandstone and took a crackling draw before she went on, "Couldn't believe my eyes. It was a nightmare—I come to find if my poor boy is alive and here's hell spread out for acres in front of me. That devil locomotive picks up one set of wheels, puts down another, turns itself around, and goes rolling off into the sunset as slick as you please. They took one of ours, too. Some poor soul who must've been less dead than he looked." She frowned at the glowing end of the cheroot in her fingers. "It don't make sense. Why take one and shoot all the others? But then, I'm thinking Californios don't make a lick of sense to start with. They take one of ours and leave a bunch of theirs and not a word about a ransom or nothing."

"We don't have anything to pay a ransom with," Bonita pointed out. "Just our feminine charms, and they don't seem too interested in those."

"They're busted up, you goose," Lorraine reminded her. "They're men, same as any other men. They'll come around. But before they do, we'll be gone."

"Gone?" Evan repeated.

With a final draw, she tossed the end of the cheroot away. "Come along, Bonita. You too, mister. I forgot your name. The freight from Santa Fe goes through at midnight and I aim to jump it when it slows for the switch. I got no obligation to play nursemaid to folk who killed my man."

"When that locomotive comes back for them, I don't imagine they'll feel much obligation to us, either. Probably shoot us as soon as look at us," Bonita predicted unhappily.

Lorraine nodded. "They think they can lock us up, but they're mistaken. I told the girls to put belladonna in that whiskey. I'm done with this place. Figure I'll take my chances back east."

Despite her invitation to come along, she didn't stay to see if he would. And by the time Evan came out of his thoughts, night had fallen and both women were gone.

Material facts, at last. Two of them, which rocked the world back onto its axis and allowed him to think once more.

The locomotive could travel on both rail and land. The Californios had taken one of the pirates. Lorraine was right—it didn't make sense, unless that pirate was not a pirate at all, but Gloria Meriwether-Astor, the one person outside his own force of mercenaries who was personally known to the Ambassador commanding the fight. Somehow she had come to their attention, been recognized, and been taken away—the very thing he and Alice had gone to such great lengths to prevent.

So now the questions he had to answer for himself numbered two, as well. One, should he find Alice and solicit her help to rescue Gloria, or two, should he waste no more time in settting forth on his own to attempt it?

And how was he going to manage either one of those options? To set out on a journey, one needed transportation and supplies. Shank's mare was not going to do the job—if he made it to the main line without losing consciousness, it would be a miracle. So, he must either steal a conveyance, if one could be had, or build one.

In the dark, before he was caught and shot.

Evan frowned and moved on to the next part of the equation, which might be more easily solved. What about supplies? There stood the luxury coach; surely there was food aboard. He had not had anything to eat since breakfast ... aboard

Swan, with Gloria and the crew. Had that only been this morning? It seemed to have been a dream, lived in another life. A sweet, civilized dream in which he would never contemplate killing a man, or abandoning the injured, or looting someone else's train.

But looting was the only sensible course of action when he needed sustenance—if only to dim the buzzing in his head and to keep up his strength.

Inside the car, he found exactly what he had imagined—and a few things he hadn't. In a porcelain bowl, he bathed his scrapes and bruises in fine French brandy to prevent infection, taking a liberal swallow for medicinal purposes. A length of white damask from the table made a serviceable binding for his ribs, two silver sugar spoons made a splint for his finger, and an investigation of the sideboard and cupboards in search of a sharper knife resulted in the discovery of a switch that, when pressed, made a statue of the Holy Virgin swing out of its carved niche. In the eight-inch recess behind her he found a gold bracelet set with rubies and sapphires, and a stack of gold coins bearing the likeness of Felipe XV of Spain.

Neither were edible. Neither belonged to him. But only heaven knew how long his journey was going to be.

He untied the damask bindings around his ribs and folded the coins and bracelet into the fabric as he re-wrapped it. If a flash flood came, he would likely sink like a stone to the bottom, but at least he could pay for his rescue.

In the galley to the rear of the saloon he found bread, cheese, apples, bacon, and the cold remains of the lunch served to the Ambassador and his guests—a roast fowl, squash, and potatoes. He ate the latter and wrapped the former in another towel. The capable-looking carving knife with the chased silver handle accompanying the fowl went into his belt like that of a pirate, where he hoped he would manage not to stab himself.

Food and the excellent brandy had cheered him a little, even if it did nothing for the pain in his head. The need to lie down and sleep upon the red velvet sofa came over him in a wave, and he swayed.

No. He must rescue Gloria, and every moment he hesitated took her farther away. Surely they could not be very far ahead—no more than a few hours' journey.

All he had to do was find some means of travel.

With a deep breath, he took a final look around the saloon at all the luxury items—china and plate and boxes of cigars and cushions and books and cards—that were useless to a man's survival in this harsh landscape. Then, taking the lantern that hung outside and lighting it, he swung himself down from the stairs at the rear of the car.

He was halfway across the flat, heading toward the town and picking his way carefully so that he did not stumble in a crevasse or trip over a corpse, when he saw tiny lights glowing just at the edge of his field of vision. Startled, he swung the lamp, and a scurrying in the dirt told him he was being watched. He went on a little faster. Animals, that was all.

But what sort? Rodents? Or bigger—coyotes? Or bigger yet—could it be a puma? What *was* a puma?

And where was he headed, anyway, out here in the dark? He might buy transport from Lorraine, if such a thing now existed, but the healthy mercenaries would catch him before he could leave. Predators with two and four legs abounded here—lured in by carnage. The four-legged sort would probably enjoy the bundle he was carrying. Or one of his legs. He should have stayed in the lounge car. Or taken refuge in one of the cargo cars, where at least he could possess himself of a gun, take up a position behind the crates, and build a barricade.

Blast and bebother it! He should have thought earlier of taking a gun.

Not twenty feet away, in a cluster of scrub pine, an animal whined. Another replied, and then a host of canine voices chimed in, howling.

Coyotes.

Primal fear reared up inside him, obliterating twenty-eight years of civilized life—including the ten spent earning a medical degree and a doctorate in the studies of the mind.

Limping, hobbling, Evan clutched his bundle and the lamp and made for the looming hulk of the behemoth, closer now than the shelter the train would have provided. He was a fool to have left the lounge car. Perhaps he could get his back up against one of these metal legs and use the carving knife to protect himself.

Around him, the glowing eyes narrowed and closed in.

CHAPTER 13

Gloria fussed a little with the cushion behind her back as *Silver Wind* steamed steadily into the gathering dusk. She had managed to put the Ambassador off for several minutes with questions about how long it would take the locomotive to regain its footing on the rails, and how remarkable it was that they need not even be concerned about the position of the switch at the junction—they might simply retake the rails where they pleased.

Which was a great pity, because the notion of leaping out of the door and running into the deepening dark while they changed the switch had been extremely appealing. If it came to a choice between being marooned in Resolution with coyotes, mercenaries, and air pirates and being kidnapped by the Ambassador on a westbound train, she would take the former without hesitation.

But she was not given the choice. A man was stationed at each door—for her safety, she was assured. The locomotive settled itself over the rails, the clanking of changing ironworks underneath sounded once more, and with a huge billow of steam, they were under way.

"I confess I feel very foolish," she began at last, having no further prevarications to make. "After our lovely talk in the conservatory at Mrs. Hadley's, I had settled into the role of president of the Meriwether-Astor Munitions Works by a majority vote of the board."

The men shifted, glancing at one another.

Oh, for goodness sake. "I have been trained practically since birth to inherit the business," she said a little tartly. "It is my father's legacy, and he made sure that I would be able to manage it competently through the best education, the most comprehensive travels, and of course, his personal guidance while he was alive."

She allowed her lower lip to tremble, and dashed a tear from her cheek. It was a very real tear; she had been quite looking forward to leaping out of that blasted door to freedom.

His face creased with gentlemanly sympathy, the gunnery captain offered her a handkerchief that smelled only a little of gear grease, and she accepted it with a grateful smile.

"It was not long after the train departed that I heard it was going to be waylaid. So I immediately took ship to try to warn you—only to find myself too late—and worse, captured by those dreadful pirates."

The Ambassador leaned forward. "How did you hear it was going to be waylaid?"

Here was a poser. Then, in a flash of illumination, she had the answer. Quickly, she turned her hesitation into reluctance. "I—I find this quite the most difficult part of the tale. For you see, I was betrayed by a member of my own family—

my cousin Sydney, whom I have known and loved all my life. Oh, how could he?" Delicately, she dabbed at her eyes with the handkerchief.

"Sydney?" the Ambassador said rather blankly. "But he is the young man who shook my hand, accepted the final payment, and released the train on its journey."

"Yes, I am sure he waved you off with every appearance of comradeship before he put the money in his own pocket," she said bitterly. "For he had already made arrangements with the inhabitants of that dreadful town back there to stop the train and relieve you of your—our—cargo. With the train vanished down an abandoned spur, His Highness the Viceroy would never know its fate, nor would there be any way to discover it."

"Dreadful," murmured someone near the brandy table.

"Shocking. *El diablo*."

"It is an appalling tale," the Ambassador said, frowning. "But how did you come to be behind that rotating gun? Of all that has occurred today, that seems to me to be the most strange."

"It is not so strange if you remember my father's training," she said. "I can shoot any of the arms we make. He made sure of that."

More shifting about as the men considered how unladylike such training was. They would probably faint if they knew she had grown up riding astride, too, and it was not until she had been enrolled in St. Cecelia's in London that she learned to manage a sidesaddle like a lady.

"So naturally," she went on, "the moment I was foolish enough to try to grab someone's gun and they saw I knew how to handle one, they at once realized the most painful thing they could do was not to assault me or even to kill me, but to set me to firing upon the very people I considered my friends and allies."

The Ambassador leaped to his feet. "If we had not already done so, I should set the locomotive in reverse and return to wipe out every single man," he fumed. "How dared they? They have no honor, no decency."

Gloria glanced at the gunnery captain with what she hoped was a sort of watery flirtatiousness. "And now, thanks to you, no CG-36 rotating carousel gun," she said.

He clasped her hand. "Please allow me to express my sincere regret for firing upon you," he begged. "Had I known—"

Flushing, she tugged her hands from his before she slapped him. "All is forgiven," she said. "In the end, you saved my life, even though you thought I was a man."

"I shall not make that mistake again, *senorita*," he said gallantly. "Your beauty is eclipsed only by your talent with a trigger. My only concern is how His Highness will take the news."

"Why should it concern him?" Gloria asked.

"Because we are taking you to meet him," the Ambassador said, taking control of the conversation once more.

"To meet him!" Gloria had the sensation that she had just stepped off one of the high red mesas, and was free-falling through space with no rocket rucksack. "Are we not going to Santa Fe, now that you have so bravely rescued me, so that I may arrange passage back to Philadelphia?"

She must at least find a postal office, where she could attempt to compose the letter that would break Ian Hollys's heart. And then she must write a similar one to Claire—or better yet, she should carry the sad news in person, to comfort her friends in their bereavement.

A bereavement that was all her fault.

"Philadelphia! What would that accomplish, my dear young lady?" the Ambassador exclaimed. "No indeed, it is you who will tell this heroic tale to His Highness, and beseech his forgiveness for the betrayal of your family."

"My family?" It was a moment before she could get her stunned brain to work, and her cold lips to move. "I believe I have hazarded my life to make reparation for that betrayal already, sir."

"Indeed you have, and that will certainly be a factor in His Highness's willingness to pardon you. But it must be done. No other course is possible to satisfy the demands of honor. You must beg forgiveness, and if he grants it, then you may return."

"And if he does not?" she said, her mouth dry as the prospect of a thousand miles of Wild West between herself and any person who might have seen her being kidnapped yawned before her. Not one soul in the country knew where she was. Or cared. Or could come to help.

She had been alone before. But isolation like this was as wide and bleak and terrifying as the country through which they traveled.

The Ambassador shook his head. "His Highness has not yet become the visionary—soldier—leader that his late father was. But he is a young man, and you are a beautiful young woman. I do not think he will withhold his magnanimity."

The prospect of hanging her life upon her ability to charm a young man—considering her demoralizing record in that department heretofore—did not appeal in the least.

She fanned herself with the handkerchief. "I—I feel quite overcome at the prospect. Please, may I beg your indulgence and withdraw?"

"We will stop at the next station to take on supplies," he told her. "Our dinner will not be elegant, but we all must eat. It is a journey of a hundred miles yet, so you would be wise to rest. It has been an eventful day for us all."

One of the men showed her to a sleeping cupboard, into which she crawled gratefully, sliding the door shut and blocking out their embarrassed faces. She had forgotten she was wearing Jake's pants. Briefly, she wondered where one might wash and perform other necessary ablutions, before sleep took her.

In what seemed like a moment, there was a knock on her cupboard door and she was escorted off the train to a ramshackle inn next to the station. *Silver Wind* hissed and groaned as her water tender was filled and the engineer saw to the great engines in front of the saloon with the arched glass roof. She was not left alone for a moment, and when she had eaten a respectable amount of the dinner set before her—for heaven only knew where her next meal was coming from—she was escorted to a room with a wash basin and a commode, and no window. A man stationed himself in front of the plank door as she closed it.

Her lips thinning with frustration, she used the commode and did her best to wash her face and neck. Only one hairpin remained of this morning's coiffure, stuck in a tangle. Well, one never knew when a hairpin would be useful in a lock, so she finger-combed her hair, braided it round her head as Alice did, and used the pin to anchor it.

Somewhat refreshed, she was escorted back to the train.

Lying fully dressed in the dark of the cupboard, listening to the snores of the men, there was nothing to do but to try to fend off fear and despair by plotting ways of escape.

It would have to be at night, and near a settlement of some kind, where one of the coins in her corset might buy her transportation. And it would have to be soon, before they crossed the border between the Texican Territory and the Californias. She doubted anyone could be paid to help her once she was in the Viceroy's realm. It would probably mean death to that person, and she would not wish that on anyone.

Oh Benny. Alice. Jake. What were the odds that they had survived? Just as low, perhaps, as the odds of anyone having seen her being carried aboard the train.

Evan. Why had she not been kinder to Evan? It was clear that he was smitten with her, and with his stiff, awkward way of speaking she had put him in his place as a brotherly acquaintance. In return, he had pulled her off that gun and saved her life at the cost of his own.

After years of feeling somehow unwomanly and left out because no one had yet shown sincere interest in her, it was a blow to realize too late that she had had real affection within her grasp and had not even recognized it. Grief welled up inside her, and she turned her face into the dusty-smelling pillow and wept. And a long time later, the rhythm of the wheels lulled her to sleep at last.

Her awakening in the gray light of dawn brought an ugly jolt of fear when she thought they had locked her in the sleeping compartment. But after a moment of determined deep breathing and pressing her lips together to keep from screaming, she tried the cupboard door again and found that it had merely stuck in its track, and a tug freed it.

She would not show fear.

She would be fragile, polite, deferential—everything they expected in a woman, without benefit of skirts and petticoats to complete the illusion. And at the first moment, she would seize her chance to escape.

Breakfast was cheese and bread and very tasty olives that she was assured came from the Californias themselves; from the rancho of the Ambassador, in fact.

"You have a *rancho*?" she asked, trying not to cram the delicious cheese into her mouth, but rather eat it as though she sat at a society table. "I understand they are very large indeed."

"They are, *senorita*. I possess two hundred thousand acres near the Mission de San Gregorio, with a view of the Pacific Ocean from at least five thousand of them."

"I have seen the Pacific," she said. "From the royal city of Victoria in the Canadas. It is awe-inspiring."

"Perhaps when you have obtained the Viceroy's forgiveness, you will come for a visit. My wife will welcome you gladly—and any information about the fashion of dresses, too." Politely, he did not glance at her pants.

"Does she not see many women?" With two hundred thousand acres to cross in order to see a neighbor, perhaps the poor lady did not.

"*Si*, indeed she does, for we have many fiestas and long visits among ourselves during the winter. It is a benign climate, and the *rancheros* are a social group, for we all have sons and daughters to marry off." He laughed, and several of the men laughed with him. "There is music and dancing, and more food than you have ever seen in one place. It is a good life *el Dios* has given us, *senorita*."

"And the men and women who till the fields to grow the

food, who cook it, and who clean up once the candles go out —what of them?" she asked. "Is their life a good one also?"

He gazed at her as if trying to parse her meaning. "All our people are fed and clothed, and have valuable work to do," he said.

"Ah, so they are paid a wage, then?"

Around the table, men looked at one another. She felt rather like a monkey who had done something human-like.

"You must understand our way of life, *senorita,*" the doctor said. "The laborers on the *ranchos* are not paid. They have honest work, and live their entire lives under the protection of the *ranchero*. They want for nothing."

"And can they move about freely? What if a man wishes to take up his own business off the rancho?"

The doctor smiled. "Why should he want to? He has no education but what is required to do simple mathematics for the counting of bushels, and so on. And he can write. These are not skills with which one can establish a business. However, many second and third sons of *rancheros* do so, and sometimes the laborers will work for them."

"And what of the women? And the daughters of *rancheros*? Are they educated also?"

The Ambassador was clearly struggling with the urge to laugh at this outrageous idea. Finally, he straightened his face and replied, "They are well educated in the feminine arts of sewing, cooking, and child rearing. Many a happy child grows up on the *rancho* to take up his father's work when the latter grows unable. And many a gently bred girl looks forward to a husband and home of her own."

Gloria smiled and nodded, doing her best to keep her expression pleasant and her feelings to herself. Such tales did nothing but make her look forward to escape. For once marooned on two hundred thousand acres of land, what were the odds of getting away?

Two hundred thousand to one.

Gloria gazed out through the great glazed arches of the saloon at the desert landscape, with its red rocks, green pines, and layers of brilliant color—purple, red, orange—like a sunset frozen forever in stone. She had been imprisoned before, but she had had friends with the courage and spirit to rescue her. Now she was alone in a magnificent landscape whose beauty itself could kill her.

Somehow she had to find the resources within herself to save her own life and stop the war. Once that was accomplished somehow, she would return to Philadelphia and make her life over without her friends. It would be a bleak life—a return to the existence she had led before meeting Lady Claire, and Alice, and Ian, and Jake. And Evan.

The view of the desert blurred, and she bent her head.

All she needed was one moment.

Just one.

CHAPTER 14

Evan Douglas put his back up against the cold iron leg of the behemoth and wished for a gun, or at the very least, a firebrand—in the flickers, the brave hero brandished fire at wolves and they ran away. But this was not the flickers, he was far from brave, and he had nothing but his wits to save him from the milling, growling pack of animals who shifted in and out of the small circle thrown by the lamp. With each pass, they came closer, and with each snarl he got a clearer look at their teeth.

Iron dug into his back, a horizontal bar across his kidneys.

Horizontal. A memory flashed before his mind's eye of the gunner in the chamber where the behemoth's head might be, and the crew working frantically in the chamber in its chest. But how had they got up there? They could not have been winched up, because the thing had been set into motion far too quickly for that.

Perhaps they had climbed up.

He held up the lantern and, keeping one eye on the coyotes, glanced up the leg against which he leaned. Sure enough, iron rungs had been constructed both to protect the mighty pistons that propelled it, and to form a ladder.

Without wasting another moment, he obeyed a gut-deep instinct to get out of reach of those teeth by any means possible. He hung his bag of food around his neck, grasped the wrought handle of the lantern more firmly, and heaved himself onto the first rung.

The coyotes rushed in, as though they had sensed he was escaping, and he was barely able to pull up his second boot in time. Yipping and howling in frustration, they milled about the behemoth's foot, snapping and jumping as he climbed the iron monster's leg rung by rung.

It was not a monster now. It was his salvation—until dawn, at least. Perhaps he could sleep inside it, as safe as if he were in the lounge car below. After that, he could only hope the animals would give up and leave him to climb down.

At the top of the leg, there was a platform only the width of a man's boot, and a door, which hung open a little way, likely because of the haste of the crew's departure. He put the lantern on the metal floor inside and pulled himself into the chamber, then latched the door securely.

Safe inside the marvel.

For marvel it was. He removed the cloth sack of food from around his neck and, lantern once more in hand, looked about him. A control console lay under the viewing ports, with two large levers in a kind of truss arrangement that gave them rather more range of motion than levers typically had.

The controls to the legs of the machine.

A great wheel occupied the other half of the console and after a moment of study, he surmised that this must be for controlling the machine's course, for pistons and levers could only move up and down. The mighty legs must be mounted on an assembly equivalent to human hips, which would allow a lateral change in direction.

No wonder this machine required a crew, to say nothing of the gunner above, who would control the movement of the firing arms.

In a moment, as he prowled to the rear of the chamber, he saw what the bulk of the behemoth's torso protected—the steam engines that gave it its power. What would it be like to have such power at one's command? What, he wondered with a kind of dark humor, would it be like to have any kind of power at all?

He moved back up front to the leg levers and grasped one of them. They had to be operated by someone standing, and the viewing ports gave the operator a clear field of vision—so clear that Evan could see the stars, as bright as lamps themselves, thickly sprinkled in the western sky.

The behemoth was pointed toward the west. Where the Ambassador would have taken Gloria, if it was indeed she that the women had seen.

All intentions to sleep faded as his perusal of the chamber became sharper. More filled with purpose. The gauges that measured steam pressure indicated the engines were nearly cold. But again, the speed with which the behemoth had been pressed into action meant that here was steam technology much newer and more advanced than any he had yet seen.

Trust Meriwether-Astor to pour his engineering resources into a war machine instead of, say, an undersea dirigible or an airship. But perhaps they might serve his daughter now.

For the first time, Evan wondered if the studies of the mind had been a wise choice for a student anxious to make his mark in the fields of science. Such study had certainly not done him any good, if the many nights he had dined on hard-tack and cheese because he could not find a patron interested in his abilities were any indication. And his wealthiest client, who had kept him in roast beef and Yorkshire pudding for months, had turned out to be a criminal and a traitor, tricking him into nearly killing his cousins Lizzie and Maggie.

Well, he had come to the Americas to find a way to make reparation for that error in judgment, hadn't he? If rescuing Gloria was not that way, he might as well climb down, invite the coyotes to dinner, and be done with it.

He took a deep breath of gear oil–scented air and filled his lungs with determination. Then he bent to the gauges, checked the coal and kerosene levels, and began the ignition sequence. The engine was not the Daimler he had become familiar with aboard *Swan*, but one manufactured by Gloria's company. The principles of operation were the same, however, whether one was dealing with a steam landau, a locomotive, or a war machine that the world had never before seen.

The pressure gauges responded, the needles tilting out of the blue, into the yellow, and finally into the orange, where they held, waiting for the action on his part that would release the steam pressure into motion. It was borne in upon him rather belatedly that he only had one chance to do this properly. One error in the timing of the levers' movement and the behemoth would topple over on its massive face, killing him. He must keep it in motion, turn the wheel to change its direction, and be prepared to adjust the length of its stride so that it did not plunge into an arroyo and pitch him forward to his death.

No wonder the crew had looked so frantic. Had they had much training before they were thrust into battle? And there had been four of them at least, not including the gunner. He was only one man.

You have the brains of two men, one of his professors at the University of Edinburgh had told him. *You'll do well in medicine and mental science—but you would do better in mechanics, my boy.*

He should have listened.

But if he had, he would never have met his cousins, and through them, Alice and Lady Claire and Gloria. If he survived this and rescued the woman he admired, he would make changes.

But first things first.

He saw now why the levers floated on their truss. If one imagined the legs below, picking themselves up as they moved forward, the way a human did, one would have to build them this way. He grasped the rightmost lever and slowly lifted it as he moved it forward.

Nothing.

The behemoth stood, leaning on its rightmost arm, the pilot's chamber level. It clearly possessed an assembly that allowed it to swing to level while at rest. Of course. He smacked his forehead.

"One straightens up before one takes a step, Evan, you idiot."

What he wouldn't give for Maggie or Lizzie's assistance right now! Or Benny Stringfellow's. The lad knew his way around an engine. Jake, he rather suspected, thought Evan was only a little short of useless, but he would welcome help from that quarter even if it were accompanied by silent disdain. But

Evan was alone, and he would do this. Gloria's life depended on it.

A push lever marked Vertical proved to be the solution. Slowly, steam pressure fed itself into the behemoth's metal muscles and tendons, and the chamber swung into position once more as it straightened to full vertical. A switch marked Cannon Housing bent the arms and pulled them flat against themselves, much in the manner of a housewife expressing alarm at the sight of a mouse.

Once again, he activated the leg levers, and this time, the world in the viewing port rocked from side to side as the behemoth lifted its foot, took a single step forward, and paused.

"Left foot."

Rock. Forward. Pause.

"Right." Rock. Forward.

Oh, no, no, no. Mistake!

The behemoth's foot slid into a hidden arroyo. It wasn't deep, but just enough to throw off its forward momentum. The monster wobbled—creaked—tilted—

His heart kicked in his chest and with the jolt, Evan realized that his own body was creating the solution—bending his knees to recover his balance.

All his focus lay on the ground below, all his senses funneling down to balance and touch. He grasped the vertical lever to redistribute the torso's weight, and bent the rightmost leg. It was utterly eerie to feel the machine respond and repeat his actions of a moment ago, saving itself in the process.

Rocking slightly, the behemoth regained the vertical. Evan did not, until his heart stopped pounding and he could breathe again.

"Left," he croaked, as much to reassure himself that he was still alive as anything else. "Right. Pick it up, out of there. Yes, that's it."

His chest felt tight, and he hauled in a deep breath before he caused himself to faint. But he could not stop. He must keep going—only much more carefully this time.

"Left. Right. That's it, you beautiful monster. Left. Right."

In an astonishingly short time, he had left behind the valley, the promontory, and even the twisted and burned remains of the spur. The thing's stride had to be twenty feet long—he felt a little like Jack up the beanstalk, riding on the shoulder of a giant. But as holes in a pasture could be a horse's undoing, so could the weathering of the landscape be that of this machine. While it had running lights powered by electricks in its arms and legs, the light was not cast very far ahead, so he must be vigilant.

On the other hand, what in all this unfriendly country was as level as a lawn and always provided the shortest distance between two points?

The railway.

Why could he not follow the railway tracks, with their artificially level ground? The difficulty there would be to get the machine out of the way if a freight should come along, before it frightened the engineer and brakemen half to death. For they would certainly tell everyone they met what they had seen, and he had no desire for the news of his coming to reach the Ambassador's party before he did.

He had never known before the relief that a workable plan provided. Evan slowed the machine as the switch gleamed in the running lights. A few minutes of experimentation with the turning wheel revealed that for each degree of movement of the wheel, the hip assembly would turn exactly the same amount. So one could not simply spin the wheel and hope for a looping turn, but must remember that metal responded in increments, unlike flesh.

Before long he was striding westward—awkwardly, hesitantly, but definitely striding—along the main line, not on the rails or ties, for they would be crushed beneath the weight, but to one side of them, where the ground had been leveled in preparation for laying the iron. Where there were hills, they had been blasted through, and where there were arroyos, gravel banks had been reinforced with iron to form bridges. And as he went, he spotted darker masses of rock in the starlight that might serve as camouflage if he had to abandon the track—which he would have to do soon, in order to get some rest.

He traveled until his eyes began to close in spite of himself, in spite of his urgency to catch up to the locomotive. He must stop, for he would be of no use to Gloria if he fell asleep and the machine walked itself off course and fell face down in a canyon.

A mile or two in the distance, a light winked on. The midnight freight from Santa Fe, perhaps, cresting a hill and coming toward him? The one that Lorraine had said she was going to jump when it slowed for the switch?

Regardless of its destination, he must not be seen. He forced himself to breathe calmly and turned the behemoth off the line, moving slowly and carefully despite the growing size of the oncoming locomotive's lamp. Several hundred yards away lay an outcropping of rock. He brought the behemoth closer, until he realized that the rising ground was more of a danger to him than the safety provided by the rocks.

So, he would become a rock himself, in the darkness.

He reversed the process he had begun hours before, tilting the torso forward and lowering the arm to form a tripod, that most stable of ancient configurations. By the time he had assured himself that he would not tip over and turned to shut down the boilers, the freight had gone by in a thundering rumble, ragged clouds of steam torn from her stack with the speed of her going.

She did not so much as slow to acknowledge the presence of an oddly shaped rock formation off to the north, nor stop to investigate in the dark. She had a destination and a schedule to keep—and, Evan supposed, would soon have a few more unticketed passengers to boot.

Silently, he wished Lorraine and her girls well, before he ate a little of his cheese and an apple. Then he found a piece of canvas to roll up under his head for a pillow, and made himself as comfortable as he could on the metal grille that formed the floor of the pilot's chamber.

Like a bird in an iron eyrie, he thought with a combination of exhaustion and satisfaction, as the wind whistled through the behemoth's legs and arms and he pitched into sleep.

CHAPTER 15

Dear Captain Hollys,

It is my sad duty to inform you that Captain Chalmers was wounded during a battle with the Californio forces at Resolution. She took a bullet to the shoulder and the doctor at the fort here in Santa Fe done his best, but he wasn't too happy with us for taking so long to get her here. He ought to try flying an airship with only half a crew.

Jake told me to mind my own business—that the captain wouldn't like me writing this, but the Lady taught me the difference between right and easy, and I thought you ought to know. You can come or not as you choose. But some things got to be said, no matter what Jake thinks.

Sincerely,
Benjamin Stringfellow
Gunner 2nd Class
Swan

Lady Claire Malvern smoothed the crumples out of the stained, blotted letter and folded it tenderly, as though it were the collar of a favorite child. She handed it back to Ian Hollys.

"Of course you are going to her, Ian—though it concerns me that Benny does not specify whether Alice is living or—never mind. Will you take *Athena*?"

Ian knew what it cost her to offer her personal vessel for such a long, uncertain journey—a ship that was such a part of her it was difficult to think of it and Claire separately. But the fact that she made the offer without hesitation told him volumes about her regard for Alice, and also her fear. The fact that she was not offering to go—that she acknowledged it was not her place, but his—told him volumes more.

He tucked the letter into the pocket of his tweed jacket. "I am so ashamed."

Andrew looked up from the fire, which he was poking into a blaze against the January cold. Not that Carrick House was cold. But the snow was blowing horizontally past the windows and the iron gray of the clouds sulking over Wilton Crescent suited Ian's mood perfectly. "Why should you be ashamed, man?"

"I cannot forget our last conversation." His heart hurt at the thought of it. "She asked me to go with her, and I told her I had to see to the estate." Sinking into a chair whose very comfort seemed to mock him, he said, "What a fool! How could I have put such concerns before the safety of the woman I love?"

"That is not the way I remember it at all," Claire said briskly. "You offered to come and she laughed and told you she'd been sailing the skies long before you ever met. Which was true then, and is true now. We all knew the journey had its risks, especially with her letter saying she was going to Resolution to stop that train."

"I should have lifted the moment I received it."

"We all should have done things that we realize only in hindsight," she told him more gently. "The question is, what are you going to do about it now?"

"I must go to her, of course. But I cannot crew a ship alone, and I will not ask the two of you to take me in *Athena,* when you have barely been married a month." Claire's mouth opened in protest, but he hurried on. "How long do you imagine it will take if I purchase a berth on *Persephone,* and then the train from New York to Santa Fe?"

"Too long," Andrew said, the voice of experience. "That is a fortnight's journey, in the best of circumstances. And travel in the winter is not what I would call the best."

"What of the Dunsmuirs?" Claire said. "If you will not have us, their ships ply the air constantly between continents. Mightn't you find a berth on one of them?"

He looked at her in admiration, amazed he had not thought of such a thing himself. "You are quite right. I will send a tube to Hatley House at once."

"They are joining the Queen and the Prince Consort at Balmoral soon—I would not waste any time. Davina says the men will be stalking some sort of poor creature over the hills, but I think in actuality they will all be enjoying Scots whiskey while she and Her Majesty confer about the Californio problem."

"I do not understand how that involves England," Andrew grumbled. "It is for the colonials to sort out."

"I believe the difficulty lies in the thirst for gold," Claire said. "After the discovery of gold to the north fifty years ago, it is a miracle the western territories of the Canadas were not annexed at that time, Davina says."

"Why does it concern Her Majesty now?" Ian wanted to know. "She has enough to do managing the empire she already rules, does she not?"

"I think the unmasking of Gerald Meriwether-Astor as a threat to the peace of the empire's borders may have revealed this new danger to her," Claire said. "When Maggie brought us the information about Sydney Meriwether-Astor's plans on Twelfth Night, little did we think that it would cause such ripples in Whitehall and Buckingham Palace."

"Does she mean to send ships to defend the borders?"

"I am not privy to that information," Claire said primly. "But Davina let something slip the other day that caused me to believe the Walsingham Office had been rather busy."

Which was a veiled way of saying that someone had kicked the anthill inhabited by Her Majesty's network of spies. "I do not want Alice mixed up in English politics," he said grimly. "I do not want her away from my side at all."

"You may find that difficult to accomplish once she has recovered." He noticed that Claire resolutely took the optimistic view—that in assuming Alice was still alive, it would prove to be so.

Silently, he prayed for the same. "I know. But while she is injured, my place is to care for and protect her. May I commandeer a piece of paper and a tube? A missive from Wilton Crescent might be read faster than one from Hanover Square."

Claire did not comment further, for which he was grateful.

She simply supplied him with brand new monogrammed stationery and a pen.

John—

I must beg your assistance. Alice has been injured and is at present in a hospital in Santa Fe. If one of your airships were to pass within a thousand miles of that place, I would be most grateful to be aboard it. I must go to her at once.

Ian

A tube came back before Andrew had even poured him a second glass of sherry, the brass cylinder dropping into the chamber in the wall with a pneumatic hiss.

Dearest cousin Ian,

Of course you must go, and take dear Alice our fondest wishes for her speedy recovery. Lady Lucy and her crew are at your disposal for as long as you need her. She is moored at Hampstead, crewed and ready. John will inform Captain Yau of the change in plans.

We will fly to Balmoral in another ship, and then return to London for my confinement. You could be in the Americas until spring, for John will not allow me to travel for some months after the baby is born. He is a dear to fuss, but I confess I will enjoy being at Hatley House for more than two minutes together.

Do not worry for Alice. She is a strong woman, one who is your equal in every way. I cannot wait for the day when we can claim her as our cousin, too. When are you going to set a date? May is a lovely time of year, is it not?

With my love,

Davina

TIME HAD LOST ITS MEANING, swirling in a miasma of fever dreams and darkness and fear. And pain. Alice had had her share of bumps and breaks, but she had not realized that pain like this could exist—the kind that blotted out consciousness and reduced intelligence to a gibbering vacuum, begging only for relief.

A century ago she had slid beneath the waves and had not expected to surface again. Had hoped she would not, in fact, if it meant surcease from pain. But here she was, swimming slowly up through glimmering levels of awareness, like those poor convicts in their diving bells beneath the canals of Venice. Sunlight wavered upon her eyelids like the water in the weeds, and a sudden fear stabbed her that she was back in Venice—with a price on her head and no way out.

She opened her eyes. Was blinded, and flinching, squeezed them closed again.

Cautiously, she separated her eyelashes and squinted up. White walls, a white ceiling punctuated by beams of pine. Crisp white sheets. White bandages against her pale skin. Clean skin. When had she been bathed? And by whom?

"Alice?" said a voice she had thought never to hear again. "Are you awake? Can you hear me?"

She turned her head and winced as a headache that had been lying quietly at the back of her skull pounced into the front of it and began to chew. "Ian?"

Her hand was clasped in his warm one, and he pulled a wooden chair closer to the cot on which she lay.

"Thank God," he whispered, pressing her fingers to his

lips. "I didn't know until this moment whether you would—" He choked.

Her mouth was dry and her tongue felt thick. "Water."

He slipped a hand behind her head and she drank from a mug—cool, wet, and tasting of gravel, but unbelievably good despite that.

"Where am I? England?" She tongued a droplet from the corner of her mouth, loath to let any of it escape.

"The Ranger hospital at the old fort in Santa Fe." Alice sucked in a breath of alarm and Ian's tired face—when had he last slept?—clouded with anxiety. "What is it, dear? You mustn't exert yourself. You've had a very narrow escape."

"Ranger hospital?"

"Jake tells me this is the only place in this part of the territory where there are doctors skilled enough to repair the damage done by that bullet."

"Must get out."

"You must lie still."

"No—no—can't be here." She tried to lift her head from the pillow and roll out of bed, but the pain in her shoulder slapped her nearly insensible. All she managed to accomplish was a groan.

Ian looked at someone coming in. "Jake, she says she can't be here. What is going on? We can't have her so agitated—she will open the wound again."

Her gaze found her navigator, and something in his eyes, in his lack of concern, told her that he knew what the problem was and had already taken steps to solve it.

"Don't worry, Captain," he said to her in a low voice. "When we brought you in, I told them your name was Lady

Alice Hollys. It wasn't a lie—or it won't be soon. Close enough for me."

A long breath went out of her and she relaxed a little upon the pillow. "Good. Pay raise."

"It's the reason you've got such nice digs and the doctors have been falling over themselves to patch you up," Jake confided. "And now that his lordship is here, it all looks as it should."

"I'm not a lordship," Ian managed, looking as though he wanted to laugh—or hit something. "Merely a baronet."

"Texicans don't know the difference." He dropped his voice to a whisper. "Alice Chalmers, you understand, had a hand in wrecking, consorting with criminals, and springing a convicted felon from prison. Then she escaped. Wouldn't want her name getting out."

Ian stared at him. "So there really is some danger of her being arrested here?"

Jake looked a little uncomfortable. "Some. It's been five years, so not a lot, but some."

"Great Caesar's ghost. What felon?"

"Mr. Malvern."

Ian's mouth dropped open. "I see there are depths to my fiancée's past to which I have not been privy. I look forward to hearing these tales on our journey back to England."

England? She couldn't even manage to roll over, never mind cross a room—or an ocean. As crazed with pain as she'd been for the past eternity, it was a wonder that she hadn't accidentally revealed her identity long before now.

"Alaia," she said to Jake.

"As soon as they let you up, Captain. I sent Benny with a

message first thing. He says she's feeding him much better than I do. Ingrate."

"What's this?" Ian wanted to know.

"Friend. Healer. But—Gloria? Evan?"

The color faded from Jake's face even as he did his best to sound reassuring. Anxiety congealed in a pool in her empty stomach. "Not sure, exactly. I thought Gloria was aboard *Swan*, but with trying to lift in the middle of a battle I didn't check until we were halfway here." He swallowed. "She wasn't aboard, but—"

Alice made an inarticulate sound and struggled to push back the blankets.

"Dearest, compose yourself," Ian exclaimed.

"Evan was fighting. We must—go back for—" Pain stabbed her and took her breath, and she collapsed on the pillow once more. Tears leaked from the corners of her eyes. "Jake!"

"I'm sorry, Captain." If her own sight had not been so blurred, she might have thought there were tears in his eyes, too. "We thought you were going to die—and that Gloria was aboard—after carrying you across that hellish valley over my shoulder like a sack of potatoes, all I could think of was finding help. It was the shortest flight of my life—and the longest." His voice cracked, and he cleared his throat.

Poor Jake. It must be such a struggle to always appear in control, to always be the man when he had never been a child.

"It's all right," she whispered. She lifted her free hand and took his. "We'll go back for them—as planned. Lorraine took a shine to Evan. He'll be fine, and he'll look out for Gloria."

Neither of them stated the obvious—that if she had left the safety of the ship, there was no telling if either one was even alive. *Oh, my friends.* The pain in her heart was almost worse than the one in her shoulder, and in her head.

Ian tipped the glass of water to her mouth once more, his face grim.

"The sooner we get her out of here, the better," Jake said to him in a low tone, turning to practicalities to cover his lapse into emotion. "Before someone recognizes her—the Rangers' command post is just across the square."

But the doctor, while he was delighted to make the acquaintance of such an august personage as Captain Sir Ian Hollys, Baronet, would not be moved on this point. "When she can sit up on her own, she can be moved to the home of your friends, your lordship, but until that time, I must insist that she remain in my care. It is not often that I am called upon to minister to ladies of quality. Usually my bullet wounds are Rangers and brawling aeronauts from the airfield outside town."

"We were set upon by air pirates," Jake offered in an accent that reminded Alice vaguely of Ian's, but suited him far less. "We're grateful for your care of her ladyship."

"And I am honored to be of service," the doctor said with a smile. "We cannot have Her Majesty thinking we are inhospitable to her subjects. And now you must let Lady Hollys rest. Your visit is most welcome, I am sure, but I do not wish her recovery to be impeded by fatigue."

It was the first time anyone had called her Lady Hollys, and for a dazed moment Alice thought the doctor meant Ian's mother. She had a feeling that pretending to be someone she was not—yet—might be more difficult than healing from the bullet.

But that was a fret much less important than the imminent

one staring her in the face—literally, for the hospital room's window looked out toward the Ranger command post across a broad parade square of hard-packed reddish dirt. How long did she have before someone in authority came up with the notion of paying his respects to Captain Hollys's injured wife?

And if she did not get out of here soon, how long would Gloria and Evan survive in Resolution?

CHAPTER 16

When Alice next woke, she found her wits to be functioning better, and while her shoulder still hurt like the devil, she did not practically lose consciousness every time she moved. And the headache was gone. She reached for the mug of water on the rickety table next to the bed and drank thirstily.

Honey, and the taste of sun-warmed grass. A familiar flavor she had known since childhood. Blinking, she focused on the figure by the window. "Alaia?"

The Navapai woman turned from her contemplation of the parade ground with a smile. She was dressed, not like a Texican, but in the clothes of her village—a white long-sleeved tunic with a one-shoulder garment over it made of a brightly patterned blanket she'd woven herself. Her hair was wound up in two high buns on either side of a center part, and finely worked silver earrings hung from her ears. Her boots were soft, pale leather, and wide silver bracelets enclosed her wrists.

"Alice, my friend, well met."

"You're well. I'm shot up."

"You will heal. The doctor knows his bones, and I know the flesh. Between us, we will see you well again."

"Where is Ian? And Jake? And how is Benny?"

"Benny and Jake are well. They are with me. The other—" Her long lashes fell, then rose to meet Alice's anxious gaze. "He has gone to make his bows to the Rangers. I do not think that wise."

Alice's breath went out of her. "What has he done that for?" It was the very opposite of what he should have done, which was to listen to Jake and lie low.

"Men of authority band together and speak of great things, while women work over fire and field." Alaia dimpled. "Without us, they would have no strength for greatness."

"But he knows that it's dangerous," Alice whispered. "He knows I could be recognized—and tossed in gaol."

"Perhaps he believes that if great men band together, their protection will extend to you."

"Or they'll have me arrested."

"Do you trust this man, this Ian?"

"Of course." She gulped again from the mug of liquid. "I am going to marry him, Alaia."

"Then he will protect you, and you must trust him to do so." She bent to kiss Alice's forehead. "Rest now. Here is more of my healing draught. You must drink one cup every hour."

"I will. Look after Benny. Don't let those boys of yours get hold of him."

Alaia's deep brown eyes sparkled with delight. "My boys are men now, and have made me a grandmother. Their days of running around are over—now they must provide for their children."

Alice gazed up at her with affection. They'd known each other since Alice was a girl, for Alaia had been a friend of Nellie Benton's—though how they had met was a story Alice had never heard. But the Navapai woman had offered them shelter five years ago when they'd been in dire straits, with no questions asked. This grassy golden drink had brought Claire around then, too.

"I wish you'd been my grandmother," she said suddenly. "Those children are lucky."

"It is not luck, it is family," Alaia said softly. "You will begin yours some day, and be a woman your children and grandchildren will praise."

Alice had to chuckle at that. "Let's not get ahead of ourselves. It's taken me a couple of months to get used to the idea of being a wife. I never thought—" *He would be interested in me. He would think me worthy of him. But he does. And I am.* What a gift it was to know that. Silently, Alice marveled at how her thinking had changed course since she'd left Hollys Park after Christmas. Primarily because Gloria could not keep her opinions to herself. Thank goodness.

Gloria ...

She must get well, and soon, and go back for Gloria and Evan. Maybe as soon as tomorrow.

"He is a noble man?"

Alice brought herself back to present company with an effort. "He is. Good, loyal, capable. He flies airships, like me."

"And he is very handsome."

"That too." Alice felt her cheeks heat up as Alaia's face dimpled with merriment at her embarrassment. "And if you say one word about handsome children, I'll throw this drink at you."

"That would be a waste, and one does not need to state the obvious. I will return later, dear friend."

When she had gone, moving gracefully and with the confidence of one who knew her place in the realms of man and nature, Alice drained the mug and slowly, painfully, made her way over to the heavy glazed thunder mug behind its curtain.

Yesterday it had been impossible to contemplate getting out of bed. Now it was impossible to imagine walking out of this room and through the door at the end of the ward. But at least she could put her feet on the cold flagstone floor and walk four steps, and though it hurt, she could survive it.

That was progress.

She had barely made it back to bed and covered her bruised self—spectacular bruises they were, too, like purple sunsets splotched all over her legs and body—when the door opened and Ian came in.

He was not alone. A man wearing a lieutenant's bars on the sleeves of his blue wool uniform and the gold eagles of the Texas Rangers on his collar points came in behind him. Alice pulled her blankets modestly up to her chin, as she imagined a fine lady might.

Ian bent to kiss her on the forehead. "My dear, this is Lieutenant Bautista, who is in charge of a detachment of Ranger airships based here. Lieutenant, my—wife, Lady Hollys."

Alice offered her right hand, and rather than turning it over and kissing it in the European manner, he shook it gently. "Lady Hollys, it is my pleasure. I trust Doctor Acosta has given satisfaction?"

"Indeed," she said weakly. "I have every confidence that I will be able to use my arm again."

He eyed her with interest. "I hear by your accent that you are not English. Do you hail from this side of the sea?"

And here she'd thought she'd given a pretty good approximation of the way Claire and Ian spoke. She probably sounded as unconvincing as Jake. "Philadelphia." Perhaps that would explain it.

"Ah. Do you know the Philadelphia Hadleys? My wife is a cousin and would be delighted to know of the connection."

"N-no." Lying about Philadelphia was a sandpit she'd just as soon avoid. "But I have met Mrs. Rose Hadley, briefly, in—in a large company. She would not remember."

"I am certain that is not true. It would be difficult to forget a lady as fair as yourself." He bowed gallantly. "My wife will be delighted. Perhaps when you are better, you and his lordship will honor us with your presence at dinner, and you might give Mrs. Bautista some news of home and family."

"We would be very happy to accept under ordinary circumstances, but I am afraid that as soon as Lady Hollys is well enough, we must cast off for England," Ian said with the smooth courtesy that came from generations of good breeding. "I am most anxious to continue her recovery in the safety and quiet of our own home."

"I do not blame you." The lieutenant looked disappointed. "But … I hope this does not mean that you do not feel safe here in Santa Fe? I can assure you that the Rangers' presence here is the heaviest in the territory. We are in no danger."

A short silence fell, before Alice cleared her throat delicately.

"I have heard rumblings that the Royal Kingdom of Spain and the Californias is preparing for war," Ian said as though there had been no prompting at all. "In fact, perhaps we might adjourn to your office to discuss the matter."

"War?" If Bautista had been the sort to wear a monocle, it would have fallen out in his astonishment. "Where on earth have you heard this? We are on the best of terms with our neighbors to the west, despite their reluctance to adopt modern means of transportation and industry."

Alice struggled to a sitting position, and Ian bent to plump the pillow behind her shoulders. "I have it from the Californio ambassador to the Fifteen Colonies himself, whom I met at Mrs. Rose Hadley's home during a ball," Alice said, neglecting to include the fact that it had been Gloria, not she, who had done the meeting. "He has spent a fortune in gold to arm his supporters with fighting automatons, mechanical horses, and contraptions that can charge a cavalry at speed, with no injury." Rapidly, she told him what she knew, omitting the part about Resolution. Under no circumstances could that name come into the conversation.

When she finished, the lieutenant's ruddy complexion had become even more suffused in his agitation. "I cannot believe it," he said. "It is impossible. We have ships patrolling the borders regularly, and have seen no such massing of weaponry and arms."

"Have they seen trains?" Alice persisted. Somehow, after what they had been through, it had never occurred to her that persons in authority in her own Texican Territory wouldn't believe her. "For the cargo cars drawn by the train I saw in Philadelphia were unusually large, no doubt to conceal the machines inside."

"One cannot tell how large they might be from the air,"

Bautista said. "The trains come and go all through that country, and have for decades."

"And, apparently, the Californios have a civilian militia, taught the arts of war from boyhood," Ian put in.

"Arts are one thing. Boys another. But knowing one's way around a trigger comes from actual experience on the field, and the Californios do not have that." He sounded on firmer ground here, as though he was quite convinced of his facts.

"Can you be quite certain?" Ian inquired. "I might drill the men on my estate to my heart's content, with no one the wiser. Are these nobles not possessed of large holdings in the hundreds of thousands of acres?"

"I—we—from all accounts, that is so. But of course our ships cannot cross into the foreign fields of air for surveillance, and there are few indeed other than at the highest levels of government who have actually visited."

"Then it is impossible to obtain that intelligence unless one goes afoot," Ian conceded. "Do the Territories have spies capable of such reconnaissance?"

"Certainly not!" The lieutenant tucked in his chin in affront. "We do not employ spies. It is underhanded. Despicable."

Alice exchanged a glance with Ian. Now would not be the time to inform him of the splendid use to which Her Majesty put the brave men of the Walsingham Office. After her escape from imprisonment by one such man, Captain Barnaby Hayes, Gloria had become quite spirited in her recounting of his efforts to capture her father, with Alice and Claire and the others listening raptly.

Quite spirited.

"I beg that you would look into these rumors by any means in your possession," Alice said earnestly. "The Ambassador himself explained to me the late Viceroy's insatiable need for gold, and I observed the Ambassador's personal resolution to see his plans through at any cost, even if it means invasion."

The lieutenant trained his gaze upon her. "And why should he tell a gently bred lady these things? These are not the kinds of secrets that one usually lets slip at balls."

"You would be surprised," Ian said mildly. "My cousin's wife, Lady Dunsmuir, is one of Her Majesty's closest confidantes, and an astonishing number of state secrets are bandied about over dessert, and decisions made between the polka and the waltz."

"Your cousin is Lord Dunsmuir?" It was clear that even in the Wild West, that name commanded attention.

"Yes."

The lieutenant recovered himself under this fresh information. "Very well, then. Regardless of its believability, out of courtesy to you and your family, Lord Hollys—"

Ian winced at the incorrect title. "Sir Ian, please."

"—I will give this information to Admiral Robert van Ness, our superior officer."

Alice drew in a quick breath, and before she could cover it with a cough or some other distraction, both men were bending looks of concern upon her.

"Are you in pain, dearest?" Ian asked gently, easing her down into the pillows.

"Yes, I—I fear I have exceeded my strength," she whispered.

"I do apologize," the lieutenant said in a tone that told her he had weightier subjects on his mind. "Lady Hollys, perhaps tomorrow you might be well enough to receive Admiral Van Ness, and relay to him the things you have told me."

"I can perform that task," Ian said. "I do not wish to tire her."

"I am sure you could, but he will wish more information that it appears Lady Hollys possesses." He bowed to them. "Until tomorrow, then. I wish you a speedy recovery, ma'am." He departed with long strides, as though he were in a hurry.

Ian pulled up a wooden chair and took her hand. "What startled you, Alice? Are you truly in pain? You turned rather white."

"It doesn't hurt—no more than it did before, at any rate," Alice assured him. "But Ian, it's Van Ness."

"He knows you?"

"Not only me, but Claire and Andrew, too. He won't have forgotten that they gave him the slip and we rescued Andrew from the pinnacle cell on which they'd condemned him to death."

Ian's eyes widened. "What in heaven's name is a pinnacle cell?"

"You have seen the spires of rock jutting up all over Santa Fe? Some are used for moorage, and some … well, once a man is up there, there's no way for him to get down outside of suicide or in bits and pieces in a bird's beak."

Now it was Ian's turn to look aghast, and then positively ill. "Our friend Andrew Malvern was condemned to such a fate?"

"By this very Robert van Ness that the lieutenant is so anxious to bring for a visit tomorrow. He was a lieutenant himself then, and a more spineless individual convinced of his own capability you'll never meet. You should hear Claire on the subject."

"Perhaps I will, when we reach England. Which I plan to do with all speed. Alice, I hope it will not pain you too much, but we must get you out of here. Do you think you could walk if we spirit you out tonight?"

"I thought you'd never ask," Alice said. "Feel free to spirit me out this afternoon."

He smiled into her eyes, and despite the winter chill in the stone walls of the hospital that the braziers could not altogether dispel, her skin warmed. "I would carry you out in my arms this moment if it would not result in a hue and cry and far too many explanations. No, we will wait for the cover of darkness, and Jake's assistance."

"He and Benny are with Alaia, in the Navapai village up on the cliffs to the west of the city."

Ian frowned. "They are not aboard *Swan*, at the airfield?"

"My dear, in this country you must never miss an opportunity to renew connections among friends. Alaia saved Claire's life five years ago, and brought the Mopsies back from the brink of death by dehydration and exposure. Jake took Benny there straightaway. She has been a friend to me for years, and I would like you to know her. She is expecting you, and she's a wonderful cook."

"That is no doubt why those rapscallions chose her over their duty," Ian grumbled, but she could see his heart wasn't in it. "Very well. Between the three of us, we will come up with a plan."

"I already have." Pulling him close, she kissed him, and then whispered into his ear what they must do.

CHAPTER 17

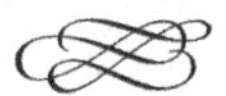

Though *Silver Wind* was an extraordinary locomotive, full of technological surprises that made her unique, her greater weight and size meant that she was no faster than an everyday freight. Endless eons passed while Gloria was borne against her will farther and farther west. The desert was vast and lonely, but despite its vistas, the track was narrow and singular, and the locomotive had to pull off into a siding periodically in order to let the freights pass.

Had she any hope of rescue, she might have rejoiced at their middling speed and these delays. As it was, she spent them trying to disguise her fuming impatience and fear, and doing her best to appear ladylike, obedient, and of all people the least likely to attempt an escape.

The result was that her captors began to relax their vigilance. After all, where would she go, a young woman with no resources, alone and on foot?

The temperature warmed as they descended from the mountainous heights of Santa Fe into what the doctor explained was the enormous basin of a river.

"It is the Rio de la Sangre Colorado de Christo, and stretches for hundreds of miles, *senorita*," he explained, his finger moving along a map that had actually been drawn by hand at some time in the previous century—when the Royal Kingdom of Spain and the Californias had ruled the entire continent west of the great Mississippi River, it appeared.

Gloria suspected the map, like the man who carried it, had exaggerated its successes just a little, for she was quite certain that the Louisiana Territory lying between the Fifteen Colonies and the Texican Territory had been settled by the French, not the Spanish.

"The river passes through canyons that are nearly a mile deep," he explained. "Our route takes us very near, so you may be able to see it, perhaps, in the distance."

"Is it so large?"

"*Si, senorita*. She is mighty, the Sangre Colorado, and deep. But we keep her at a distance, until she reaches our borders and becomes tractable and civilized."

Gloria let this pass. "At a distance? Is the river not used for commerce and shipping?"

He shuddered. "No, *senorita*. It is far too dangerous and unpredictable. The flash floods, you see, they magnify her power so that she cannot be controlled or harnessed. And then there are *las brujas*—the witches." He crossed himself.

"Witches." She could not help it if her tone was a little flat, for that was the last word she had expected to come out of his mouth.

"Devout men do not speak of them, except to say that in years past, the brave have sought to conquer the Sangre Colorado de Christo and failed. Entire expeditions have met their doom at the hands of these savage beasts, *senorita,* and now you will find it impossible to persuade the captain of any Californio vessel to ply the waters upriver of our borders." His gaze rose to meet hers, and in his brown eyes she saw not humor, or teasing, but utter conviction. "It is part of His Excellency the Ambassador's mission to reconquer the lands east of ours," he said in a low voice that trembled with emotion. "To sweep the country clean of witches and superstition and death, as Holy Mother Church did hundreds of years ago in Spain. We know the evil beings inhabit the caves and cliffs along the river. We suspect they cause the wrecking of steam ships and take pleasure in the killing of crews and the looting of cargo. It is certain they possess knowledge of the lost mines of legend—El Dorado, Victorio Peak, the Salvación. With the help of your father's arms, once His Excellency secures these territories under the Viceroy's flag, he will invade and extract the information as a miner himself extracts gold."

Gloria knew her medieval history as well as anyone. She swallowed, and delicately moved the subject to one less dreadful. "And once he has done so?"

"Then the late Viceroy's plans may proceed under his son's guiding hand—to build a series of shipping canals that link the Sangre Colorado with the rivers to the west and north. And eventually to the east. Between railroads and shipping, the Royal Kingdom of Spain and the Californias will enjoy such a time of prosperity and riches that the rule of His Highness Felipe XVI will become the stuff of legend."

Gloria took a moment to get her thoughts in order before the grandeur of such thinking carried her away screaming. "And all that stands between the Ambassador and his plans to change the world are the peaceable inhabitants of the territories and … witches?"

"Do not mistake me, *senorita,*" the doctor said soberly as he rolled up the map. "They are real. But they will not be for long."

"But—" There was no such thing as witches. Surely he meant some kind of natural phenomenon. Flash floods were very real, as were sheer cliffs and winds and any number of hazards in this country. Perhaps superstition might attribute these things to some feminine power, some female entity. A goddess, even.

But witches?

"I must attend to the dressings of the wounded men, *senorita,* if you will excuse me." The doctor bowed, put away the map, and turned to bend over a man in one of the bunks. She took up the place that had become hers—the corner of the sofa closest to the glass of the great arch above their heads.

Witches, real or otherwise, did not matter. They came second to stopping the Ambassador and his mad invasion of the Territories. She must first do that, and as far as she was concerned, *las brujas* would be welcome to haunt whomever they pleased.

The closer they came to the river, the warmer it became under the glass, until finally Gloria and the other men were forced into the corners of the saloon until the sun passed its meridian. Still, when they stopped in mid-afternoon to take on water and coal and Gloria was allowed out to take the air, it was almost a shock to feel the warmth on her face.

She was positive it was still January, but the gentle touch of the breeze felt like May. Even the red rocks thrusting from the ground looked as though they might burn, so intense did their color become—or perhaps they were merely reflecting the heat across the desert floor.

"You may take exercise for ten minutes," the Ambassador said, as though he were bestowing a gift. "Please stay within sight of the train. This is no country in which to become lost."

"Is it always this warm?" she asked. She had been using one of the blankets from her bunk as a shawl, and was tempted to leave it behind. But the uncomfortable glances of the men at her form clad in a boy's pants and shirt made her wrap it around her waist instead, in an approximation of a skirt.

"Not always," he said, standing ramrod straight at the foot of the iron steps, hands clasped behind his back, and surveying the land as though the Viceroy's flag flew over it already. "The temperatures can change between one moment and the next. Snow can fall where moments before there was a cloudless sky. See there?" He pointed back toward the mountains, where clouds had massed as though they were pinned against the slopes by some greater force. "It is raining there, and not here. We Californios are used to a moderate climate—one less changeable. I fear that here it is a symptom of a greater spiritual deficiency."

But Gloria did not want to debate theology with a man who could believe in witches yet in the same breath denounce the airship as being the tool of the devil for allowing man to fly in the face of God. Who seemed to believe that he alone had a God-given right to mount an invasion upon a territory that had exercised the will of its people and seceded of its own volition.

What were the odds that the young Viceroy, fresh out of school and mourning his father's death, had any idea of the plans of said father's right-hand man? For all she knew, the young Viceroy's plans for his kingdom could include peaceable trade and treaties. His days could be numbered while the handsome, power-hungry individual before her gathered more and more of the reins of government into his hands. As her father had so amply proven, nothing drew a country together faster than war. And without a ruler, who would be the obvious choice to lead?

"I thank you for the opportunity for exercise," she said, sidling away, "and shall make circuits about the locomotive until it is time to be on our way."

But her agitated circuit took her some hundred feet north of the engine—close enough to hear it huff and sigh, but far enough away that she could turn her back on it and pretend it was not there. Under her boots the soft red soil crumbled and puffed, though it was pitted with millions of tiny holes, as though there had been rain recently. Spiny plants grew here, and twisted, hardy bushes that breathed out the scent of sage as she brushed past. She breathed deeply of the scent, trying to calm herself. Jackrabbits hopped away, and buff-colored lizards the length of her palm darted here and there, frightened at her shadow. Above, three large black birds that might be eagles or might be ravens circled and croaked to one another, no doubt discussing the possibilities her person might hold for a meal.

Gloria climbed a gentle rise to a pile of red rocks that looked like a stack of pies that had been knocked over. The rough sandstone was warm to the touch, and she leaned on it, gazing out into the red and gold rocks, the landscape scored by arroyos and water, and the lavender haze in the distance.

Was that the river, perhaps? But no, it was deep in a canyon, the doctor had said.

Too much distance. Too little hope.

Or was there? Who was it had once said, *The enemy of my enemy is my friend*? What if the witches were not witches at all, but ordinary men and women who resented being treated as lesser beings by people like the Ambassador and the doctor? What if their destructive tendencies came not from a murderous urge to destroy everything that invaded their territory, but from a healthy sense of self-preservation? What if they were simply the original inhabitants of this land, like the Navapai of Santa Fe, and did not appreciate the incursions of other peoples on the ancient cliffs and rivers of their homes?

Might they not be sympathetic to a prisoner of their enemy, and render her some assistance?

Gloria measured the distance between her knob of stony pies and the lavender haze. It must be twenty miles—though the air was so clear here that often distances were deceiving. Could she walk twenty miles with no water or food?

Probably not.

She could not hide in these rocks, or climb the mesa without being spotted. *You must catalogue the resources at hand and use your intelligence,* Lady Claire said in her memory. That was all very well for Claire, who seemed to have endless resources. But unless a Gatling carousel sprang out of the ground, at present Gloria's resources amounted to exactly nothing. What a pity her education had not extended to the operation of locomotives. If Claire could steal an airship, Gloria might have been able to steal a train.

Well, then, what remained? Up was not a possibility, nor

forward or back. Her gaze dropped to the ground. A cave, perhaps? Or any other hiding place? Other than rocks and brush, there was nothing visible but a small crack in the earth a little way off, screened from the view of anyone on the train by the knoll on which she stood.

A crack in the earth—deep enough to conceal a slender form unencumbered by skirts?

It was painfully clear that unless she did something to help herself soon, her chances of escape before they crossed the border were shrinking with every mile. Walking twenty miles to find the witches was utterly mad, unless one considered the alternative, which was apologizing to a prince for losing his mechanicals, and likely being executed for her effrontery. At the very least the Ambassador would not permit her to leave the kingdom until she had promised to resume cordial relations between his country and its supply of arms—and that she was not prepared to do. She would die first.

So ... die at his hand, or at her own?

She could already hear the puffing of the locomotive increasing in its vigor, and a glance over her shoulder confirmed that the men were performing their final duties before they boarded the train once more. She had nothing but the clothes on her back and her blanket—but that was more than she had come with.

She must be mad.

Gloria plunged down the slope on the other side, heading for the crack in the earth.

Mad and angry and desperate.

A man shouted. Panting, she ran between two rock formations and onto a solid shelf of sandstone that tilted down to the desert floor. And there it was—the crack—barely wide enough to admit her feet. All she needed was two or three feet of depth, just enough to conceal her body until night fell.

For her good sense had at last caught up with her. She need not find the witches or walk twenty miles. All she needed to do was hide, and when the next freight stopped at the siding for water and coal, she could leap aboard and conceal herself among its crates and sacks. Once she reached Santa Fe, she could inform the authorities about the impending invasion, go to a bank, and arrange passage on the first airship back to Philadelphia.

A plan at last!

She shuffled sideways in the narrow miniature canyon, now up to her knees. Then her thighs. Would this be deep enough, if she were to wriggle between the walls and lie on her side on its sandy floor? Ought she to go farther? What if there were spiders? Or worse—scorpions?

Another shout galvanized her into motion, and then several voices rose in argument—no doubt concerning the last place she'd been seen. She stepped farther in, and realized that its floor sloped downward. What luck! In a moment, with a scrape of stone over breast and derriere, she was fully entombed in the ground.

With her next step, the sandy floor fell away more steeply under her soles and she landed on her backside, slipping ten feet down a chute of rock before she got her boots under control and stopped herself. Goodness. She must be more careful. Cautiously, still sitting with her feet braced against a curve in the rock, she craned her neck to look up.

Above, like an inverted river, the cloudless sky was sandwiched between rippled banks of red and purple rock, allowing plenty of light to see by. The chute in which she sat was more of a sandy riverbed, and the more she looked about her, the more astonished she became. The walls curved and fluted, as though at some time they had melted like ice cream and then frozen into rock again.

The curve in the chute that had allowed her to stop also blocked her view of the crack through which she'd come. That meant it would block the view of anyone looking in, too. She didn't dare go farther in case she couldn't get out again, so she tucked herself up in a ball against the cool red wall, wrapped the gray wool blanket about herself, and prepared to wait out her captors.

How long would it take them to abandon the search?

Everyone aboard was well aware that the young Viceroy was waiting for the appearance of his train and ordnance. Would they abandon her here in order to keep the schedule? Or would the Ambassador decide that the recapture of his scapegoat was well worth the prince's anger at their tardiness? It could go either way, but Gloria was inclined to favor the latter. In which case, she was concealed as well as it was possible to be, and there was nothing more she could do.

A shout sounded from above, and now she could hear the scrape of boots on stone as the search party approached. She hardly dared to breathe, though she was at least eight feet underground and it wasn't likely they would hear.

"Senorita!" someone shouted. The doctor? Perhaps they thought she had fallen and injured herself. *"Senorita,* call out so that we might help you."

She buried her nose in the blanket.

She was not familiar with any more of the Californio tongue than she had managed to pick up over the past few days, but after some discussion, it appeared that someone may have suggested she had not fallen at all, but had vanished on purpose.

"*Senorita* Meriwether-Astor!" came the call again, more sternly this time. "Reveal yourself at once or the consequences will be most unpleasant."

More unpleasant than a public pillorying by the Ambassador? She doubted it.

More scraping of boots, urgently this time, as the search fanned out to encompass not the search for an injured woman, but the pursuit of a running or hiding one.

The sounds faded, and Gloria dared to take a normal breath. Was it possible her ruse had succeeded so easily? Whether it had or not, she wasn't moving until she heard the racket of the locomotive's departure, even if that were two days from now.

A flicker of black wings drew her attention to the opening above, as a raven landed on the edge of the precipice and teetered there. It cocked its head and observed her with interest.

No, I am not your next meal. Lips pressed together, she glared at it as though it might understand her by sheer force of will.

Footsteps approached, and the raven flew off, croaking in irritation at being thus interrupted, and Gloria huddled into her blanket once more. Boots scraped, and she heard a whispering sound. The sound the sand had made around her own boots.

Her stomach plunged into a cold pool of fear.

Someone had seen the raven and made a most intelligent guess. He had found the crack, and in moments he would find her. He shouted something rapidly, and other voices responded as footsteps pounded toward him across the stone above.

No, no, no!

Gloria scrambled to her feet and used the blanket to erase the evidence of her rest in the sand. They would find no trace of her. She rounded the curve of the wall and nearly pitched over the edge as the chute ended abruptly.

A cave opened up around her, though the narrow opening of the crack above did not widen. It was as though a giant had scooped it out by blowing from one end, as a Venetian glass-blower might create a vase. Frantically, she scanned the smooth red walls below for a way down. How far? Twelve feet, perhaps? Could she scale them—and having done that, climb back up again?

There was no time to speculate.

She wrapped the blanket around her waist and lowered herself over the edge. A foothold here, a handhold there—

The excited voices of the men told her they couldn't be more than twenty feet from her, around the curve of the chute.

Her exploring foot found purchase on a sandy ledge —slipped—

Gloria scrabbled for a second handhold, but the fluted curves provided none, and her own weight was too much for a single hand.

With a gasp, she slid ungracefully off the rock face and plummeted into the void.

CHAPTER 18

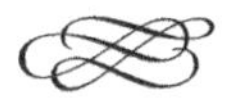

By sunset on the second day, doubt had begun to plague Evan Douglas quite as much as hunger, to the point that he felt nearly paralyzed by indecision.

As a result, he and the behemoth remained motionless even after the sun rose, while he attempted to decide whether he had been right in pursuing Gloria based on hearsay, or if he should give her up for dead and return to civilization while he still had the strength to pilot the machine.

For as carefully as he had hoarded his apples and cheese, they were now gone. One of the unfortunate results of a lack of fuel for the body was a lack of clarity in the mind, and for him, this was the greater problem. As a young man of much intelligence but few prospects other than those he created himself, he was no stranger to stone soup. But what if his guess had been right, and Gloria was at this moment being carried westward, with no hope of rescue but for him?

But what if his guess had been wrong, and in the horror of the battle's aftermath Lorraine had mistaken one fallen pirate for another? If the coyotes and pumas had already done for

Gloria, there was nothing for it but to make his way east, and attempt to scratch a living at some trade until he could pay his fare back to England.

In the pilot's harness, Evan studied the desert, brightening into color with every moment as the sun rose. Put like that, even a fool's errand stumping across the desert to rescue a woman who might not even be there held more appeal.

Right, then. He had committed himself this far. He must go on until he either found her or found himself—

Until he found himself.

Evan set the behemoth into motion as his mind seized upon a new direction.

He might be without food, but he could drink from the boiler. That would give him a day or two more of his pursuit. And he was not without resources. He had a behemoth. How many behemoth operators were there in the world, after all? Perhaps he was now the only one. Granted, it didn't do much besides shoot and crush, but perhaps it could be modified and he could hire himself out for more useful work.

If he repaired its arm, it could be used for—for construction. For building bridges and trestles. Or for setting rafters into place in tall buildings. For that sort of work, though, one needed a destination where things were being built. There must be towns out here with aspirations. Once he had calmed the townspeople's initial alarm at the behemoth's appearance, he could give them assistance.

Feeling somewhat less hopeless—for he now had two reasons to be traveling west—he increased the length of the behemoth's stride.

Hours later, after two nasty-tasting draughts from the boiler and many miles of walking, the sun had dropped nearly to the horizon, and the pilot's chamber began to cool. Evan had fallen into the habit of approaching crests and dips in the landscape with caution, so as not to frighten the trains should there be one, or in case he saw the locomotive he pursued. Now he slowed as the track passed between two towering mesas that gave him no visibility ahead, even though the pilot's chamber was so many feet in the air.

He moved the behemoth through the gap, and a fresh vista opened before him. It contained the same sere hills and red rocks, the same railroad track, the same endless sky.

It also contained a large and familiar locomotive, resting at a siding and puffing contentedly.

He'd caught up at last! His heart leaped, and Evan allowed himself a grin of triumph before schooling himself to caution. In his weakened state, he was no match even for the Ambassador's secretary, should he have one, to say nothing of any mercenaries that might still be aboard.

The first order of business was to find out if Gloria was inside. Oh, if only he'd had some food today, he could think clearly! He forced himself to drink a little more from the pressure relief spigot, shuddered, and despite the taste in his mouth, felt somewhat refreshed.

He could not simply go stumping up to them, point an arm at the locomotive, and demand they hand her over. While this plan had the benefits of directness and simplicity, the people who had ordered the behemoth were no doubt aware of its limitations, and could very well shoot the legs out from under him before he could say Jack Robinson.

After some minutes' gazing at his quarry, it became puzzlingly apparent that it was simply sitting there, unmanned. Where was everyone? Were there men inside, having lunch? Was Gloria inside, watched by twenty armed guards? They couldn't have abandoned their only transportation, so they must be about somewhere.

There was nothing for it. He was going to have to reconnoiter the situation on foot. Even if he were taken prisoner, at least if Gloria was there, they would be together.

And perhaps the Californios might share their provisions.

Evan pushed levers and controls, and the behemoth bent into its now-familiar night resting position, sheltered from view in both directions by the gap in the rocks, and off the main line behind an outcropping. Then he opened the exterior door and cautiously climbed down the off-side leg.

His own legs felt rather wobbly, but he steeled himself to ignore the sensation. His body needed fuel, and that locomotive undoubtedly contained it. Moving from rock to scrubby pine to hillock, he crossed some hundred yards of ground, until at the last he abandoned caution altogether and loped up to the rear of the locomotive.

No one shouted to alert the others of his presence. For goodness sake, why had they abandoned the train? Were they out hunting jackrabbits?

He eased up the ironwork steps and opened the door just enough to put one eye to the crack.

The saloon was empty of men, but he could smell food. That was enough to lure him inside, like some scavenger animal, his hunger overpowering his fear of man. The table did not boast the luxury of the saloon car he had looted back in Resolution, but he was not fussy. Bread and hard cheese went into his mouth with no regard for utensils or finesse. When he was satisfied, he found a haunch of what must be roast rabbit, and ate that too. A long draught of water followed by one of wine went a long way to restoring him to himself.

At which point the absence of the locomotive's occupants began to weigh more heavily on his mind.

Had Gloria been here?

A quick search of the saloon turned up no evidence of her ... until he rifled through the sleeping cupboards and found a single metal hairpin lying on the bare ticking where a head might have been.

He held it up. Only a woman would possess one of these, and to his knowledge, there had been no women accompanying the Ambassador's party. It had to have been Gloria. A wave of relief passed through him at this confirmation that he had done the right thing in pursuing her across so many miles of desert. But now what?

A thick iron door led through to the business end of the locomotive. Taking a deep breath, he leaned on the lever and eased it open. Voices immediately came to his ear—Californio voices, speaking idly in their musical tongue. The engineer and the brakeman, no doubt, bound to stay with their engine no matter what the rest did. There was no sense of danger, simply two men talking until the Ambassador saw fit to come back.

Evan closed the door with infinite care, wincing as the iron latch clicked into place. Perhaps it could be mistaken for the sound of the metal all around them, expanding and contracting with the temperature. When they did not raise the alarm, he moved back into the saloon and went out the door. He descended the steps and took refuge at the rear of the great engine to think.

The two men up front were waiting for the rest. Gloria must

be with the others, but only one sensible reason for them to be perambulating about the landscape seemed likely. They must be hunting, for the locomotive could not have been stocked with food the way the lounge car had been. Their departure had been too precipitate, and now they must supplement their stores.

Very well. He could not trick them into giving her up, but now that he had eaten, he wondered if perhaps the direct and simple plan might not be best after all. What if he brought the behemoth here and refused to let them board their train until they sent Gloria up to join him? The rotating firing apparatus would not work, but there was nothing wrong with the cannon in the other arm.

He had no time to waste in formulating any other plan. He took off at a ground-eating pace, confident he no longer needed to worry about being spotted. Within ten minutes he had regained his former position in the pilot's cabin, and set the behemoth into motion toward the locomotive.

The siding was built in a flat pan that might once have been the bed of a small lake, now overgrown with scrub and grass. Evan took up a position ten yards in front of the stair into the locomotive's saloon, his rotating arm trained on the engine.

The locomotive squawked in alarm.

It took a moment for Evan to realize that he was being hailed by the engineer through a speaking horn. The man clearly recognized the behemoth—did he think its original operator was still aboard?

A moment's startled perusal revealed that he had his own speaking horn, there on the side of the viewing port. "Throw down your arms!" he said in his most businesslike tone.

"El capitan?" the engineer said. "Is that Captain Escobar? State your name at once."

"I'm the one with the gun, and I will ask the questions." Never in a thousand years would Evan have imagined those words coming out of his mouth. He felt rather as though he were in a flicker. Perhaps he should not have had that wine.

"We bear no arms, senor. We operate this locomotive only."

They could be lying, but even if they were, his guns were bigger than theirs. "Where is Gloria Meriwether-Astor?"

"She is taking the air with the Ambassador's company, to the north of the track."

Another wave of relief. She was here. Unharmed. Thank the good Lord.

"I have come to fetch her back," he informed them. "Do nothing to prevent me, and you will not be harmed."

"But senor, who are you?"

"I am the operator of this machine. That is all you need to know."

"As you wish, senor."

He was rather pleased at their civility. Either they were wily as foxes, and were armed indeed, or they were men who focused upon the task they had been set, and were no threat to him. He turned the behemoth about so that his viewing port faced north, and discovered that next to the speaking horn was a lever that opened two grates on either side of the port, to admit air.

He wished he'd known that earlier, when he'd been sweating and losing moisture copiously in the warmth of midday. But it had not been warm for an hour at least, as clouds had massed up against the mesas and skeins of rain were falling from their bellies.

Since the behemoth could not climb about in the rocks, he must wait, so wait he did.

An unconscionably long time.

When the skies clouded over completely—so completely it became almost twilight—and rain fell in earnest, pounding the desert floor in sheets that bounced and bubbled, unabsorbed by the soil, he watched the rocks anxiously. What on earth was taking them so long? Gloria would be soaked to the skin. Perhaps the engineer had been lying, and she wasn't here at all. But that would not explain the disappearance of at least a dozen men.

And now the speaking tube squawked once more. "Senor! The rain!"

"Yes, obviously," he said into the tube. Did they think he was blind up here?

"Senor, there may be a danger of the flash flood. You must take refuge in the locomotive."

And put himself at their mercy? He thought not. "I doubt there is a danger, sir, but I thank you for your concern."

This was surreal—polite remarks exchanged between two metal machines so large they could form their own hill.

And then he became aware of a sound he had not heard before. A sort of whispering thunder that he would not have heard had he not opened the air vents.

"Senor!" was all the man in the locomotive had time to say before there was a sound like a thunderclap, and a plume of water leaped over the rocks to the north.

"Great Caesar's ghost!"

There was nothing he could do but watch a torrent fling

itself out of what must be a canyon below, splashing up on the rocks. How could so much water appear so suddenly in the desert?

Too late, he remembered the rain that had been falling all afternoon in the upper elevations—rain that had nowhere to go but dry courses it had carved into the earth over the centuries. A dry course such as a lake bed in which a siding had so foolishly been located because it was conveniently flat.

And now figures appeared on the rocks. Half a dozen, dressed in short black uniform jackets and silver-trimmed trousers, running as if their lives depended on it. Evan counted them off one by one—and found among them no slender figure in a boy's buff canvas pants.

The puffing of the train had increased, and now its whistle screamed with urgency. The brakeman hung out the window, urging his compatriots on with sweeps of both arms, shouting for them to hurry.

And with horror Evan realized that the torrent would not be contained in its canyon on the other side of the hill for long. Clearly both locomotive and behemoth were in danger.

In a moment he was proved right. With a sound like an explosion, the water crested the hill and began to pour down, heading for its level in the lake bed. If they did not want to be marooned, they would have to move, and they had only seconds in which to do it.

Half a dozen men flung themselves up the stair of the locomotive, leaving two bringing up the rear—the Ambassador and one other. Shouting encouragement, a man hung off the stairs, waving, but it was clear the Ambassador was not going to make it ahead of the torrent of water bearing down upon them.

This man knew where Gloria was, and Evan was not about to allow him to drown before he told him where.

He set the behemoth into motion, and when he reached them, he shouted into the speaking horn, "Climb the legs!"

And just in time, too. The men leaped upon the metal legs of the behemoth, clawing their way higher while Evan turned it about.

The water hit so hard it nearly lost its footing, but the machine was heavy, and he knew its capabilities well now. He set one huge foot in front of the other, water foaming around them and up to the knee joints. The locomotive was already steaming away. Once he regained level ground, he set off after it, trying to ignore the shouts of the two men clinging to the metal rungs below, for there was no time to stop.

They traveled for a good two miles, Evan grim in his harness and the men outside soaked and cold. At last the locomotive came to a halt where the ground opened out and it seemed that flash floods were not in the habit of rearranging the landscape. He brought his machine to a stop within hailing distance and sat back against the metal webbing, breathing heavily.

Men descended from the locomotive to assist the Ambassador to the ground. Dripping, with a man on either side to hold him steady, he looked up at the pilot's chamber. "Senor!" he called. "That was very well done. To whom do I owe my life and the life of my companion, *el doctor*?"

"Never mind that," Evan said, throwing his manners to the wind. "Where is Gloria Meriwether-Astor?"

The Ambassador staggered a little. "Would that I knew."

"What do you mean?" he shouted. His stomach churned

and his lungs felt as though a great hand were suddenly pressing on them. "What have you done with her?"

The Ambassador gazed up at him. "Please come down, senor. This is not a conversation to be shouted at the tops of one's lungs, even if one had the breath to do so."

"I shall not. Not until you tell me what happened. She was supposed to be taking the air with you." His voice cracked.

"And so she was. Until the flood came. And now—now I fear we must form a recovery party, for her and—several of my men." His gaze locked with that of Evan. "Your help would be invaluable—I had thought that only two men on this earth could operate this machine. One is in Philadelphia, and the other is now dead. But I see that I was wrong. Please come down. You need not fear—I owe you my life, and yours therefore has as much value among us as my own."

He hadn't a choice—a search party of one wouldn't be of much help to Gloria, and until the floodwaters receded, nothing could be done. He needed information, and sustenance, and manpower, all of which the Californios could provide. He needed to control himself, to rein in the urge to hit something in his fear and grief, and show them nothing but a man confident in his own abilities.

So he bent the behemoth into its resting position and climbed down its iron leg-rungs to the ground.

He was the only one in the company besides the engineer and brakeman who was still dry. The Ambassador extended a cold hand. As Evan took it, beside him, his shorter companion's dark-eyed gaze searched his face, and widened in recognition.

"Madre de Dios," he breathed, putting a hand on the Ambassador's arm and indicating Evan. "I know this man."

CHAPTER 19

It was fortunate that Alice was female, for it meant that other than a woman out on the ward recovering from pneumonia—asleep at the moment—there was no one near her room. Alice did regret the necessity of having the window open, in case it affected the lady's health, but Ian had promised to close it after they were gone.

A slight commotion erupted among the saltbush and chamisa outside. Alice sat up, checking that her buttons were all fastened, her canvas pants were belted and ready, and her lightning pistol was still in her pocket. Ian had had to lend her a shirt, which was several sizes too large, to replace the bloodstained one in which she'd arrived, but he'd had everything else laundered, and recovered all her property.

It felt good to be clean. Sore and slow, but clean. Ready for whatever the day would bring, as long as she could share it with him.

Fingers gripped the sill, and in a moment Jake's eyes appeared above it, marked her location and that of Ian, who was standing by the window, and vanished below. It was a good six feet to the ground, and in her current condition the most she could do to assist them was to cross the room by herself.

A wide board tilted up and through the window. Ian grasped it and balanced it on the sill. "Your chariot awaits, madam," he said, his smile just for her, but his gray eyes worried all the same.

She hoped devoutly that they would not drop her. It was the best they could come up with on short notice, for she could not be lowered by her armpits because of the shoulder wound, nor could she jump lest she land badly and cause the bleeding to start again.

She arranged herself along the board in a fashion reminiscent of an effigy upon a tomb, and reminded herself that she could trust her men.

With Ian handling it from inside, and hands reaching for it on the outside, Alice gripped the board for all she was worth with her good hand, and slid out of the hospital window. She was lowered to the ground and in moments engulfed in the rustling, scented shrubbery.

"All right, Captain?" Jake asked, his eyes pinched with concern. "Did we hurt you?"

"I'm just fine," she assured him and Benny. "Help me up, would you? Ian will meet us at the ship."

He would pretend to take leave of her empty bed, then bid the matron good afternoon as he had done every day of her stay here. Meanwhile, Jake and Benny helped her through the garden to the wooden gate in the adobe wall at the rear, where a hired conveyance waited driven by one of Alaia's sons.

He grinned at her, his dark eyes sparkling with enjoyment

of one more prank. “Alaia will have my head,” she murmured to Jake as he climbed in next to her, with Benny on the opposite seat. “Involving her boys in my scrapes again.”

“He volunteered,” Benny informed her. “Besides, this mechanical contraption is a marvel—it would be wrong for you to miss it. See how it goes?”

It looked to her like a combination of a galloping horse and a pair of scissors, but its workings moved too fast to follow. And since they covered ground at a terrific rate, she could do nothing but close her eyes and concentrate on staying upright.

Half an hour later, they passed through the gates of the airfield and found Ian waiting for them at the base of *Swan*'s gangway.

He was not alone.

“Who on earth—” Alice leaned forward. “Great heavens, is that *Perry Connelly?*”

“If it is, I'll have satisfaction from him,” Jake snapped. “I don't take kindly to jumped-up boys keeping honest folks prisoner and enjoying it.”

“Get in line, Navigator,” she said wryly. “Help me down out of this machine, will you?”

They made their farewells to Alaia's son, and bade him convey their thanks once again to his mother. As they approached *Swan,* she could see it was indeed Perry, struggling futilely in Ian's grip. “For goodness sake, Ian, where did you find him?”

“In your galley, helping himself.” He shook Perry like a rat. “Explain yourself to the captain of this vessel, you wretched excuse for a man.”

“Alice—you know I didn't mean any harm,” Perry gasped,

for Ian's grip on his shirt was forcing the collar up around his chin. "With Ned, you ain't got a choice but to do what he says."

"Are you referring to your imprisonment of me on my vessel?" she demanded, though it was difficult to sound stern when he looked so miserable. Tears stood in his eyes, but that could be from chagrin at being apprehended as much as from regret for his actions.

"I am. I'm heartily sorry for it, Alice." Ian shook him violently. "Ma'am! Captain!"

"Captain Hollys, please release your prisoner, but remain on alert," she said, gripping Benny's shoulder rather more firmly in order to remain standing.

When Ian did so, Perry rubbed his throat and shook himself into order. "I stowed away, ma'am. Captain," he said hastily, when Ian growled. "When I saw your boys load you on the ship there in Resolution, I followed fast as I could. They was undermanned and didn't see me sneak into the hold when they lifted."

"Why?"

He gazed at her blankly. "So's I wouldn't be shot—why else? I been with your ship all this time. Guarding it until you was well. I'm heartily glad to see you ain't dead, Al—Captain." He glanced at Ian. "This gentleman caught me off guard, is all."

"This gentleman is my fiancé, Perry, and you're lucky he didn't put a hole in you a raven could fly through."

Perry blanched, and bobbed his head at Ian. "Thank you, sir. Pleasure to make your acquaintance, sir."

"You imprisoned my fiancée?" Ian said with dangerously enunciated syllables.

"Ned Mose told me to!" Perry's voice cracked with desperation. "But I'm a changed man, I swear. I come with the aim to sign on with your crew, Captain. You won't find a truer man than me, I promise."

"As true as you were to Ned?" Time was when Perry had been her only friend—a few years younger, and with an unlikely innocence and faith in people—unlikely considering he was Lorraine's son.

"*More* true," Perry said. "I'm volunteering to sign on with you. With him, it's obey or get shot. Ma told me I'd better obey because she didn't go to all that trouble to bring me into the world just to have Ned Mose use me for target practice."

He'd been brought up with the desert flowers same as she, and forced to work for Ned just as she had. Alice supposed she ought to give him a chance rather than turning him loose here in Santa Fe, where he'd probably fall in with bad company out of habit, and be irretrievably lost.

Lorraine had done right by her, back there in Resolution. Perhaps it was only fitting to return the favor—before she returned him to his mother.

Alice studied him a moment longer. "Did you look after my garden like I asked you to?"

His eyes widened eagerly, and for a moment she saw again the boy he had been. "I sure did, Alice. I swear the pumpkins the autumn after you left were the biggest Resolution ever saw. We had a grand Christmas, with pies and everything."

Maybe there was hope for him yet. A man who kept the small promises was likely to keep the big ones, too. "Did Melvin come with you?"

A shadow passed over his face, and he dropped his gaze to the ground. "He got shot. Ned, too."

Jake shifted as though a chill had run up his back, but Alice was conscious only of the relief that welled up inside her. "I can't say I'm sorry. And your mother?"

"I don't know. But if Ma can survive Ned Mose, she can survive anything. Plus every girl in that house is armed to the teeth. Ain't nothing coming in there they don't want there."

"Then we'll go and see."

"What?" Jake said. "Back to Resolution?"

"Aye," she told him. "Have you forgotten that Gloria and Evan are still there? If Ned's dead, maybe they had half a chance of surviving. Get ready to cast off, Benny and Perry. We're pulling up ropes as soon as Captain Hollys helps me aboard."

ALICE HAD FLOWN into Resolution many a time, but she had never seen it like this. They had come in low, on a long approach, in order to spy things out before they moored. Wreckage strewed the wide flat where the spur had been blown up, and around the line of train cars lay the ravaged bodies of men, right where she had seen them last.

Days ago.

"No one's buried them," Perry said. He might pretend to be a man of hard experience, but in that murmur Alice heard shock and pity. She had done the right thing in hiring him on.

"This ain't right," Jake said, peering out the viewing port.

"I'll say. *Swan*, slow engines for landing. Descent at five degrees." After a moment, the Daimlers responded, and they floated closer.

"Not about the bodies, though that ent right, either.

Captain, where is the locomotive? And the behemoth? They're gone."

"That's impossible."

It felt strange not to be at the helm, but she could not imagine her ship being in more competent hands than Ian's. But no matter how she wiped the isinglass or strained her eyes, all she saw was the impossible, large as life. The two biggest machines she had ever seen had simply vanished.

Ever cautious, Alice directed Ian and Jake to moor on the same rocky hill where they had found such brief refuge on their previous visit. Then she fetched her second best flight jacket—she had not quite got over the loss of the first one during the battle—thrust her good arm into the sleeve, and bade Ian fasten the toggles over the sling.

"You are not going with us," he said in disbelief. "Alice, your shoulder—"

"I'm not going to be walking on it, dearest," she assured him, shrugging the jacket into a more comfortable position.

"But we do not know the situation here." Reluctantly, he fastened the toggle that kept the fleece-lined flight hood closed at her throat.

"All the more reason to have as many people familiar with Resolution as possible in our party. I can shoot one-handed, don't you worry. We have one job, don't forget—to find Gloria and Evan as fast as possible. After that, maybe someone will tell us what in the Sam Hill happened to that locomotive."

Jake checked his pistols again. "I'm not easy about this, Captain. I could maybe see the behemoth being packed away into whatever crate it came out of, but not the locomotive. It beggars reason."

Alice didn't tell him that reason had not been a feature of life in Resolution before this, so there was no use expecting it now.

She nodded at Ian and Perry to take the lead. She and Benny followed, and Jake brought up the rear to make sure they weren't taken by surprise.

The dry creek bed they'd used as a road before was now running with water—which was only to be expected. She'd seen the clouds massing in the west and north, and could only hope that Gloria and Evan had had the sense to get into one of the buildings before the water hit. There was a reason all the lower floors in town were made of stone and for the most part left unused.

As they approached the town, she could see Ian taking note of landmarks and changes since his last visit five years before, when he too had been a prisoner of Ned Mose. "The floods have not been kind," he murmured over his shoulder. "But should there not be some people about? Why have they not buried the bodies?"

Perry's face had set in hard lines that Alice would wager concealed his fear. "Captain, permission to find my mother?"

"Granted," Alice told him. "If Gloria and Evan are there, send one of the girls to tell us. I don't like the look of this one bit. And watch out for animals. Those poor souls' bodies will have brought them in from all over the mesa."

Ian thumbed his lightning pistol into the charging position. It began to hum. Prudently, Alice did the same.

The doors to the saloon swung loosely, creaking in the wind, and when she pushed one open to look inside, no one stood at the bar or dealt a hand of cards at the table. All the bottles behind the bar and the mirror that had hung above it were smashed to bits. A shiver of cold air ran down the back of her neck.

They checked inside the first house they came to, but Alice could tell by the silence as she climbed the stairs that there was no one in residence on the second floor. An odd smell hung in the air, and it wasn't from the three chickens who had taken up residence on the iron bedstead. The remains of two eggs lay in the middle of the mattress, smashed and eaten. The hens, it was clear, had had no one to feed them in some time.

"We're going to Lorraine's," she told her companions. "I know the battle was bad, but even if all Ned's men were killed, where are the Ambassador's men?"

"They left on the train," Benny said sensibly.

"Except the train couldn't leave, ye numpty," Jake told him, ruffling his hair. "Our Alice blew up the spur."

"You did?" Ian glanced at her. "Rather rash of you."

"I hadn't much choice, with Ned holding Evan hostage until I did. Oh, where is Evan? I hope he's all right."

They had nearly reached the Desert Rose, trailed by the hens, who apparently had decided to gamble on the prospect of food, when Perry staggered out of the door and sat rather abruptly on what was left of the raised sidewalk constructed of boards.

"What's happened, man?" Jake demanded.

Perry looked up and met Alice's gaze. "Don't go in there. It ain't a fit sight for a lady."

"What is it? Is your mother—"

He shook his head, turned away, and vomited into the street.

Ian vaulted up onto the sidewalk and pushed into the

house, Jake on his heels. "Benny, keep an eye out," Alice ordered tersely, and followed them inside.

Not Lorraine. Granted, the woman was as hard as a stone, but she had been Alice's mother's friend, and had been kind to her as a child.

The smell was ten times worse here, and this time she recognized it. Blood, feces, and urine had created a noxious cloud that was nearly visible. The house seemed to have been pressed into use as a hospital, but every patient's throat had been cut, seemingly as he slept, for the bedclothes were not disturbed. Near the door lay the bodies of two men in black uniforms, blood stiff and congealed from a fatal head wound and a gunshot to the back.

Upstairs they found the same, the rooms where the girls had plied their trade only tombs for dead men now.

"Is no one left alive in the entire town?" Ian wondered, his voice leached of sound. "Who could have done this?"

"Someone who hated a black uniform," Jake said. "Captain, I'm worried for the desert flowers. And our friends."

"I am, too." Alice's stomach felt as though it might follow Perry's example. "Go down and see if Perry knows where his mother might have gone. Someone has to be alive. The whole town can't have been murdered, or pulled up stakes—and even if they did, where are Gloria and Evan?"

Alice didn't have the will to look any further. When she went downstairs, she saw that the chickens had come in. The ragged little scraps of life never gave up, did they? She followed them into the kitchen—empty of dead men, thank heaven—and with squawks and beats of their wings, they launched themselves upon a spilled sack of corn as though they could not get to it fast enough.

"You poor things," she murmured. "A whole town dead around you and no one left to see to you. I suppose the coyotes have done for the rest of your flock."

In the middle of the scratched and damaged kitchen table lay a scrap of paper with a name scrawled across the top. She snatched it up and took it outside, drawing a grateful breath of clean air.

"Perry," she said, "here's a letter for you."

Still pale, he straightened and took it as Ian, Jake, and Benny joined them. In halting syllables, he read it aloud.

Dear Son,

I don't know if you will ever find this but I can't think what else to do. I searched the battlefield and don't got any body to bury but Ned's, so I can only hope you're alive somewheres. Maybe with Alice. God don't pay us much mind here, but I pray so.

Them Californios took their abomination of a train overland and headed west, but they left all their munitions and their wounded, so they'll be back. Me and the girls balanced the books and now we aim to hobo on the eastbound freight and seek our fortune elsewhere. That nice boy who come with Alice lost himself in the dark looking for someone. I expect the varmints got him.

If you're alive, I hope we'll meet again some day. I'll check the post office once a year in New Orleans. Maybe you'll send a letter.

Your loving ma,

Lorraine Connelly

Carefully, Perry folded up the letter and pushed it into the pocket of his shirt. He did not speak, merely gazed toward the horizon in the south and east.

"Balanced the books?" Young Benny sounded puzzled. "They did their arithmetic before they left?"

Alice exchanged a glance with Ian. "I suspect she meant that they took the Californios' lives in exchange for those of their men," she said gently to the boy. "The wounded were all abed in there, dead as doornails."

"Oh," he said, the color draining out of his face. "If they're all dead, what's that racket in the kitchen?"

"Those chickens followed us in."

"Chickens!" With the resilience of thirteen, he brightened. "Can we have chickens aboard *Swan* like Lady Claire does aboard *Athena*?"

"Certainly not," Ian said.

"Benny, those birds are next door to dead themselves." She stopped, undone by the hope in his eyes. "But they're the only things who managed to stay alive in Resolution. You're quite right. We can't leave them on their own."

"Alice—" Ian began.

"They'll be good company for those stuck-up French hens in the garden at Hollys Park." Her throat closed up unexpectedly. "They're brave, and gallant, and I'm not going to leave them." Tears started in her eyes, and to her dismay, Benny's began to fill, too. "They're in the kitchen," she told the boy. "Gather up the corn and bring it as well."

Too much death. Too much horror. And there were three chickens, standing innocently in the face of it, the way poor Evan had when Ned Mose had sent her off to reconnoiter that train.

"Evan can't have been eaten by varmints," she whispered fiercely. "I won't let him. We have to search."

Ian seemed to have learned a thing or two about women in

general and about her in particular in the months since their adventures in Venice. "Of course, dear," he said, more gently. "While Benny wrangles the chickens on to the ship, the four of us will form parties of two and search town, battlefield, and train carriages for any sign of Evan and Gloria."

"I wish they'd just stayed on the ship," Alice moaned. "Gloria in particular. Why did she leave it? Where did she go?"

"Why, Captain? Because of Evan," Benny said, reappearing in time to hear, a red hen in his arms. He dashed a tear off his dusty cheek. "They—the pirates—they were making him shoot that big Gatling carousel and Miss Gloria, she could see through the spyglass that they'd put it together wrong. So she ran to stop him killing himself, and they made her fix it and shoot it at the Calfornios instead."

Alice stared at him. "Why didn't you tell us this before?"

"I haven't seen much of you, Captain," he said reluctantly, adjusting his grip on the bird. "And I just remembered."

"Never mind, Benny. Then what happened?"

"That behemoth took aim at them and shot the gun off the top of the hill. Everything went flying, even the wagon it stood on."

The contents of her stomach heaved again, and Alice struggled to breathe deeply. She must not lose control in front of her crew.

"But just before it did, Evan must have seen what it was going to do, for he pulled Miss Gloria off the pilot's brace and —and after that I couldn't see because of the smoke and dust, but my orders were not to leave the ship, and then Jake came back carrying you, and—"

"Thank you, Benny. We know what happened after that. Carry on. Ian, Jake, do you agree we ought to begin our search on the far side of that hill, if it was the last place either of them was seen?"

"I do," Ian said. "And following that, we'll search the train for any survivors. At the very least, we'll know what armaments are left so that we can report it to the Texican Rangers."

"They didn't pay any attention to us, remember?" Alice reminded him as they walked across the field toward the hill where the big rotating gun had been set up.

"Perhaps they might if we bring them one of the mechanicals," Ian said grimly. "For it is clear to me that the Texicans must take possession of these arms before the Ambassador comes back with a larger party—or an army—and be ready to defend themselves."

"And if they don't?"

"Someone must. Even if it is only you and I."

"*Swan* is a military-grade airship, Captain," Jake said thoughtfully. "She's built to carry munitions. I wonder how many mechanicals she could fly? And what about that behemoth?"

"You'll need an articulated train car to load one of those on her," Alice told him. "Never mind that. First we need to find some trace of our friends."

It wasn't difficult to see what had happened to the equipment on top of the knoll—it had been scattered for an acre or so down the slope and into a dry arroyo. Wagon wheels, shells, human remains, and bits of the carousel assembly, including the pilot's brace, led them downhill and into the sandy bottom.

There, they found bloodstains on the rocks near the wall of the arroyo, but no bodies. For which Alice was devoutly grateful.

"Ma's letter said your friend got lost looking for someone," Perry ventured. "So he survived. Maybe she did too."

"But why would he be looking for her if he was close to her when the explosion happened?" Alice gazed up at the hill. "Say you're knocked down here together and you land hard. One doesn't wake up and leave the other to go wandering around in the dark. Not with coyotes about."

"One might if one believed the other to be dead," Ian suggested.

"Evan didn't believe Gloria was dead, then," Jake said. "She must have been gone when he woke."

"She wouldn't have left him," Alice said firmly. "Not Gloria. Not if she could help it."

"Maybe she couldn't help it," Jake persisted. "Maybe she was taken. For ransom. Or something."

Alice drew in a breath. "The Ambassador knew her. Maybe he recognized her."

Something caught her eye in the dirt, and she bent to brush the sand away. "Look."

A hairpin. She turned it in her fingers. It was just like the ones in her own hair at this moment. Because Gloria had lent her some of hers for the board meeting.

"She was here. And then she wasn't, and Evan set off to look for her."

"The Ambassador's men would have left her to lie if she'd been dead," Ian said. "Therefore it follows that if someone recognized her and brought her to the Ambassador, she was alive."

"And Ma said they went off in their train," Perry put in. "Though it beats me how."

"That can't be what happened." Alice's strength had begun

to flag, and she sat rather suddenly on a rock. "She can't have been taken out West by those people. What would they want with her?"

"It seems to fit a limited set of facts," Ian said, "but there are great holes where we have no information. Come, Alice. We must get you back to the ship."

"We have to find Evan."

"You will not be able to find so much as a hairpin again if you do not rest. Please, my dear. Perry, Jake, and I will continue the search once I have you aboard."

Much as she wanted to protest, she felt as though she would faint if she didn't lie down. And in the end, Ian had to carry her the last hundred yards to *Swan*. When the search party came back two hours later, it was to report no sign of Evan.

Nor was there any evidence to tell them what had become of the behemoth, which was neither in pieces in the empty crates in the train carriage, nor anywhere near it. But by then, the sun had fallen and it was too dangerous to be out on the treacherous, pitted ground any longer. For the predators had indeed come in to feast on the bodies, and while there was not much left to bury, it was clear they had not finished yet.

They set fire to the Desert Rose, turning it into an enormous funeral pyre for the remaining men. It was the only decent thing they could do so that they would not meet the fate of their companions.

Alice turned from the fiery glow and gazed instead at the three chickens roosting on the rail in front of the viewing port in the dining saloon. They had shared the crew's dinner and drained a soup bowl full of water, and now fluffed their feathers and blinked contentedly as night fell outside. They made a picture of safety—a red hen with a white tail, a black-and-white speckled individual who looked as though she had been marked with Morse code, and a black one so glossy that her feathers glinted green in certain lights.

The only survivors of the Battle of Resolution.

Outside, the dark bulk of the mesa rose behind the ruins of the town. The only survivors but two. And she wouldn't rest until they were all together again.

CHAPTER 20

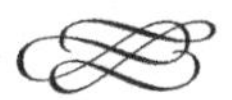

Evan Douglas gazed at the Californio doctor, who may have recognized him, but whom he was quite certain he had never clapped eyes on in his life. "You have the advantage of me, sir."

"It was after the battle," the man explained, more to the Ambassador than to Evan. "His body lay near that of the senorita, and we left him for dead. My deepest apologies, sir."

Evan restrained the urge to remark upon his inability to diagnose such a grave condition. Tensions were running too high for levity, and if the truth were told, he felt very small and vulnerable outside his movable iron fortress.

"I regained consciousness some time later, having sustained a blow to the head that was not fatal," he told them. "I was told that you had offered hospitality to Miss Meriwether-Astor, and determined to follow her—she is the only one left of my traveling party, you see."

"Ah." The Ambassador eyed him. "You are among those who assisted her in attempting to stop the theft of the armaments by those members of her family who have betrayed His Highness's trust?"

"Er—yes." He hadn't quite followed that, but chalked it up to the lingering effects of having had only one real meal in several days. "But sir, while we are standing here discussing the matter, Miss Meriwether-Astor is in considerable danger. Would we not be better employed in coordinating our rescue efforts?"

"Indeed."

Evan could not decipher the expression on his face, but then, he was notoriously poor at the sort of communication that did not require words and images. Hence his ill luck with members of the fairer sex. But Gloria had not seemed to mind. In fact, being understood by her had been quite a novelty.

"You are quite right, Senor ...?"

"Douglas. My name is Evan Douglas. I was a passenger aboard *Swan,* the vessel that carried Miss Meriwether-Astor here, before we were captured by air pirates."

"You also?" The Ambassador's eyebrows rose. "I will dispense with remarks upon the wages of sin in connection with airships and ask merely this: Were you also pressed into service against your will by these pirates, and forced to fire upon us?"

Also. They could only have heard such a twist upon events from Gloria, so he must play along. "Yes, sir. For which I hope you will in turn accept my apology. We have not, apparently, left one another for dead, for which I am most grateful."

The Ambassador smiled beneath his moustache. "It has resulted in the creation of an operator for our *Gigante de la Guerra* to replace the man so recently lost, so we may grieve but not regret the past. *En verdad,* sir, your assistance in the rescue of Senorita Meriwether-Astor is a gift from God."

"Then let us set off," Evan said eagerly. "The waters may have receded by now."

The doctor shook his head. "The sun is at the point of setting, and *el Gigante* cannot be operated safely in the dark. Nor can we see our fair quarry, who may be injured or even unconscious. We must wait for morning."

"But the cold—"

"We can do her no good from this elevation. The wisest course is to direct our journey to the nearest river crossing, and search the banks upriver from there, where her—where she may have been able to swim ashore."

The Ambassador stiffened. "Doctor Escobar, you are not suggesting—"

"I am, Excellency."

"But *las brujas*—we cannot—"

"No, we cannot. But Senor Douglas and *el Gigante* can, without let or hindrance. He may give them a taste of what is to come while at the same time mounting the search for the senorita—at no loss to His Highness's remaining forces."

"Speak English before assigning errands to me," Evan said crossly. "What are *last brouhas?*"

"*Las brujas.*" The doctor spelled the words so that he could see them in his mind. "Witches."

Evan nearly asked him to spell that, too, so incredulous was he. The doctor explained to him what they knew of these beings, and then informed him with a smile that Gloria had not believed him at first, either.

If she had not convinced Evan and the crew on the flight across the territory of the madness of the Ambassador concerning his plans for invasion, he believed it now. First an insane plan to invade a country for gold that did not exist, and now a fear of witches that did not exist, either?

But it seemed he was to have a look firsthand at them, whatever they were. He did not care. The sooner he could get down to the river and find Gloria, the happier he would be. Once they were both safely ensconced in the behemoth's pilot's chamber, no one could stop their escape. He rather looked forward to showing her how well he had learned to operate it.

He held fast to that thought through the rest of the night—which he prudently spent inside the behemoth, accepting only the gift of another blanket from the doctor, and an excellent breakfast in his company the next morning.

The locomotive set off at dawn, with the behemoth stumping along behind, and switched to a northbound spur that took them lower and lower in elevation until finally the red rocks took on a purple cast as they plunged into canyons deeper than any Evan had yet seen. The spur terminated in a dusty town where the river was shallow enough for a horse and rider to cross, and where commerce and trade could proceed unhindered. The Californios took on provisions and possessed themselves of a map of the river much more recent than the relic that had been open on the table in the saloon.

"The word will have gone to the witches already," the Ambassador said in a low voice as he traced the route the river took between the spot where they had lost Gloria and their current location. "We must retreat to the main line to avoid capture. Your search will encompass a distance of only ten or fifteen miles, as the raven flies, but you see here the bends and breaks in the Sangre Colorado's course. The river has cut deeply into the stone and it may force you into the water, so steep and plunging are these cliffs."

"How deep is it?" Evan asked. "Can the behemoth be submerged without injury?"

"It can, for short distances, as long as the exhaust piping is not submerged and air remains in the pilot's chamber. If the water comes in through the piping, it will destroy the steam engine."

Evan nodded. The river would have to be twenty feet deep before he was in any danger of that. But he could not quite believe they meant to leave him here. "I cannot go alone. Surely you see that a search of this magnitude requires every man you can spare."

"Senor." The Ambassador's face seemed to stiffen with the effort to control his emotion. "The battle cost the lives of eighteen good men. We left eleven injured and two whole to guard them in that cursed town, awaiting our return, and eight more were lost to us yesterday during the flash flood. It is a miracle that the doctor and I, the engineer, the brakeman, and three of my escort remain to bring news of these dreadful events to His Highness. I have no more men to spare, I assure you. I am only thankful to God in Heaven that we have you to assist us, or Senorita Meriwether-Astor's life would be forfeit for certain, if it is not already."

Put like that, Evan could see the man's reluctance to risk any more lives for that of one woman. That left only Evan with both the courage and the resources to come to her aid.

"We will not leave you entirely alone in this effort," the Ambassador went on, laying an encouraging hand upon his sleeve. "At the next river crossing, we will deploy ourselves to search, in case the waters carried her farther than our estimates have allowed. We will wait for you there. If we are not successful, you must continue the downriver search and *Silver Wind* will proceed to the great southward bend, where *las vegas*—the river meadows—are wide enough to permit a town to grow, and there is a hospital. Whichever party finds the young lady first will bring her there with all speed, and meet the others."

An excellent plan. He could hardly wait to be on his way. "All right. But tell me, sir, where were you taking her to begin with? It is the one thing that I do not understand. Why should the survival of one young lady from Philadelphia mean anything to His Highness?"

The Ambassador exchanged another unreadable glance with the doctor. "For the simple reason, senor, that she is a heroine. We were acting as a kind of honor guard, conveying her to His Highness so that he might bestow upon her the royal favor merited by her father, his own father's personal friend. She acted as a true ally of the Viceroyalty, and it is my personal belief that His Highness might even have gone so far as to confer a title and lands upon her in his gratitude."

Evan's face went slack in his astonishment. Had Gloria really fooled them? Had she not meant to stop the war at all, but to encourage it? Had he somehow managed to get everything backward? He could hardly credit it, but neither could he imagine her going willingly all the way to San Francisco.

No, that could not be right. She had believed in her mission to stop the war her father had begun—that was why he had risked his life in support of it. There was no way on earth she could be a collaborator—not the woman who had nearly been killed saving his life.

The facts did not match this new information, but neither

could he fathom why the Ambassador should think these things—unless Gloria had merely been playing along. Yes, that must be what had happened. So he must play along, too, until he found her.

The Ambassador, apparently, had not missed his thoughtful expression. "You see why we are stopping at nothing to recover her, and why your ability to assist is so very important."

"I do," Evan said at last, for there was nothing else he could say. "Well, then, allow me to bring this discussion to a close. It seems I have a very great deal of work to do today."

HOW LONG WOULD it take to search fifteen miles of river? Evan had no idea, but erring on the side of caution, he took enough food for three days, and memorized the location of the water meadows on the map, where the search parties would meet. Then, to the astonishment of the few people out in the single road through the town, who dove in fear into doorways and alleys, he guided the behemoth down to the shallow, graveled banks of the river and turned it eastward.

The banks here appeared to have been carved out in flat loops wherever the river took a bend, so there were maybe fifty yards of walking room and his progress was rapid. Gloria had been wearing buff-colored canvas pants and a brown flight jacket, so it would not be as easy to spot her as it would have been had she been wearing her lavender or even her blue gown.

Nonetheless, his gaze raked every yard from bank to bank, and sometimes twice, when a human-sized rock or the sudden movement of a foraging animal made him snap to attention.

Toward mid-afternoon, the banks narrowed to the point that he must take to the river. Narrowed and stretched higher and higher, their red, gold, and purple faces sheer and forbidding on either side.

The colors and striations in the rock made a fascinating display, almost as though a giant hand had laid down layers of sandstone, and then for a diversion had added layers of some chalky white substance that broke and crumbled more easily, like frosting on a cake. On top of that were rippled layers that looked oddly like the rocks where Gloria had disappeared, and another layer of frosting. Perhaps that was a good sign that he was going in the right direction, if the two landscapes shared similarities.

As he progressed, the current swirling around the ankles of the behemoth rose to its jointed knees, and then halfway up the struts and pistons of its thighs. Its feet were large enough that the rocks of the riverbed did not overset him, though the thought of that was frightening enough that he proceeded with extreme caution despite his gnawing anxiety.

By sunset on the second day he had lost all interest in the colors of the cliffs and simply concentrated with a sort of grim endurance on continuing his march. When he could, he guided the behemoth to walk on the banks. When he was forced to take to the water, progress was much slower—though in one way it was easier, for he did not need to search. No human could cling to the sheer, plunging cliffs.

Or could one?

On the third day, the landscape slowly took on a different aspect. In the sandstone cliffs, wind and water appeared to have carved out elongated openings from which dark stains descended on the rock faces. And within the openings he could swear there were buildings—blocky stone houses, towers, even rounded granaries. Evan could not imagine how one reached these dwellings, for they were far above the head of the behemoth. There appeared to be no signs of life in any case, other than ravens and jays flying in agitated circles at the sight of him.

A lost civilization, perhaps, though the buildings seemed in good enough repair. A sense of wonder at the thought of being perhaps the first person in centuries to see such evidence of a lost civilization overcame him, and the urge to explore, to get out of his cramped harness and walk about in the fresh air, was overwhelming.

But he could not. Gloria's life depended on it.

He'd seen no other signs of human life except for the completely incongruous sight of a riverboat emerging from a tributary and chugging merrily upstream, the sounds of music and the clatter of its steam engine utterly out of place in the majestic loneliness of the canyon.

He had climbed down and been resting in the sun on a wide bank, trying to decide whether or not he should turn back, but the riverboat had not stopped or even seemed to notice the odd configuration of iron resting on its arm behind him. Before he had thought to leap up and hail them to ask if they had seen a young lady in the course of their voyage, they had rounded a bend, leaving nothing but the music of a banjo and fiddle and the sound of laughter in their wake.

Blast. His exhaustion must be affecting the workings of his mind, for he had lost an excellent opportunity to ask for assistance. For his food supplies were once again running low.

He must turn back. There was no other option, though everything in him urged him on. She could be around the next bend, shivering on a rock and equally ignored by the riverboat, never knowing that he had been within shouting distance.

He dashed tears of frustration and weariness from his eyes, and climbed once more into the pilot's chamber. The trip back downriver went a little faster, not least because he knew the vagaries of the riverbed now, and where to avoid the rapids and deeper pools in favor of the banks.

By the evening of the fourth day, he had passed the first town and reached the second river crossing, where a man in a short-jacketed black uniform had been posted to watch for him. *Silver Wind* rested at a proper train station on a siding, and the Ambassador met him eagerly when he set the behemoth to rest and climbed wearily down.

Taken aback by his exuberant greeting, Evan could hardly understand him. "She has been seen, senor!" he said, grasping Evan by the upper arms and embracing him.

His heart leaped in his chest. "Seen? Where? For I have seen no sign of her in miles and miles."

"It is as we feared—the river carried her much farther than this. A pair of traders pulled a young lady from the water three nights ago and took her by boat to the hospital. We must leave at first light, after you are rested, for the water meadows. It is a journey of two days, and you must be exhausted by your unfruitful search."

He was. He was so weary he could barely think, and spent the next twelve hours in an upper room of the station house, where the bed was so comfortable he never wanted to get out of it.

Gloria was safe. In the hospital, being cared for. His mind had no more room for anything but those two facts, and so on a deep wave of thankfulness, he allowed his body to succumb.

Two days later, he was still exhausted by the constant movement in the harness necessary to make the behemoth walk. But joy was like a fuel that kept him going even as his limbs screamed for surcease.

The railroad descended out of the ironlike, spiky rocks of the mountain range into a massive valley spread wide by the loops of the river. The water meadows were marshes on the margins of old loops and crescents where the course had been carved over centuries. The very sight of water behaving in a civilized manner was a balm to the soul, and Evan's relief at climbing down from the behemoth came at least in part from the softness of moisture in the air.

He hurried aboard *Silver Wind,* which rested, steaming gently, at a much larger station than he had yet seen in this country. Around him, adobe houses with graceful ironwork gates and window shutters stood along orderly streets, the walls bright with climbing vines and bougainvillea. In the distance, he could see the blocky brick steeple of a church. Inside the locomotive, the Ambassador and his men were in the process of toasting each other with delicate glasses filled with a tawny liquid. He accepted one with alacrity.

"Shall we proceed to the hospital immediately, sir?" he asked the Ambassador when he had tossed back the liquor and it had burned its way down to his stomach. "Have you sent a messenger to inquire after Miss Meriwether-Astor's health?"

The Ambassador shook his head, gazing at Evan sadly. "She is dead, senor."

Evan felt as though the man had punched him in the stomach. "What? How is this possible? Have you had word from the hospital so quickly? What happened?"

"There has been no word. I am sorry to have deceived you, senor, but there is no hospital here, either. Only an apothecary." He nodded at the man he had called *el doctor*. No wonder the man had not been able to tell the difference between a dead man and a live one with a head wound. Evan felt very stupid in his turn, as though the Ambassador were speaking a language he'd thought he knew, but using words he had never learned.

"It is impossible that the senorita could have survived the flash flood that took our men," the apothecary chimed in sadly, pouring himself a second glass. "But it was of the utmost importance that *el Gigante* should cross the border into the Royal Kingdom of Spain and the Californias so that he may lead our forces in battle."

Still Evan did not understand.

"You are the only operator who could have brought him here." The apothecary patted his sleeve. "I regret that it was necessary to use your hope of finding the senorita to compel you to make the journey, but there was no other way to transport our behemoth. You have our gratitude."

"Welcome to the Viceroyalty, Senor Douglas," the Ambassador said in tones as smooth as silk, accepting a second glass and lifting it in a toast. "I am obliged to inform you that you are now a prisoner of war."

CHAPTER 21

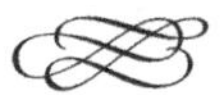

Several days previously

Gloria landed in a heap in a drift of sand at the bottom of the rock wall, the breath knocked clean out of her. In the moments that it took for her lungs to begin working again, sand and gravel rained down upon her from above as the Ambassador's search party clustered on the edge of the precipice and muttered among themselves.

Could they see her? No matter—they had certainly heard her, for no one could have prevented a shriek of fear as she plunged into the abyss, however short the fall may have been. Perhaps they were making a plan to pursue her.

In a moment, her fears were confirmed as a rope snaked down the stone and practically hit her in the face. Biting her lips together to prevent herself from crying out a second time, she scrambled along the wall and around a curtain of stone that thrust out into the passage.

A man shouted the alarm, and in a moment someone called, "Senorita! Stop at once! Are you hurt?"

No, no, no. Tightening her blanket about her middle, Gloria ran along the passage, which undulated this way and that, its solid walls not walls at all, but ripples and flutes and ruffles of stone thirty feet tall. Light from the sun glanced off the curved walls, turning them pink and orange and purple, and beams struck down through holes in the roof in glowing pillars that turned the sandstone gold and looked like the fingers of God.

She could hear her pursuers now, scraping and sliding down the rope. She must escape! The fingers of God must not point them to her. If she were recaptured, she was quite sure she would die of despair, and what would Claire think of her then?

In the distance, she could hear a kind of hollow roar, increasing in volume, as though there were a waterfall. A big one. But a waterfall meant a river, and a river meant witches, and witches meant safety.

She hoped.

She plunged on, becoming a little disoriented now. The walls would not stay put. They curved and swirled, and when she put out her hand to regain her balance, they didn't seem to be where they suggested they were, but curled playfully away so that she staggered like a drunken woman.

Here and there, passages branched off, but she followed the ribbon of blue sky far above her head, trusting that the largest passage might lead her to safety more quickly.

"Senorita! Come back!"

The voice seemed farther away, thank heaven. Perhaps she could outdistance them yet.

The roar seemed louder now, booming and crashing, and

on the heels of a particularly heavy explosion she thought she heard a man scream.

Heavens! Were they firing on her now? In this undulating enclosed space? Were they mad?

She dodged around a rock formation that looked like an angel, complete with spreading wings, and skidded to a stop with a muffled shriek.

A skeleton stood in the passage.

Gloria felt her knees give out.

It had no eyes, only black cavities in the skull set upon its neck. Black and red dots outlined where eyes should have been, and it had no mouth, only bony teeth in a grinning row, surrounded by more dots. Gloria was too frightened even to scream. She was frozen, staring, as the figure ran toward her.

Trapped between death and imprisonment—oh, how had she come to this!

But … but … skeletons did not wear skirts. Dazed, Gloria gaped at the very ordinary tiered skirt and black boots the creature wore. And at the white cotton blouse with a red jacket that matched the roses in her twisted-up hair.

Dead people might wear roses, but they certainly did not run about in skirts and boots, or take the trouble to put up their hair.

Gloria made up her mind. She had been knocked unconscious when she'd fallen from the rock wall, that was all. This time she really was dreaming, and in dreams, things did not hurt you. Skeletons could dance upon your head, and you would come to no harm.

The creature grabbed her hand. "Run! The water—it will kill us!"

No, it wouldn't, but Gloria had no objection to running

down the passage with the witch—for witch it must be. Its skull had spoken in distinctly feminine tones.

They pelted down the passage, Gloria imitating the witch in dodging and ducking ... and splashing. For now the sandy bottom of the canyon was running with water, first a trickle, then a runnel, and soon a creek, up over their ankles.

"Faster!" the skull shouted over her bony shoulder.

Gloria couldn't go any faster—was out of breath, in fact—but the water frightened her. Even if this were a dream, she had no intention of letting it get her. Screams echoed down the canyon, and now the roar of the water was so loud she couldn't hear her own splashing footsteps.

Then, in a moment of horror, she realized there was no waterfall. The water was coming down the canyon passage behind them—a maelstrom, a monster, exploding through the passages like a dragon intent on death.

"Jump!" the witch screamed, and Gloria had no choice, for the creature's bony fingers did not let go of her hand as she launched herself over the precipice feet first.

Thank heaven one could do this safely in dreams.

Gloria leaped after her, and not a moment too soon. The water exploded out of the hole they had just vacated like a projectile from a cannon's mouth, leaping and spewing out over their heads and washing them willy-nilly down a slick slope of rock.

The witch lost her grip on Gloria's hand, but there was no way on this earth that Gloria was about to lose her in the maelstrom. She flung herself forward and grabbed the creature's skirts with one hand, her blanket locked in the cold fingers of the other. Together, they slid over the precipice and plunged forty feet into the river.

The cold was as savage as a blow.

Gloria kicked for the surface, blinded by bubbles and swift water, hardly conscious of anything but the fabric in her left hand and the need to hang on to it no matter what. Their two heads broke the surface together, gasping, and when Gloria felt the other pulling away, she kicked in that direction, the tug of the skirt the only thing tethering her to reality.

For this was no dream. This was so painful it had to be real. One did not feel stabbing cold like this in dreams, nor was there this much water in all the world of imagination.

Far away, she heard another scream, but her companion did not so much as turn her head. Instead, she seemed to be swimming strongly for a black opening in the cliff on the other side. They hadn't much time. Gloria could feel her lungs seizing up, and her limbs no longer obeyed the commands of her brain.

Her companion must have felt the increasing drag on her garments, for she turned and snatched the blanket from Gloria's hand, passed it about both their bodies, and formed a kind of sling so that even if Gloria lost consciousness, she could still pull her along.

But she was not going to lose consciousness. If she was to be saved by a prehensile skeleton only to be made into the witches' dinner or sacrificed to a pagan god, she was going to be awake and conscious to see it, by George.

The witch was a surprisingly strong swimmer. Gloria did her clumsy best to assist, but the current did a much better job at swinging them around and pushing them toward the opening in the rock. The witch yanked her under the water before she bashed her head against the stone lintel, and in a moment Gloria was crawling and sloshing up a gentle slope of stone and out of the freezing river.

She refused to allow herself to faint.

All the same, she could not rise from her hands and knees, either. Shivering, a dreadful mewling sound coming from her mouth, she crouched in the sand at the top and concentrated grimly on remaining conscious.

Into her limited field of view came a wet pair of boots and a sodden skirt, and then a dry edition of the same. "Help me get her on her feet."

"Have you lost the boat, Ella, and brought us a drowned rat? Not a fair exchange."

"Boat's still tied up, far as I know. Flash flood came through the church. I was running for my life, when I turned and there she was, running hellbent for leather after me. Couldn't very well leave her there, could I?"

"I was—b-being pursued," Gloria gasped. Straightening, she staggered between them, one hand on each skeleton's arm, the sum total of her ability being to put one foot in front of the other.

"Not drowned after all." The dry witch peered into her face. "Pursued by what?"

"Californios—the Amb-bassador's m-men."

The hands on her upper arms became rigid as bone as the grips of both witches clenched involuntarily. "Here? In our church?" They picked up their pace. "Mother Mary needs to hear about this. She ain't going to tolerate Californios in church. The nerve of them!"

Gloria found her circulation coming back out of sheer necessity. Her brain was still not working properly, for she had no idea what church they were talking about. No matter.

From the indignation of both, the enemy of her enemy had just become her friend.

For now, at least. Until she could find her way back to Santa Fe … and once she had done her duty, on to an airship going east.

Her companions guided her along one passage and then another, until the light ceased to come from torches set in holders along the wall, and came instead from the light of the sky coming through a broad oval opening. They emerged on the back side of a village set in the cliff some twenty feet above the river's surface. The village wasn't large—ten or eleven stone houses all attached to one another, with a long, semicircular piazza fronting the river behind a wall just tall enough to keep a child from falling in.

On the piazza a skeleton lounged in the sun, whose long golden rays told Gloria it would soon sink behind the cliff at a turning in the river downstream. At the sight of Gloria and her companions, the skeleton swung her feet down from the wall and stood.

With one look at Gloria and the wet witch—Ella—she snatched up a brown bottle from a perfectly unmagical wooden table, and poured a healthy amount of amber liquid into a clay cup. "One shot, each of you," she ordered.

The liquor burned down Gloria's throat and hit her stomach like a curl of flame. Ella coughed and handed Gloria the cup a second time, indicating she should drink the last of it. Oh, why not? She tossed it back and did her best not to shudder. It certainly warmed her insides, though it did nothing for her swimming head.

"Come into the sun," the witch ordered. "Ella, where did you find her?"

Gloria staggered to the wall and sat, gripping the edge with both hands so that she wouldn't topple over backward. One more plunge into the river would certainly kill her.

"Running from a flash flood and Californio men, in church," the girl said with admirable brevity. "I couldn't leave her there. She'd have died."

"Of course not," the witch agreed. She bent to examine Gloria's face. "*Mi'ja,* can you tell us who you are and how you came to be in our church?"

But Gloria needed to be certain of something before she answered anyone's questions. "Are—are you *las brujas*?" she croaked.

"Have you heard of us?" The witch seemed pleased.

"The men who took me prisoner … are afraid of you," Gloria said slowly. Each word had to be formed separately, so cold were the muscles in her face. "I escaped them and hid in a crack in the desert. They pursued me, and I fell. But they kept coming. If it hadn't been for the water—and Ella—they would have captured me. Again."

She rubbed her face and tilted it up to the blessed warmth.

"Why are you this deep in the desert?" the witch asked. "We are not used to intruders in our church."

"On a train. From Resolution. The tracks are half a mile from the crack in the earth."

"Resolution!" squeaked a witch in the growing number filtering out of the houses and into the piazza. "I lived in Resolution. Worked at the Desert Rose, until Bert Blake busted my arm and I ran away."

Gloria couldn't tell them apart, so similarly did their skull faces and hollow eyes look. But she had to ask, "Did you know Alice Chalmers?"

The woman blinked, her eyes brown and sparkling with interest. "I sure did. She stole Ned Mose's airship and disappeared. I heard she was dead."

Gloria shook her head. "As of a week ago, she wasn't. I came to the Territories aboard her ship."

"You don't say. Alice Chalmers," the witch said in wonder. "I'm glad she ain't dead. She was always kind to me."

"I'm happy to hear of kindness among mutual friends. That's a good sign," said the tall, buxom witch to whom everyone deferred. "What's your name, girl?"

Fuzzy and non-operational as it was, Gloria had made up her mind. As far as she was concerned, any connection to the Meriwether-Astor name was no longer a benefit, but a liability.

"Meredith Aster," she said.

"And what about you is so interesting to the Californios that they'd chase you into a slot canyon and get themselves killed by a flash flood? We seen a body or two come by here after Ella pulled you out. Ain't many Californios with the courage to come near the Sangre Colorado de Christo unless they were forced to."

How much of her tale ought she to tell? Would the truth gain her sympathy, or have her tossed over the wall to join the dead men in the river? Abruptly, Gloria's courage failed her, and her determination to be brave fizzled away as suddenly as water on a hot rock. Her eyes filled, and wordlessly, she began to cry.

The witch gazed at her for a moment as Gloria slid from the wall to curl up in a weeping ball on the flagstones. "Looks like our guest has been through enough for one day. Ella, take her to your room and the two of you get some rest. Mother knows you've earned it. We're expecting Captain Stan and the boat tonight. We'll feed her and have the story then, when everyone can hear it."

With encouraging murmurs, the witches helped Gloria to her feet and led her into one of the stone houses, where Ella showed her a pallet laid on a bench and helped her out of her filthy clothes. When she would have clung to her sodden blanket, Ella pulled it gently from her hands and made her lie down.

And there the darkness claimed her even as the tears dried on her cheeks.

GLORIA WOKE hours later to the sound of music and conversation, and the chug of an engine. A fire crackled cheerfully in the hearth of the room in which she lay, and as she pushed herself to a sitting position, she saw that her clothes had been laundered and lay dry in a neat pile on a chair. Even her corset. As she fastened its hooks, she felt surreptitiously for the gold coins sewn into the corners.

Still there. Those coins represented her ability to someday return to her own life, once the task she had set herself was completed. If the corset had been slit and the coins removed, she was not sure she would have been able to stand the blow.

She was becoming very tired of other people controlling her life. If only she could figure out how to regain the autonomy she had once taken for granted! But then, it seemed that said autonomy had been the product of wealth. Without that—or without people about her who respected it—she was no more and no less than what she could prove herself to be.

Thoughtfully, she pulled on her pants over clean bloomers.

Jake's shirt, evidently, had not been deemed satisfactory, for the blouse she found on the pile had the gathered neck, cheerful flowered embroidery, and puffed sleeves worn by Ella. It was probably hers. Gloria would have to express her thanks at not having to go about in company in pants and a corset and not much else.

Even her boots were dry, a miracle she would not have been able to pull off even in Philadelphia. How had they done it? Magic?

Clean clothes did amazing things for the spirits. Gloria sallied forth, only to meet Ella on the steps coming up. "You're awake," the girl greeted her, looking pleased.

"Thank you for seeing to my clothes, Ella. And for the loan of a blouse."

"You're welcome. Keep the blouse—I can always make another. Come. Mother Mary is waiting."

The whole village, it seemed, was waiting, along with a crew of ramshackle men who toasted the witches and laughed at something one of them said. When the woman turned, Gloria saw that it was the witch in charge. Mother Mary.

Awkwardly, not knowing what else to do, she curtseyed. "I neglected to thank you before for saving my life, you and Ella," she said. "And for seeing to my clothes so quickly."

Mother Mary regarded her for a moment. With the paint and the dots along her eye sockets, Gloria couldn't be sure, but she thought an eyebrow might have been raised. "I like courtesy in a visitor. It ain't often we see it in these parts. Come along, Meredith, and have some supper."

It took a moment for Gloria to recall this was the name she had given, and then she crossed to a pair of trestle tables, which had been set up by a roaring bonfire and were laden with roasted meat, squashes, potatoes baked in their jackets, and round, flat bread in which everything appeared to be rolled up in lieu of plates. Some sauce was splashed on the top, and when Gloria bit into it, fire roared along her tongue.

"Oh my," she choked. "I have heard of this, but never tasted it."

"The plants are called chiles. We grow them up on the mesas," Ella said. "The sauce—*salsa*—takes some getting used to, but capsaicin is good for a body, especially after the dunking you took."

"If you say so," Gloria gasped, having taken a second bite. But she could not stop, despite the spicy heat. Nothing had ever tasted so good, and she devoured not one, but two of the meat- and vegetable-filled rolls, and prepared a third one for later, just in case they ran out. There were juicy oranges for dessert, and cinnamon-flavored pastries filled with honey. Gloria had one of everything, and came very close to giving up the thought of Philadelphia if she could only eat like this forever.

During the meal, she became aware that several of the men were watching her—and one in particular seemed to be enjoying the spectacle as much as she enjoyed the food.

Hmph. She gave him her shoulder. It was probably because she was the only woman not wearing face paint. For that, she could see now that she was in her right mind, was how the witches achieved their skeleton-like appearance. If he was a friend of the witches, an undisguised woman was likely a novelty. Still, it was rude of him to stare, and so boldly, too!

"Come," Mother Mary finally called. "If you've all had enough, gather around. I have a powerful need to hear Meredith Aster's tale."

"Might I be properly introduced to your friends, and your other guests?" she asked the witch.

"What good will that do?" called the bold man. "These ladies all look alike."

"Indeed, they do not," she said, feeling a little huffy on their behalf. "Ella looks nothing like Mother Mary, who looks nothing like the lady who prepared the roast, though I was not told her name."

"Clara," that lady said, laughing. "How can you tell me from Ella?"

"By her voice, Ella is ten years younger at least," Gloria said. "And you have a flower pattern at the corners of your lips, while hers is between her brows. Your skirt is blue, and cotton, while Mother Mary's is as red as her velvet jacket."

Mother Mary let out a shout of laughter and slapped her knee. "Not only polite, but observant as well," she said, smiling. "Not one witch in a hundred could do that on first meeting."

"She's no witch," the man said. His eyes sparkled green in the dancing firelight, and under his disreputable bowler hat with the pilot's goggles on the brim, his hair curled against his neck and shoulders, black as a crow's wing. A leather holster ran over his chest and under one arm to hold a pistol, his low-slung belt was decorated with silver brooches similar to those of the Californios, and a revolver was strapped to his thigh. Had his firearms been made by M.A.M.W.?

He bowed and swept the hat from his head. "Captain Stan," he said. "Pleased to meet you, Miss Aster."

"We're all friends and equals here, Stan," Mother Mary reminded him. "Call her Meredith, same as we."

"Let me introduce my crew, then, Meredith—Mike, Jim,

Carlos, Sully, and Miguel, serving aboard the riverboat *Colorado Queen*."

"I am very pleased to make your acquaintance, gentlemen," Gloria said to them, and was rewarded with a toast from various glasses and bottles. One of them—Sully?—plucked a fanfare from his banjo in lieu of a greeting.

Next she was introduced to the witches, a feat of memory that had her concentrating hard to put decoration and clothing with names. There were at least thirty in the company, including several children. Perhaps it would take a day or two before she could address someone correctly, but all the same, she felt better for knowing at least a few.

"Now that we're all friends, let's hear your tale," Mother Mary said, settling onto the wall as though a chair were too confining for her. Captain Stan took a seat not far away, while those who did not find chairs arranged themselves on the stones and steps leading down from the houses above.

Gloria took a breath to calm a heart that suddenly beat hard in her chest. "I came from Philadelphia to stop a war," she blurted.

If she had thought this bombshell would elicit some surprise, she was mistaken.

"Lofty ambitions," Captain Stan said, "for a young lady of gentle upbringing."

"Shut up, Stan, and let her speak," Mother Mary said with greater asperity than politeness.

"I hired Captain Chalmers to fly me and a friend to Resolution, where we convinced Ned Mose and his men to waylay the train on which many tons of armaments were being shipped to the Royal Kingdom of Spain and the Californias."

"Why would you do that?" Mother Mary asked, the dots

between her eyes practically meeting as she frowned. "What business was it of yours?"

"I believe it is everyone's business," Gloria said steadily. "The Ambassador to the Fifteen Colonies, who seems to have aspirations above his station, has encouraged his young and inexperienced sovereign to spend hundreds of thousands in gold on arming his own supporters for an invasion of the Texican Territory. This train carried mechanicals of war—metal horses and missile-bearing cats to be used as cavalry—and a great behemoth with a rotating gun in one arm and a cannon in the other that could destroy half a village in one shot. All of it is to be deployed—first, to wipe out the witch population along the Sangre Colorado de Christo, and once that is achieved, to take for himself the gold he is convinced you are hiding."

Half a dozen people swore in as many languages, the babel breaking out and spreading in a wave through the crowd.

"Us!" Mother Mary said when she could be heard again. "*We* are to be this man's first objective? What madness is this?"

"Yes," Gloria replied. "With the gold, he can finance a push deeper into the Territories, all the way to the Mississippi and beyond. At the very least, he—or perhaps the Viceroy, I am not certain—plans to build canals and water courses from the Pacific Ocean to the Sangre Colorado, using the rivers to ship weapons and men more easily." She gazed at her hostess. "So you see that the only things stopping this man—Senor Augusto de Aragon y Villarreal is his name—are you … and me."

"I'd be very interested to know where you're getting your information." Captain Stan's gaze was no longer flirtatious. In fact, he might have looked upon her in just this way had she been a rattlesnake or a scorpion.

"Yes," Mother Mary agreed. "What proof do you have?"

She had no proof. But someone had to listen. Someone had to believe her, or the entire country would be convulsed by one man's madness.

"You will find that all the armaments were built by the Meriwether-Astor Munitions Works. The reason I was captured during the battle at Resolution is that I can fire anything that company makes. I am—I was closely allied with the company and until its owner died, was very familiar with its workings. The owner, unfortunately, allied himself with the countries with the deepest pockets. Until his death, he had been inciting wars all over the world to promote the sale of armaments." Her throat closed, and she swallowed. "This war is the last of which I am aware, and since I could not live with my knowledge, I determined to do what I could to stop it."

"And so you were captured for that knowledge." Captain Stan's gaze lay on her with steady disbelief.

For she was a woman, of course, and what knowledge could a woman have?

"I was to be taken to the Viceroy because of it and, I suppose, made to fight on their side—if I was not executed first. Or, being a woman, perhaps I would have been set to training their troops." She glared at him. "I was able to lull them into believing I meant to do so, until we reached the siding some distance across the country, there." She waved a hand across the river. "I escaped and thought to hide myself in a crack in the earth. But as I was pursued deeper and deeper into the caverns, I realized it might lead to the river—and that I might find allies among you."

"And that was when we heard the flash flood coming," Ella put in. "It swept away the men chasing her."

"Leaving us that many less to fight, if what you say is true," Mother Mary said.

"I do not know how many are among your number," Gloria said earnestly, "but if somehow we can return to Resolution to collect the armaments left aboard the train, at least you would have a fighting chance—and they would have lost their investment, which can only work in our favor. I certainly—I cannot imagine the company will want them back."

Mother Mary looked astonished. "Do we look like the sort to ride a mechanical cavalry? Unless it can swim, I can't see the use in it."

"You look like the sort to use any means at hand to protect your homes," Gloria retorted. "If you are to be the first under attack, do you not think it would be wise to have some form of defense?"

"We've done just fine depending on the river for that," the witch called Clara said from where she sat near the table. "Californios don't come any more."

"They are afraid of you," Gloria allowed. "But de Aragon—he is not afraid. He loves the gold he thinks you have. He is a man willing to take the risk and is completely confident that he will win."

Mother Mary and Captain Stan exchanged a look that Gloria could not read.

"I will think about what you've said," the witch said at last. "Spend some time in church praying for guidance from the Great Mother. This invasion—it's not likely to happen tomorrow, is it?"

"No," Gloria said slowly. "But the locomotive—*Silver Wind* is its name—will arrive in San Francisco without its cargo and without me. Reinforcements will be sent to Resolution to collect the mechanicals and armaments, and then it will begin. You have less than a month, and that is a generous estimate."

"A month, eh?" Mother Mary's gaze lay on her, cool as water. "What luck that you washed out of that chute to bring us this news."

She was losing them. Gloria scrambled to find proof that would convince them—without revealing who she was. Only one thing presented itself.

"I think perhaps the Great Mother might have had a hand in it," she said. "For I certainly felt myself in the presence of something otherworldly in your cathedral—and she did not allow the Californios' feet to walk on sacred ground, did she?"

"She certainly did not. That is why we will allow you to stay, since clearly you have her blessing." Mother Mary clapped her hands. "Enough of wars and rumors of wars. Let us have music, and dancing—and who is with me for a round of cowboy poker?"

The crowd broke up as the banjo and a fiddle players found their way into a tune. Someone shouted, "Longways, for as many as will!" and several of the men grabbed a witch for a partner while other witches partnered each other. Two lines formed, and Gloria had a moment to wonder how on earth they knew the contradance, this far out in the wilderness, before she was whirled into line.

She found herself partnered by Captain Stan, but that would never do. He did not believe her, and while she was not convinced that Mother Mary did, either, she would certainly not subject herself to his control in anything, even a dance under the stars. She pretended not to hear when he attempted to make conversation, and at the end of the first figure, she accepted another partner with wounding alacrity.

And then she was invited to waltz, and then to sing, and then to play cowboy poker, at which she proved herself so adept thanks to Claire's and Alice's excellent tutelage, that she earned herself twenty dollars in silver. By the time the witches had plied her with drink and the third boatman had proposed marriage, she was breathless with laughter and amazement at finding such camaraderie in such a place.

And then Captain Stan swept her out for a waltz, his arm so strong about her waist that it would cause more difficulty to refuse than to accept. So she did as she had been taught at St. Cecelia's, and leaned back against his arm as he whirled her across the flagstones, her hand properly upon his shoulder and the stars so close above that they seemed to burn in the night sky.

"You've been very elusive," he said, drawing her closer to speak into her ear, and guiding her as expertly in the turns as any London gentleman in a Mayfair ballroom, though his accents were colonial.

"I may be as elusive as I please," she informed him, her chin tilted.

"And you're very good at cowboy poker. Better than I am, and that's saying something."

"I had very good teachers."

"I could offer you a job fleecing passengers, if you'd like it."

"No, thank you. I have a war to stop."

"So you say."

"So I mean. I do not care if you don't believe me, Captain.

If I must do it myself on the back of a mechanical horse, then I shall."

He gazed down at her, and she was compelled to meet his gaze, for to avoid it would have put her at a disadvantage.

"Who are you, really, Miss Meredith Aster?"

"Someone who hates war," she replied, "and the destruction and loss of homes and families that goes with it."

"But you are more than that," he said. "I wonder how long it would take me to find out?"

"What business is it of yours, sir?"

"None," he said baldly.

"I should as well wonder why a gentleman of such skill upon the dance floor and in conversation should find himself on a riverboat in forbidden territory instead of in a fine house among good society."

"I have plenty of good society, present company included."

"But you have not answered me."

"Nor shall I." His eyes creased in a smile. "I can keep secrets as well as you. But I'm quite sure that mine will not affect the outcome of a war like yours will."

She did not miss his choice of words. "So you believe me after all—that it is coming and your friends will be among the first to see it?"

"I believe that you did not happen here by chance. That a young woman washed up by the river does not have eyes like yours and yet make up such stories for her own entertainment. I believe in whispers on the wind, and in little birds, and in the overturning of rocks. All of which tend to add up when great changes are afoot in the world."

"Great changes are set into motion by ordinary people," she murmured.

Look at Claire, and Alice, and Andrew, and the Mopsies. Her friends had affected the course of history. She would never have believed even six months ago that she might follow in their footsteps, but it seemed that she was destined to play a similar part.

No, that was not right. She had *chosen* to play a similar part the moment she had discovered her cousin Sydney's betrayal. And now she must see the course she had set for herself all the way to its conclusion.

"I agree with you on that score, at least, Miss Aster," her partner said, and whirled her across the flagstones with such grace that she almost felt as though she were flying, her laughter carried away by the changing wind.

EPILOGUE

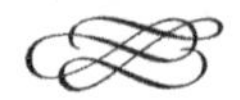

Dearest Claire,

I am writing to tell you that Ian and I were married yesterday at the church of San Francisco de Asis in a tiny village in the mountains north of Santa Fe. We would have done the deed in Santa Fe itself, except that Robert Van Ness is now in charge of the Ranger outpost there, and we felt it was best to get as far as we could from anyone who might recognize me.

I am sorry that you and Andrew could not be with us, but life being uncertain, we thought it best to seize joy when the good Lord offers it to us, and not quibble about invitations and toast racks. Jake and Benny made admirable witnesses, and three chickens formed my bridal party. The padre tells me St. Francis would have approved. What a lucky thing you made me buy that silvery silk dress! Ian assures me that we will have a reception at Hollys Park when we return to England—and that he will personally guarantee the absence of royalty.

I don't think I have ever been so happy. I have a healing hole in my left shoulder and a heart sore with worry, but in spite of all that,

I could never have imagined feeling like this. I can't think why I was such a baby about being married. It's completely wonderful.

On a more sober note, our plans have gone awry. Ned Mose betrayed us and is dead. Evan and Gloria are both missing. The only Texican survivors of the Battle of Resolution are the aforesaid bridal party, and Perry Connelly, whom you might remember. We believe the Californio Ambassador has taken Gloria, so our first task is to find and rescue her. Perhaps she may have some clue as to poor Evan's whereabouts.

I had hoped to be back in England by now, but I know you'll be the first to agree that we must stay the course and recover our friends. I am deeply grateful that Ian feels the same way. Jake quite likes Gloria, and has taken her disappearance rather personally. We will do our best to send news as we get it.

Jake and Benny send their best regards. They are building an aviary like the one on Athena for Soot, Mrs. Morse, and Rosie. Apparently the red one is very similar in looks and temperament to your bird of fond memory.

Ian sends his love, and begs me to assure you that no harm will come to me. I don't have the heart to remind him that I'm a better shot than he is, but all the same, I wouldn't want anyone else at my side, save perhaps you, my dearest friend.

And now I will stop before I embarrass myself.

Affectionately,

~~*Alice, Lady Hollys*~~

Your loving Alice

P.S. COULD you inform the Admiralty that Benjamin Stringfellow has been promoted from Midshipman to Gunner, Second Class, effective January 20, 1895. If anything happens to us, I want that on record, at least.

A.H.

THE END

AFTERWORD

Dear reader,

I hope you enjoy reading the adventures of Lady Claire, Gloria, and the gang in the Magnificent Devices world as much as I enjoy writing them. It is your support and enthusiasm that is like the steam in an airship's boiler, keeping the entire enterprise afloat and ready for the next adventure.

You might leave a review on your favorite retailer's site to tell others about the books. And you can find print, digital, and audiobook editions of the series online. I hope to see you over at my website, www.shelleyadina.com, where you can sign up for my newsletter and be the first to know of new releases and special promotions. You'll also receive a free short story set in the Magnificent Devices world just for subscribing!

And now, for an excerpt from *Fields of Iron*, the next book in the Magnificent Devices series, I invite you to turn the page.

EXCERPT

FIELDS OF IRON © SHELLEY ADINA

Somewhere in the Wild West
February 1895

The witches who inhabited the canyons and tributaries of the mighty Rio de Sangre Colorado de Christo had controlled its sandstone fastnesses for fifty years. *La bruja* who went by the name of Mother Mary had been the first child born to a member of the original band of runaways, escapees, and criminals, and had grown up knowing no father, but many mothers, sisters, and friends. Her biological mother, a former dance-hall girl who had run away from an abusive employer and a worse lover, had accumulated a number of whores and Navapai laborers and even a Canton scientist who had been forced to be a laundress as companions along her journey to freedom. They had found the river and its bewildering series of canyons, tributaries, and caverns, to say nothing of its ancient, abandoned cliff dwellings, to be a more welcoming home than the towns of the Texican Territory, and had taken up residence in a country where no one would find them.

Slowly the word spread among the abused, the dispossessed, and the destitute in the desert reaches of the Wild West that if one could only get to the river, one could find safety and food and employment. For the witches did not merely haunt and hide. They built. What they lacked in physical strength they hired or invented. The Canton scientist specialized in steam-powered engines, and was only too delighted to teach any who cared to learn about how to control the flow and speed of the river, how to go up and down the seven-hundred-foot cliff faces with the ease of a house spider, and how to construct the underwater traps with which they inspired terror in the hearts of the invaders from the west. These were men from across the sea who coveted the power and commerce the river could make possible if they could only get their hands on it.

Oh yes, they coveted it. But the witches had no intention of giving up their fierce independence or their arrangement with the small but cheerful armada of steamships plying the races and reaches of the river. No one outside of those echoing canyons could understand how the steamships could navigate the rapids. Most believed the boats to have been wrecked years ago. Some believed there had been powers of magic or time travel at work.

But the witches knew, and smiled, and counted the gold that bought more iron and more supplies and seeds for their crops and the occasional pretty gown.

Gloria Meriwether-Astor sat upon a wonderfully carved stool made of silvery driftwood and tilted up her face for Ella Balboa, Mother Mary's daughter and the girl who had saved her life the week before. With one fingertip, Ella rubbed white paint into her skin from hairline to chin, and then picked up the paintbrush with its load of black.

The bristles tickled as she traced whorls and webs and flowers around Gloria's blacked eyes, a pattern that, when it was completed, would look like lace upon Gloria's skin and render her completely unrecognizable in its very uniqueness.

"So what happened to the Canton scientist?" she asked, doing her best not to move her lips.

"Jiao-Lan climbed the starlight stair about fifteen years ago, but before she did, she was able to teach two generations of girls what she knew. Stella, Clara's daughter, is probably the smartest of all of us. She'll be heading upriver soon to add some improvements to the original mechanisms that control the rapids. She's been teaching the younger ones, and they'll take over when the time comes." She added a final flourish to Gloria's nose, and tilted her head to examine her handiwork. "Red lips, I think, to set off these gold roses, and I have a silk crown of roses for you. I think yellow goes better with your hair, though tradition tells us red, for love and blood. Oh!" Her brown eyes, starred with long lashes, widened with an idea. "We could play brides!"

Gloria laughed, and was surprised to find that the paint did not stiffen or crack. Considering the hour and a half that Ella had taken to create her work of art, she was grateful that a single smile would not spoil it all.

"My dear friend, while I confess to having been the unwilling recipient of a number of proposals, it seems that playing brides will indeed be as close as I will ever come to that happy estate."

"Oh, no," Ella said quite seriously as she applied gold paint from a tiny pot to this spot and then its opposite on Gloria's cheeks, where presumably there were roses. "You are so beautiful. I am quite sure that had you not left your former life, you would have been married within the year."

"And I am quite sure that you are sweet to say so."

Gloria could not tell if the other girl's color changed under the paint, but her gaze dropped in embarrassment at the compliment.

Gloria went on, "Fortunately, there is more to marriage than beauty on one side and wealth on the other. My friend Claire Trevelyan Malvern has found love and companionship with a man who is her equal in intelligence. While my standards in that regard must be set considerably lower, I aspire to such a union, too." She paused, gazing past Ella's shoulder at the wide ribbon of brilliant blue visible from the stone veranda on which they sat, where the canyon walls admitted a view of the sky above. "I am willing to wait for the right one," she said softly. "And to remember that a man's worth is not measured by social skills or wealth, but by temperament, and generosity, and courage."

"Men aren't the only ones with those qualities." Ella carefully applied red from another pot to Gloria's lips, and then stood back to admire her handiwork. "Could you not make a home among us? Because you know, there is plenty of generosity and courage and intelligence among our ranks, if that is what you're looking for."

"I have seen that already," she agreed. "May I see what you've done?"

Ella waited a moment, as though she expected Gloria to say more, and then got up to fetch the mirror. It was silver, with a chased handle, and could have held its own on any dressing-table in Philadelphia. Gloria held it up and gazed upon the wraith it reflected.

"My goodness, you're talented. No one would know me—all they can see is your beautiful art, Ella. Now I truly feel like one of you."

The other girl dipped her head. "*Gracias, amiga.* It was my pleasure. Will you have the crown and veil now?"

"Oh, why not? In for a penny, in for a pound."

The much abused canvas pants in which Gloria had spent much of the past two weeks had finally given up the ghost when she had climbed the hidden spiral stair up to the witches' main palace in the cliffs a few days ago, and she had been obliged to raid the coffers in the storage rooms here. Nothing would force her to part with her custom-made corset with the gold coins sewn into the lining, but now she wore a ruffled, bleached cotton skirt with several layers of point lace, and the embroidered blouse Ella had given her on her arrival, cinched at the waist with a corselet of tanned and polished leather. Along with the gray wool blanket and boots she had brought with her, she also now possessed a chemise edged in lace, a linen shirtwaist, and a brocade waistcoat with no fewer than four hidden pockets, as well as a short canvas duster against the night's chill. If she could only come across another pair of pants that fit, she would have nothing left to wish for.

Now, her white blouse and creamy skirt would have to do for playing brides, a thought that made her want to giggle. She had never played brides in her life. But with Ella, who may have been past the age of making her debut but still possessed the innocent joy of childhood, it seemed like just the thing to while away a warm February afternoon while they waited for

Captain Stan and his crew to come back with news of the war brewing in the west.

Ella climbed the stone steps and Gloria heard her opening and closing a chest in one of the rooms above. She came down a moment later bearing two veils over her arm and two crowns of silk roses.

"Where did the veils come from?" she asked curiously, dipping her head so that Ella could lay the large square upon it, with one long point falling over her face. It was edged six inches deep in the most beautiful embroidery Gloria had seen since— "Why, this looks like Burano lace, from the duchy of Venice."

"I don't know." Ella fitted a crown of yellow and black roses over the veil and handed Gloria the mirror once more. "Things come on Captain Stan's boats and we never know where he gets them. Sometimes I believe it's better not to know. Oh, don't you look like a bride, to be sure!"

Gloria gazed at her reflection. She certainly didn't look like any bride she had ever seen before—not like Claire must have, in the Worth ivory satin Gloria had sent as a wedding gift two months before. But all the same, the lace was delicately sumptuous, and the rose crown made her feel rather regal, if one overlooked the face painted to look like a celebratory death's head.

"For we are the dead," Ella had explained to her the other day. "Many of us have grown up on the river, but many have come here to leave their lives behind and be reborn as the dead. So we celebrate both death and life. Besides, it frightens the stuffing out of the Californios if they get a glimpse of us."

"Your turn." She set a smaller veil on Ella's glossy brown curls, and crowned her with red and white silk roses and trailing black ribbon. "I think we make a beautiful pair of brides, don't you?"

Ella turned this way and that, then brought the mirror over so they could look into it together.

"Dearly beloved," Gloria said, laughing, "we are gathered here today in the presence of this lizard and that pair of eagles to witness the union of … who? Ella Balboa and …"

Gloria couldn't see Ella's eyes very well behind the embroidered mist of her veil, but she could see a glimmer of a white smile.

"Never you mind. It's a secret."

"Ah, a proxy wedding," Gloria said. "Very well, let us proceed. Ella Balboa and Meredith Aster, standing as proxy for a person unknown. Do you, Ella, take this—" A chugging sound echoed up the canyon and Gloria stopped. "Is that the boat?"

"I think it is. Finally! Come, let's go meet them." Ella pulled off her crown and veil, and headed up the steps at a run, Gloria right behind her. "We may keep the crowns, but we mustn't let Mother Mary catch us soiling these veils. She's saving them in case there's ever a real wedding someday."

Gloria contained her impatience as Ella carefully folded the squares into their trunk, then smoothed her hair and set the rose crown back on it as they ran down the passage.

The others had clearly heard the *Colorado Queen*'s engine, which had a distinctive wheeze Gloria suspected needed a mechanic's attention. She and Ella were joined by several others streaming out onto the lowest of the terraces, where the dock was. A few yards upriver was a stone building containing the engine that controlled the great underwater chain that ran from here to the opposite bank. The wreckage of a number of the Californios' attempts at invasion lay along the banks and submerged in the deep waters of this section of the river.

Captain Stan leaped across the gap between deck and stone dock without waiting for a gangplank, and waved his shabby bowler hat at the witches waiting on the terrace above. "I have news!" he shouted, pushing his steering goggles on top of his head. "We'll just tie her off and be up shortly. How about something to drink? Spying is dry work."

Clara snorted and turned away to chivvy her usual helpers into setting up tables and bringing out food. It wasn't until everyone had helped him or herself to flatbread, spiced meat, and vegetables, and had a tin mug to hand containing anything from cactus juice to lemonade to whiskey, that Mother Mary finally said, "Well, lad? You've kept us on tenter-hooks long enough. What is the situation downriver?"

Captain Stan swallowed his whiskey with the air of a man who believes that mouthful to be his last. "It ain't good, Mother, to be blunt. What Miss Aster tells us seems to be true." He glanced at her, and Gloria primmed up her mouth.

Of course it was true, for heaven's sake. If he had been so foolish as to think she was making it all up, and had wasted precious days going downriver with the intention of proving her wrong, that was on his head. She had never misled them in any way … except perhaps in the matter of her real name. That she was not prepared to divulge to anyone.

"The Royal Kingdom of Spain and the Californias has somehow got hold of a massive piece of machinery they call *el Gigante*," the captain went on. "We had not been in the water meadows an hour before we saw it stumping along in the distance. The entire town is talking of it."

"What is that?" Mother Mary asked. "The Giant? Is it a train?"

"No, far from it. In shape it looks like a man as tall as a building, and in purpose it is a weapon."

Gloria sat bolt upright as though lightning had passed through her. "Yes, it possesses a cannon in one arm and a rotating Gatling gun in the other. I told you about it before. It has a pilot's chair in a window in its chest, room for a crew of two, and great hydraulic legs."

Captain Stan gazed at her with a mixture of astonishment and annoyance, his mug dangling empty from slack fingers. "You are quite right. What else do you know of it?"

"I did not know its present location," she said. "If it is the same one, the Californio Ambassador to the Fifteen Colonies brought it out here on his train, having purchased it and all the other armaments and munitions I told you about from the Meriwether-Astor Munitions Works in Philadelphia. I last saw it firing at me, moments before I was blasted off the top of a hill near a town called Resolution, in the Texican Territory."

Eyes wide, Ella covered her mouth with her fingers, and Clara and Mother Mary exchanged a glance.

"The soldiers called it *el Gigante,* but in practice it is a steam-powered mechanical behemoth, operated from within by its crew. But—" She fell silent as a new thought struck her. Who could the operator be, if the man who had had that responsibility was now drowned? How had it covered all those miles between Resolution and the water meadows known as Las Vegas? It had not been on the *Silver Wind* when she was taken from Resolution by the Californios as a prisoner, so how had something so enormous been conveyed here?

Frankly, it was impossible.

"There must be two of them," she murmured. "This must be the first, sent out in a previous shipment."

Then why had it not been among the manifests she had seen before embarking on this godforsaken journey?

"Anything else you can tell us, Miss Aster?" Captain Stan inquired with silky politeness.

"It cost ten thousand pounds to build," she snapped and, too late, realized her mistake.

"My, my, what a lot of unusual knowledge our drowned kitten possesses. I wonder what else she knows?"

Now Mother Mary and Clara and half the women in earshot were staring at her. Oh, if only she could wind back the last thirty seconds and take a single moment to control her temper!

"That is all I know," she said stiffly, controlling the urge to leap to her feet and run up the steps to the room she shared with Ella. "With the behemoth and the cavalry of mechanical horses, the Ambassador's troops will be difficult to fight, indeed. That is why I have been encouraging you all to ally yourselves with the Texicans. They possess airships—and bombs—that are our only hope of overcoming these mechanical menaces."

A moment passed in which the only sounds Gloria heard were the gulps of a riverman slugging down his whiskey, and the rush and gurgle of the torrent below.

At last Mother Mary turned back to the captain. "What other news have you?"

"Miss Aster's previous information about the war has

proven correct. The Royal Kingdom is mobilizing, and not everyone is happy about it. There are acres of tents pitched between the town and the river as the ranchos send troops. But many are not there willingly. While some share the late Viceroy's dream of regaining the Texican Territory and its supposed caches of gold, others have no interest and are content to raise their families on their farms in peace."

"On the backs of their tenants' labor," Clara said sourly. "And that of their captives."

Gloria had learned that Clara's younger daughter Honoria had been captured during a raid, and was now somewhere on one of the massive ranchos, forced into servitude until she escaped ... or died.

Captain Stan acknowledged the lost member of their company with a lift of his tin mug, and someone obligingly filled it.

"What of the present Viceroy?" Mother Mary asked, gripping Clara's hand in support. "Does he share his father's dream? Word has it that he's barely out of the schoolroom, and the studious sort. He would have gone to university in the old country had his father not died and he not inherited the throne."

"All true, from what I hear. One wonders how a bookish boy could be convinced to go to war."

"It is part of their culture," Gloria said bitterly, still stinging from the experience of her own capture. "The boys are trained to war from infancy—though from what I understand, no one has actually fought in two hundred years."

"Remember what she told us—they bought these mechanicals to do the fighting for them," one of the rivermen said. He was the mechanic who ought to be looking after the boat's engine, but what was he doing? Drinking. If a captain cared about his boat and its crew, Gloria thought sourly, he ought to have words with the man.

"Would that we had one of the Texicans' airships, and could travel to San Francisco in a matter of hours to ask him," Captain Stan said with a laugh.

The only airship within five hundred miles that Gloria knew of was Alice Chalmers's *Swan,* and she and Jake and Captain Hollys were probably back in England by now. Evan had to be dead. A hollow feeling opened up in the region of her heart. Another missed opportunity. Another reminder that she was achingly alone, with a monumental task ahead.

At the same time, sound business practice dictated that when one needed something, one began at the top. "How far is San Francisco from here?" she asked.

"It must be six hundred miles of mountains and desert and wildcats and well-armed *caballeros,*" Mother Mary said. "Why? Are you going to see the Viceroy? Shall you ask him to abandon his war?"

"Someone must," Gloria said. "Why should it not be me?"

I hope you'll continue the adventure by purchasing *Fields of Iron.*

Fair winds!

Shelley

ALSO BY SHELLEY ADINA

STEAMPUNK

The Magnificent Devices series

Lady of Devices

Her Own Devices

Magnificent Devices

Brilliant Devices

A Lady of Resources

A Lady of Spirit

A Lady of Integrity

A Gentleman of Means

Devices Brightly Shining (Christmas novella)

Fields of Air

Fields of Iron

Fields of Gold

Carrick House (novella)

Selwyn Place (novella)

Holly Cottage (novella)

Gwynn Place (novella)

Acorn (novella)

Aster (novella)

Iris (novella)

Rosa (novella)

The Mysterious Devices series

The Bride Wore Constant White

The Dancer Wore Opera Rose

The Matchmaker Wore Mars Yellow

The Engineer Wore Venetian Red

The Judge Wore Lamp Black

The Professor Wore Prussian Blue

The Lady Georgia Brunel Mysteries

"The Air Affair" in *Crime Wave: Women of a Certain Age*

The Clockwork City

The Automaton Empress

The Engineer's Nemesis

The Aeronaut's Heir

The Texican Tinkerer

The Wounded Airship

The Regent's Devices series with R.E. Scott

The Emperor's Aeronaut

The Prince's Pilot

The Lady's Triumph

The Pilot's Promise (novella)

The Aeronaut's Heart (novella)

~

REGENCY ROMANCE

The Rogues of St. Just by Charlotte Henry

The Rogue to Ruin

The Rogue Not Taken

One for the Rogue

A Rogue by Any Other Name

~

PARANORMAL

Immortal Faith

ABOUT THE AUTHOR

Shelley Adina is the author of more than 50 novels published by Harlequin, Warner, Hachette, and Moonshell Books, Inc., her own independent press. She writes steampunk adventure and mystery as Shelley Adina; as Charlotte Henry, writes classic Regency romance; and as Adina Senft, is the *USA Today* bestselling author of Amish women's fiction. She holds a PhD in Creative Writing from Lancaster University in the UK. She won RWA's RITA Award® in 2005, and was a finalist in 2006. She appeared in the 2016 documentary film *Love Between the Covers*, is a popular speaker and convention panelist, and has been a guest on many podcasts, including Worldshapers and Realm of Books. When she's not writing, Shelley is usually quilting, sewing historical costumes, or enjoying the garden with her flock of rescued chickens.

Shelley loves to talk with readers about books, chickens, and costuming!

www.shelleyadina.com
shelley@shelleyadina.com

Made in the USA
Las Vegas, NV
22 December 2023